I0600334

RESCUED BY LOVE:

LATER IN LIFE BOOKS 1-5

DEBRA ELISE

HEA
production llc

Debra Elise/HEA Productions LLC www.debraeliseauthor.com

Publisher's Note: This is a work of fiction. Names, characters, places, and incidents are a product of the author's imagination. Locales and public names are sometimes used for atmospheric purposes. Any resemblance to actual people, living or dead, or to businesses, companies, events, institutions, or locales is completely coincidental.

LOVE AT EVERMORE & 39TH —1st ed.

LOVE AT SECOND & 49TH—1st ed.

LOVE AT FIRST & 35TH—1st ed.

LOVING GOLDIE—1st ed.

LOVE AT FOREVER AND 56TH Debra Elise—1st ed.

Print ISBN 9798992933123

CONTENTS

L♥VE at

Evermore

&

39TH

steamy

A RESCUED BY LOVE: LATER IN LIFE NOVELLA

DEBRA ELISE

ABOUT

"This is a perfect heartwarming romance for anyone looking for a feel-good romance..."

A steamy, curvy woman, sports star, later in life, insta-love, quick read romance.

"What's your game, Evan? You enter my contest then ghost me?"

Cassidy Love, a popular YouTube chef and Evan Slater, a former pro baseball player for the Idaho Outlaws, and new sports podcaster, come together via an Instagram set up that only one of them knows about.

Follow along as Cassidy and Evan come to terms with their intense attraction, sexy banter, and shared interests on their way to a new chapter in their lives ~ including a happily ever after.

Welcome to Pineville, Idaho where love always finds a way.

ONE

"WAIT, run that by me again. The guy who won a date with me hasn't responded?" Cassidy Love had recently hired her assistant, Sara, to handle her social media accounts. The *Win a Date with Cassidy* contest ended three days ago, and she was just now hearing about this.

This was why she hadn't wanted to hire someone to take over posting on her accounts and helping with her scheduling. Giving up control sucked. Cassidy schooled her features and bit her tongue. Maybe there was a good reason she was just now finding this out.

When her "*Cooking with Love*" YouTube videos landed her in the top ten worldwide of internet influencers a year ago, her life had exploded with requests to do the national morning shows plus endless interviews and cross-promoting. She no longer had the time to do everything. And the saddest part of this whole thing was this would be her first date in months, and it wasn't even real.

"I know I should have told you sooner, but who doesn't respond after five DMs? I know where he works, so my next step was to call him, but looking at his Insta, he's not a very active poster. Not sure why he even entered? So, do you want me to pick someone else?"

Cassidy pulled the scrunchy holding her long hair back. Massaging her head, then her temples, she let out a long sigh. She really needed a shorter style. "No. We still have two more days. Let me see his account." She held out her hand and admired her recent manicure. The sky-blue nail polish had seemed like a good choice at the salon, but now in her home office, she wasn't so sure. Not that it mattered, since it would be ruined in less than a day. A hazard of being a chef.

Sara handed over the cell Cass recently purchased to be used just for her social media accounts. She squinted at the screen; the image blurry. Stupid eyesight. She looked around the desk for her glasses. Since turning thirty-five, her eyesight had changed, and she'd finally given in and bought some reading glasses. At least the red frames were cute.

Whoa! And so was the guy in the photos. Really cute. Actually, handsome fit him better. His dark hair was short, with a hint of silver at the temples. The hair on top was longer, but not too long, so probably no man-bun. He had a chiseled jaw, his body lean yet muscular, and his arms—oh, my. She was a pushover when it came to well-defined biceps and forearms.

Her fingers itched to brush through the hunk of hair laying across his forehead in his profile picture. Her stomach did a slow roll as she took in his crooked smile, and the look in his eyes hinted at a fun-loving personality with a dash of comfortable sensuality.

Man, she needed to get laid.

She scrolled further, only to find a total of five pictures. The last one posted about a month ago. She looked through his profile to see how many followers he had. Over a hundred thousand, but he only followed back twenty-seven, including her *Cooking with Love* page. Weird.

"Hot, right?" Sara grinned. "Too bad he hasn't responded."

The initial hit her ego had taken faded a bit. The pictures this guy, Evan Slater, had posted were of him with friends, or maybe family. She went back and read the captions on each post and any comments. Definitely a mix of both. All the pictures were taken during an outside activity. They showed him with a group of guys at a barbeque, at the local beach, then a couple at the Idaho Outlaws stadium watching from the stands. Not one of them could be described as "selfies." Someone else had taken them. A girlfriend, maybe? But that would have been against the rules of the contest. No significant others allowed. The winner had to be single.

So why was Evan following her? And why not respond to the multiple DMs?

"Has he commented on any of my other posts besides the one for the contest?" Cassidy kept her gaze on the cell in her hand. His dark eyes intrigued her. He also seemed familiar, but she knew she'd have remembered him if they'd ever met in real life.

Her gaze flipped back up and she read his profile header: Baseball, beer and the outdoors.

Sara was busy staring and drooling over the mini carbonara quiches Cassidy had just finished making. "Nope. Just the one. Strange, I know. But maybe he thought you were cute and decided to take a chance at winning a date to the charity ball?"

Cassidy had only agreed to the charity ball raffle was because the money would go to The Children's Club, a local center dedicated to low income and disadvantaged youth. Their yearly fundraiser was just a couple days away, and with her history and ties to the center, she'd given back as often as she could.

The director, Rod Davis, had asked her as a personal favor and she couldn't say no. The kids really needed new programs to keep them busy after school, and the building had required a lot of repairs to the heating and cooling system this past year.

"Yeah, or maybe he regretted he won because of the price tag that came along with the date. I'm not letting him off the hook that easy. I'll swing by where he works after we're done filming the next segment." Cassidy took one more look at Evan's picture, then handed the phone back to Sara.

Too bad for Evan if he thought he could get out of his commitment. Instead of enjoying an evening of fine food and mingling with the celebrity crowd the event drew year after year, she'd make sure Evan not only paid the $5,000, but he'd experience the most unpleasant and uncomfortable night possible—without compromising her principals of course.

No one ghosted her, or the kids, and got away with it.

TWO

LOOKING AROUND O'MALLEY'S PUB, Evan couldn't help but feel gratitude toward Maverick Jansen and Luke Garibaldi, his former teammates and owners of the popular restaurant. He'd spent the last year wallowing in self-pity after his career-ending injury. To say baseball had been his life was the understatement of the century. Working at the pub while he got his life together and worked on his next steps was just the tonic he needed.

"Evan, there's a group who'd like a picture." Slade Johansson, the lead bartender and assistant manager, nodded toward the back corner of the pub. Loud cheers rang out, along with the sounds of back slapping and high fives. All the flat screens were streaming the hometown team, the Idaho Outlaws on the road against the LA Knights. It was another night with the typical crowd of die-hard fans.

In his playing days, he would have blown off the request. Not today. He knew his time in the United States Baseball League had been a dream for many, reality for very few, and he was done feeling lost now that it was in the past.

He didn't need this job. With his big-league salary and endorsements, he'd made smart financial decisions. Evan needed the community. A touchstone to keep him from becoming a damn statistic of former athletes who spiraled after leaving a sport that had been all-consuming since his playground days.

"Sure. I'll finish this order and head over." Evan filled the pitcher and called out to Scarlett, one of the servers. "Outlaw Special for table six is up." He pulled chilled mugs from the cooler and added them to the tray, wiped down the counter, then his hands, walking over to the rowdy group cheering on Maverick's latest shutout.

Twenty minutes later, he returned to the bar and went over the receipts for his shift. The pub's new signature microbrew from Hart's Pass Brewery had been a bigger hit than expected.

"Hey, good day, huh?" Slade pulled two drafts and handed them off to Scarlett.

Evan grinned, "Best yet. Oh, and by the way, I talked to Mav and Luke last night about the advertising spot for my podcast with Ken Abrams. They're all in. In fact, they mentioned you'd be perfect for the voiceover, you interested?"

Man, he was looking forward to his next step: *In the Dugout and Beyond with Evan & Ken* on the new streaming platform *XYZ Nation*.

"No joke?" Slade's face split into a smile.

"You know me, dude. This is for real. Think about it. I'm off till Tuesday and—"

"Excuse me. Evan? You're Evan Slater, right?"

Heat slammed into him. It began in his gut, then headed south. Rarely at a loss for words, Evan locked eyes with the furious woman across from him. Fire blazed in her eyes. Her long, dark brown silky hair swaying around her shoulders as she slammed her phone down on the mahogany bar top. She stabbed a finger toward him. "What's your game, Evan? You enter my contest then ghost me?"

Jesus, what the hell was that? Looking over to Slade, Evan raised his eyebrows, seeking help.

"Man, you ghosted Cassidy Love?" Slade shrugged, "I got nothing. Good luck." He walked away to fill an order.

Evan turned his gaze back to the gorgeous woman, who continued to shoot daggers at him with her piercing brown eyes. "Um, Cassidy? Hi, I'm not sure what you think I did... and I haven't got a clue about ghosting you so...uh, how about we go to that table over there and we can figure this out?" He didn't wait for her to respond. Pushing off the bar, he rubbed his hands on his thighs, lifted the bar gate, then guided Cassidy to a table in the back, the furthest empty one he could find.

Turning around in one smooth motion, Evan pulled out a chair for her, then turned back toward where she'd been standing. The look on her face was priceless. He grinned at the flush on her cheeks and her eyes growing wide. He'd caught her checking out his ass. Holding back a laugh, he waved his arm over the seat.

Oh, how the tables had turned. Cassidy's former bluster now replaced by what he hoped was mutual desire, because no matter what brought her to him, something about her had punched him in the gut. It filled him with a sense of, "oh, there you are," plus a zap of recognition that he'd found his person, his other half. Crazy.

Shaken by the feeling, it just wasn't about being turned on or not having sex since his injury last year. No, it was something more, something he needed to find out if it was real and not a fantasy he was creating at the moment.

"Cassidy? Please, have a seat. I'm sure we can figure out what I hope is just a misunderstanding." Evan gave her his best smile and himself an imaginary pat on the back when she straightened her back, returning his smile with a shy one of her own.

She sat down and he took a moment to savor her unique scent of lavender and something he couldn't name before walking around the table and taking his own seat.

"Sorry for the accusation. It's been a day and there's only two more before the charity event, so you not answering my DMs, well my assistant's DMs, kinda threw me. This is a big deal for The Children's Club. Your donation means a lot to me, and when you didn't respond about winning a date with me, it got my hackles up, you know?"

Evan absorbed the rapid-fire download of information. Also, who said hackles anymore? Charmed by her ability to go from pissed to pleasant, he tried to place her. Had they met somewhere, at an after party or maybe here at the pub? But he dismissed both possibilities. If he'd met Cassidy before, there would be no way he'd forget her or her body. His preference in women tended toward short and curvy and she embodied both.

As for not responding to a message, there was no way he'd intentionally snub her. She'd mentioned DMs, so there must have been a definite mix-up because he rarely used his social media accounts and when he did, it was interacting with his friends and family only, no fans. He'd learned a lesson a long time ago not to engage, even if it was a positive reply.

"So, about this date you mentioned. I'm not sure you have the right guy. That's not something I would do." Evan's gut twisted at the frown his words created on her beautiful face. "What I mean is, nothing personal. You're definitely my type, but I don't make a habit of committing to something and not following through." Sweat popped out all over his body. The last thing he wanted to do was chase her off by saying the wrong thing.

Cassidy shook her head and blinked slowly, "Oh, well, I like the sound of that. Okay, so maybe your assistant missed the Instagram message saying you won. It happens. But I'm here because you did win, and I didn't want to have to choose someone else and create a whole thing if you found out." Cassidy placed her phone on the table and began scrolling.

Evan couldn't take his eyes off her. The bright smile she'd flashed him grabbed his heart, wrapping itself around the pounding muscle, then nestled into a space that had been empty, waiting just for her.

Where had she been hiding? Pineville was a growing community, and he'd partied enough his first couple of years with the Outlaws that surely their paths must have crossed. Plus, Slade knew who she was. It tore him up thinking she'd been out there, and they'd just now met.

Cassidy glanced up from her phone. "Do you have a tux? If not, there's still time to rent one and oh, the date comes with a limo, so you won't have to drive. It'll pick you up first, then me, and drive us to the resort on Saturday. Once we arrive, there'll be a red carpet to walk, get our pictures taken, then we go inside to mingle. We'll have dinner, then there's a brief speech by the director. Oh, and a silent auction. There might be dancing, but that's about it. We should be done by ten."

Evan felt like a cement truck had hit him. He couldn't keep up. Her eyes had lit up with excitement as she spoke, and he was a goner. Only registering every fourth or fifth word. His gaze locked on her lips, then over her upper body. Cassidy was petite compared to his six-foot two frame, but she was curvy in all his favorite places. His fingers itched to touch her. He pulled his arms off the table and clenched his hands together to keep from reaching out and embarrassing them both.

His mind raced. Evan didn't want to say anything that would make her upset with him again. When was the last time he'd been so nervous, so turned on by a woman?

"So, that's it. I'll have my assistant email you an itinerary and I'll see you at five-thirty on Saturday, okay? Oh, and thank you for entering the contest." Cassidy paused. She tilted her head, her eyes filled with concern. "Evan? How does that sound?"

Shook that he'd lost himself in her enthusiasm, Evan sat back in his chair. Had he agreed to something? She'd mentioned a contest and Saturday. And a tux. Damn, he didn't wear or own one. "Um, yeah. Sorry, but what contest?"

Cassidy's eyes went wide. "The contest to win a date with me. To The Children's Club annual charity event. You won. You entered on Instagram, pledged $5,000 and were, I mean are the winner. Are you saying you don't want to go with me?"

The look of disappointment on her face slayed him. Evan opened his mouth, but nothing came out.

Instagram? What the hell?

THREE

CASSIDY COULDN'T BELIEVE the roller coaster she'd just been on. First pissed, then stunned and now confused—at the intense reaction she felt toward Evan Slater. But didn't they just clear everything up? Was he playing dumb to get out of going with her?

Last night when she'd called her bestie, Zoe Riordan, she nearly dropped the phone when I told what'd happened. She knew who Evan was. Her brothers were huge baseball fans and their dad, an orthopedic doctor, had recently taken a position with the Outlaw's, so she filled her in on the sexy former Outlaw, encouraging her to google him.

What Cassidy found was encouraging. Evan could certainly afford the required donation, so that couldn't be why he ignored her assistant's messages. But after an hour of scrolling, it had left her unsettled and achy. The shirtless photos she found of him in various advertisements for a sportswear company plus a heartbeat raising body spray commercial had her reaching for her nightstand drawer and its battery-operated content before she could settle down to sleep.

Now that she was sitting across from him, her pulse pounded once more as he politely stared at her, fully clothed. But she knew what his broad shoulders and muscled chest looked like without the Pub's branded shirt covering him up and she found herself slowly losing focus. Somehow, she needed to ignore her body's response to the sexy former USBL player.

Confronting him in person had seemed like such a good idea earlier in the day.

But his *person* was overwhelming—electric. Cassidy had been around attractive men, famous men, but Evan was...she couldn't put her finger on it, but other parts of her body wanted to, and images of his hard body pressed against hers filled her head. She tried to keep herself from squirming in her seat, but he kept staring at her like she was his last meal.

Cassidy held out her hand. "Can I see your phone?" There had to be more to the story than missed messages in Instagram.

"Excuse me?" Evan's eyebrows narrowed, then he chuckled. "You sound like a jealous girlfriend. Trust me, there's nothing on my account that I wouldn't let my mother see."

Hmm, a sense of humor. Cute, but it wasn't getting him off so easily. "I'm serious. Something is going on and I need to figure this out. I've got to get back and set up for my next video shoot. I'm making a spicy sausage and sweet potato burger for this week's video." Her palm shook ever so slightly. "Please?"

Evan stared at her like she'd lost her mind. "Wait. You're a cook?"

"Chef."

"Okay, chef. So, you do videos on Instagram and Slade knows you. And that makes you like an influencer or something."

"Or something. Your phone please?" Cassidy grit her teeth but kept her smile in place. She was beginning to believe he really didn't know who she was.

Evan rubbed his face and let out a sigh. "Yeah, sure." He took his cell from his pocket, unlocked it, and handed it over.

Her nose twitched, picking up the scent of earthy male and notes of citrus. Her stomach took a slow roll, then her breasts tingled as their fingers brushed. Warmth spreading throughout her limbs.

She opened the Instagram app, then his messages. "There. Five messages from me, well from Sara." Handing over the phone, she pointed at the screen. Cassidy hoped he wouldn't deny the evidence. Prayed he wouldn't say no. She really didn't want to choose someone else. She really wanted Evan. Charity date or not.

Cassidy allowed her gaze to roam over Evan's face as he looked at his phone. She looked her fill from his wide shoulders to his muscular arms. He wore a dark blue, form-fitting, long-sleeve shirt with the sleeves rolled up to his elbows. His forearms were dusted with fine hair and the veins popped as he scrolled. She'd never thought herself particularly attracted to ripped guys. But now she found herself fantasizing about running her fingers over those forearms, over his biceps, then onto his rounded shoulders. What would it feel like to be wrapped up in all that steel? Oh, lord she needed to stop this.

Evan lifted his head and his gaze slammed into hers. He caught her checking him out—again. She licked her lips and swallowed, but her mouth had gone dry. His gaze then shifted, locking onto her mouth, and his nostrils flared. Wow, this was not how she saw things going. "Um, so what do you think?"

A flash of something hot entered his eyes. "I think someone got a hold of my phone and entered me in your contest."

Cassidy blinked. Her confidence faltered. "Wait. What?"

"Believe me when I say this, I would remember entering your contest. Hell, I'd bypass it altogether if I'd come across your profile on my own. I'd have figured out another way to meet you."

Evan's intensity rocked her. Were the overwhelming feelings enveloping her since the moment she confronted him a result of her dating desert, or was it him? *Them?* Was he feeling that same instant connection?

He offered one of his large hands. "Cassidy, I didn't enter the contest, but I will go on the date. And I'll get you a check for the donation. You have my promise."

She didn't hesitate. Laying a hand on his, she absorbed his warmth. A zap of electricity igniting a need she immediately knew she couldn't pass up. Cassidy squeezed his hand. "I'll take it." Expecting him to release his hold, her heart thumped as he ran his thumb along the back of her hand.

"Now, tell me about The Children's Club. I get the idea it means more to you than just a place to give money to once a year."

His interest thrilled her. The club meant so much to her. Memories of feeling safe during her teenage years and finding her way through the chaos of a dysfunctional family, then a brief period of homelessness, tied her forever to the mission of The Children's Club. She'd do almost anything to ensure its continued success.

"You have no idea, but if you have half a day, I'd bend your ear off. Let's just say my love for cooking and creating content were born and nurtured there. I honestly don't think I'd be where I am today if it weren't for the club. That's one of the reasons I tracked you down. There was no way I was going to let you back out, and that was before I found out who you really are." Surprised at her confession, she'd never shared so much to someone she'd just met, Cassidy gathered her things and stood.

Evan quickly stood as well and stepped in close. So close, their bodies now inches apart. His heat enveloped her. Cassidy shivered and briefly closed her eyes.

"I think that's awesome. Maybe on our date you can fill me in a bit more?" Evan tucked a loose strand of hair behind her ear.

For a moment, she thought he was going to lean in and kiss her. Wishing for it seemed silly. They'd just met. When he pulled back, a momentary loss overcame her.

Cass sat back, adjusted her blouse, then swung her purse strap over her shoulder. "So, thanks again. I'll see you Saturday." Standing, she did her best not to stumble, but when she made it to the main door, she chanced a look back. Evan was still at the table. His face wore a goofy grin. Her stomach did another slow roll. The live and in-person Evan outdid the two-dimensional version.

If she hadn't been such a staunch disbeliever in fate, she'd almost believed that divine intervention had brought them together. But since she believed in what she could see and touch, maybe this odd Instagram connection was simply random.

Randomness or not, Cassidy was going to make the most of spending time with Evan Slater.

She couldn't wait till Saturday.

FOUR

Two HOURS after leaving O'Malley's and his encounter with Cassidy, Evan couldn't stop thinking about her and replaying their conversation. It'd been forever since his first crush on a girl, but his body's response to the sexy internet chef continued to distract him as if he was a hormonal teen. Cold shower non-withstanding, he found himself ramped up again just thinking about the fire in her eyes when she accused him of ghosting her.

He'd had to google ghosting and her YouTube channel. Starving after watching her whip up dish after dish. But it just wasn't a meal he wanted from her. He wanted a long taste of Cassidy Love, naked and in his bed. Or hers.

The videos gave him a sense of the type of person she was. Sometimes she had guests on the show, and she had an easy, personable way that shone through. Plus, she had a wicked sense of humor. It was clear why she'd become so successful. And then there was the admiration he felt toward her for continuing to give back to those who'd helped her when she was in need and long after most people in her position would have.

What really got him thinking he was crazy was when he found himself in bed that night coming up with topics of discussion. He wanted to find out her goals for the future. Had she ever been married? She looked to be late twenties, so it was a possibility. Maybe she had kids. Did she want to have kids? *Whoa...dial it back, Slater. You just met her.*

What guy worries about this stuff after spending less than an hour with a woman? He needed to get those thoughts out of his head and figure out who got into his phone and tagged him on her Insta contest. Not sure if he wanted to strangle whoever it was for invading his privacy or thank them for bringing her into his life. But either way, he would find out. Tomorrow.

He tossed for a bit, but just before he dropped off to sleep, his mind wandered from thoughts of Cassidy to who could have accessed his Instagram account. Which sent his mind to the barbeque he'd attended a couple of weekends back with most of the Outlaws right before the start of the season. He'd taken a couple of pictures, and at one point, he'd handed his cell off to someone to take a group shot.

Then it hit him who accessed his Instagram. He chuckled and fell asleep thinking of that person and her group of notorious matchmaking friends.

―――――――――

THE DRIVE to Outlaw Stadium was bittersweet for Evan. Less than six months ago, he'd been riding high as a senior member of their team, starting each game at second base, and maintaining a .345 batting average. They'd won the championship a year ago, but during the last play of the game, he'd twisted his knee as he scooped up a ground ball and heard a pop as he made the throw to put the runner out at first.

During the celebration, he was on such a high he ignored the pain, half-heartedly wrapped his knee in ice, then drank what felt like a gallon of champagne. It wasn't until shooting pain woke him the next morning that he acknowledged it and called the team doctor. He worried the x-rays would show a torn meniscus similar to what their catcher, Luke Garibaldi, the co-owner of O'Malley's, had the season before. Luke had recovered and come back, so Evan had some hope to hang on to.

But Evan's wasn't torn, it was shredded. Years of abuse and contorting his body to make plays no one else in the league dared had taken its toll. Surgery wasn't a guarantee, but it was the only option if he wanted another season playing the game he loved.

Rehab hadn't gone well, but he'd faced facts. He'd played his last game in the big league. Struggling to find balance in life after baseball had him turning everyone away and drinking way too much. That was when Maverick had come pounding on his door and put him on blast. And thank God he did. Evan had plenty of money to live on, but he had no game plan for after his playing days. Working part time at O'Malley's had given him something consistent to do and keep in touch with his friends.

It had also led him to his next chapter. Podcasting.

He had a good voice, a deep love for and knowledge of the game, its current players, as well as the experience of having it all pulled away from him. When *XYZ Nation* reached out to him about starting a show with one of the country's most popular sportscasters, Ken Abrams, he jumped on it. Evan believed in hard work and a little bit of luck.

Today, both of those things were the reason he was going to the stadium to discuss interviewing current players with the Outlaws Sr. V.P. of Communications, Kelsey Jansen and one of her top public relations coordinators, Thea Lynch.

Kelsey was married to Maverick, and Evan was friends with both of them. In fact, he'd been to their place a couple of weeks ago. But he was smart enough to realize that he had to treat this meeting, and her, like any other business associate. But that didn't mean he'd hold back all his charm in negotiating a list of players he and Ken wanted for their first season.

Evan cleared security in the lobby and entered the elevator that would take him up to the executive floor. Stepping out, the view never ceased to amaze him. It was breathtaking. Floor to ceiling windows framed the scenery across and behind the stadium. Ponderosa pine and tamaracks dotted the ridge across the Kokanee River, providing a spectacular backdrop to the retractable roof stadium.

"Evan, it's so nice to see you. Kelsey and Thea are in the first conference room to the left. There are refreshments, but if you'd prefer something different, please ask." Lois Campbell was the gatekeeper on the executive floor. And personal assistant to Thomas "TS," Scott, majority owner of the Outlaws.

"I'm sure what's in there is fine. It's great seeing you, Lois." He grinned and followed her directions down the hallway. Both women were seated when he arrived. "Please, no need to stand. I'll grab some water and we can get started."

He'd never met Thea, so Kelsey made the introductions. Noting Thea was about the same age as Cassidy, her build and coloring similar, but his body didn't respond to hers in the same way. Shaking her hand, he felt no sparks, giving no thought to lingering. Pushing the observation away, Evan took a seat, placing his right leg over his left knee. "Thanks for agreeing to meet me on short notice, Kelsey."

"Of course. This is a no brainer for us. We're excited for you, Evan." Kelsey looked to her left. "Thea is going to be your primary contact as far as scheduling the players who agree to appear on your podcast. To be honest, it's going to be harder for you and Ken to pick who you want to interview. Once the word got out, almost all the players let us know they were on board. You might just have a hit on your hands before you even start taping."

Evan's nerves settled upon hearing Kelsey's words. "That's great news. Our plans are to begin taping in about forty-five days. As we get closer, either Ken or I will reach out so we can nail down dates. If this thing takes off, we'll hand the scheduling over to someone on the production side, but till then you're stuck with us."

Thea's cheeks pinkened. The coordinator touched her hair and gave him a bright smile. "That sounds perfect, Evan. If you need anything in the meantime, just give me a call."

He knew when a woman was interested, and Thea was sending all the signals, but again, all he could think of was Cassidy. "Uh, sure." He took a swig of water. "So, Kelsey, you've got a minute?"

Thea excused herself and sent him a quick wave at the door.

"Looks like you've got another admirer. I'm not really surprised. She was pretty excited about this meeting. So, what can I do for you, Evan?"

Confrontation was not something he was good at, but he had to start somewhere. Clearing his throat, he sat up straight. "Have you ever heard of a YouTube chef by the name of Cassidy Love?"

If you'd just met Kelsey, the small lift in her eyebrow may have gone unnoticed. She almost pulled it off, but then she ruined it by grinning, confirming who'd set him up. "Something tells me you're taking her to the charity event tomorrow. Congratulations."

How could he be mad? Knowing that it was a friend who'd pulled this off and not some random hacker made the situation less stressful, and if things worked out tomorrow with Cassidy, then he'd definitely owe Kelsey a favor.

"I should be mad. What if we couldn't stand each other? Or—"

"You don't seem too mad; in fact, I'd say you look like a man in major 'like'. There was this little spark in your eyes when you said her name." Standing, Evan joined her. She looped her arms through his. "I'll walk you to the elevators. I've got another meeting in a few minutes. You're going to have a great time; I just know it. I've met her a few times. She's been busy ever since receiving that YouTube ranking."

Evan chuckled at Kelsey's explanation. It saved him from asking how she knew Cassidy. Kelsey stopped in front of the elevator, pushed the down button, then patted his arm. "Mav and I will be at the event as well, so let's plan on having drinks, okay?"

Evan laughed, "You're buying."

"Of course." Kelsey winked as the elevator door closed.

FIVE

Cassidy wiped her hands on her apron and sighed. Sara hit the stop recording icon and let out a "whoop!"

"You keep getting better and better. And that dish? We need to work on smell o'vision because if your viewers got a sniff, especially those in the male demographic, you'd be raking in the marriage proposals." Sara leaned over the counter and breathed deep. "I love my job. Can I have a bite now?"

Cass laughed at Sara's theatrics and accepted the compliment on her cooking and presentation skills. Sara's comment on marriage proposals, however, had her mind swirling with excitement over the man she met yesterday. Her attraction had been so quick and intense it had her thinking of past relationships, trying to compare if she'd ever felt this way before.

But when she did, a weird and scary thing happened. Evan's face had been superimposed over every other man she'd dated. *What did that mean?*

He had been a big surprise yesterday. A tingly head-to-toe-making-sleep-impossible surprise. How she managed to concentrate on today's complicated recipe and narration while thoughts of Evan's smile and interest in her as a person and not the popular YouTube chef she'd become filled her with a joy she hadn't felt in, well, ever.

Cassidy cleaned up and let Sara go for the day with a to-go carton that had her assistant singing. She still hadn't decided what to wear tomorrow. Her thoughts wouldn't behave and by ten that night she was exhausted from keeping herself from sliding into Evan's DM's. Tomorrow would be soon enough to find out if that connection she felt was real and find out if Evan had felt it, too.

EVAN'S NERVES FELT RAW. He was so wired from a night spent dreaming of Cassidy. He woke with his cock pulsing, images of her under him, crying out his name. He thought about jerking off, but he wanted the real person coming with him. Climbing out of bed, he took one of the longest cold showers since his early twenties, then dressed in his jogging shorts and shoes and went for a run.

He spent most of the morning taking care of minor projects around the house. The tux he rented was being delivered late in the afternoon. He still had hours to kill before the limo was due to pick him up. He needed a distraction, or he was going to give in and stalk Cassidy on social media to find out more about her. But that felt like cheating. Last night, he'd pulled up her Instagram profile and looked at her profile picture, but that was as far as he let himself go.

This strange feeling held him back from scrolling and not just because he rarely looked at anyone's social media accounts, even those of his family and friends. He wanted to know more about Cassidy, but he wanted to hear it from her and not randomly posted photos or comments made by her followers.

Man, he had it bad. But was it just straightforward lust or something more? He jumped at the sound of his cell chiming. He grabbed it off his kitchen's granite counter where it was charging. He had a brief flash of hope that it was Cassidy texting him. He wasn't ashamed to admit that he was disappointed when he saw Ken's name in the message bubble.

Instead of texting Ken back, he decided to call. "Hey, what's up? How'd your meeting with the LA Knights go?" Evan asked before giving his new business partner a chance to say hello.

"Dude, you didn't need to call," Ken admonished. "I wanted to see how your meeting went with Kelsey. I'm sure it was just routine since you've got an automatic in with the Outlaws."

"Yeah, they're on board. It seems we may have more players wanting to be on the podcast than we can handle. In the beginning, anyway." Evan grabbed a beer from the fridge.

"Same with the Knights. In fact, it's been the same with just about every team I've contacted in the last week. I can't wait to get started. How's your recording studio coming?" Ken's excitement filtered through the speaker, mingled with sounds of kids yelling in the background.

"I've got the techs scheduled for the end of next week to do the install in one day, then we can start doing our practice sessions." Evan checked the time again. Two hours to go. "Hey, it sounds like I caught you at a bad time so we can do this on Monday, if that's better for you.

"No worries. Stephanie's here. I still don't think she

trusts me yet to be on my own with the boys. The last time she left me with them, they both ended up with syrup in their hair and on their sheets. Also, did you know three-year-old's shouldn't drink soda?" Ken laughed sarcastically at his parenting misstep.

"Really? How long did it take you to get them settled down and into bed?" Evan chuckled at the image of Ken chasing two caffeinated toddlers around the house.

"They were still up when Stephanie got home. All I can say is, she's a saint when it comes to dealing with me and our boys, and I owe her more spa days than I can count."

At the mention of Ken's wife, Evan began thinking. Quite a few of his friends had married and had kids in the last few years. Were the feelings he had for Cassidy similar to those felt by his buddies when they met their eventual wives? Did other guys have this feeling of being knocked over the head by a woman so soon after meeting them?

What the heck might as well ask. "Hey, Ken, speaking of your better half. When did you know? I mean, that Stephanie was the one?"

Ken's sharp laugh echoed over the line. "You mean when you meet *the woman*, you'd delete every other woman's phone number in your contact list for? Hmm, I'd say it took a good five minutes for the angels to stop singing and the blood to return to my brain after taking a quick detour south. Then my inner voice yelled at me, 'kiss her, you fool and lock her up so no other guy gets his paws on your woman.'"

Stunned at the rawness of Ken's words and how closely Ken's experience mirrored his own, Evan rubbed his chest, then took another drink of beer.

"Slater, you still with me? Who's the woman?"

Ken's question pulled him back into the moment.

"Thanks. I guess that answers my question. She's um, she's a chef. She does this cooking show on YouTube. Her name's Cassidy Love and I just met her. It's the craziest thing, but we're going to this charity event later and I think...well, I can't stop thinking about her. I mean, like every effing minute. It's almost as if—"

"Cupid slung an arrow into your ass and now you're all moony and starry-eyed over Cassidy...hey, wait a minute, is she *the* Cassidy from *Cooking with Love?* Stephanie loves her stuff. I haven't ever watched but Steph raves about her recipes. And I happily stuff my face with the results."

Jeez, how is it everyone around him except him knew who Cassidy was?

"That's her. I won this contest for a date with her, and she came to see me at the pub and *BAM!* I'm all tongue-tied, my dick's at half-mast and I haven't been able to sleep since." Evan rubbed his forehead. He couldn't believe he just dumped all that on Ken.

"Oh, man, sounds like the bug bit you big time. Hey, have fun tonight and let me know next week how it played out, yeah? I'm getting the stink eye, so I gotta go. Good luck, man."

Evan sat holding his cell, staring out the window facing his backyard—for how long he wasn't sure. It's a good thing he set a reminder alarm, otherwise he'd still be sitting there stunned stupid at what was racing through his brain and what he was contemplating for later, after his date with Cassidy.

SIX

CASSIDY SOAKED in her clawfoot tub, inhaling her favorite bath bomb—lavender and ylang-ylang, lost in memories of her ten-year journey from the brink of poverty to a top viewed YouTube chef.

The tub was one of the few luxuries she'd indulged in from the money she earned doing her show. Most of her income went back into the business and marketing, her mortgage on the town house that doubled as her studio, and the retirement nest egg she was building. Losing her mom, then her home at sixteen, had taught her how important it was to prepare for the unexpected.

The Children's Club had been a beacon during her darkest days. A thankfully invested foster family, and the club had saved her from falling down the rabbit hole of negativity or the no-way-out attitude she'd initially been sucked into. This year's charity event meant more to her than she'd imagined.

Very little rocked Cassidy's foundation, but Evan had managed to do just that. And she had one hour left before he arrived for their date. A date she desperately wanted to be real instead of staged for the charity. Not that she wouldn't do anything for The Children's Club, but perhaps that's why she was so nervous. Because now she had someone to share the yearly event with, someone whose opinion mattered.

And now that she was thinking of him again, her body tingled. Cassidy closed her eyes and gave in to the visions that had been plaguing her the entire forty-hours after meeting him. She ran her fingers over her arms and stomach, imagining it was him touching her. When she dipped her hand under the water closer to the top of her thighs, she hesitated. Self-pleasure wasn't new to her. But something made her stop. Imagining wouldn't be enough.

If the night went well, Evan would be touching her just where she needed, wanted, and fantasized about the past two nights.

Stepping out of the tub, she wrapped herself in a fluffy white bath sheet. Cassidy was not ashamed to admit that after her initial google of Evan, she'd done another deep dive last night. Evan didn't have much of a social media presence, which was kinda refreshing. She found some articles on his baseball career and some hot pictures he'd done for a body spray line. Those photos had triggered her dreams and oh, what dreams they were.

Cassidy cleared her thoughts of Evan Slater almost naked and added a dab of perfume behind her ears and pulse points, put on earrings, then stepped back from her full-length mirror. Smoothing down the sides of her dress, she felt both comfortable and sexy. It was a high-necked, long-sleeve dress that ended just about her knees. And it hugged her in all the right places. Stepping into her new low-heeled pumps because she never could pull off high-heeled shoes. The outfit gave her a boost of confidence.

"Well, Cass. You're ready as you're gonna get." She smiled at her reflection, closed her eyes, and made a quick wish. It couldn't hurt.

The sound of the doorbell had her eyes going wide. *Ask and you'll receive.* She grinned at her reflection, grabbed her clutch off the dresser, then swiped the silver and black shawl from the end of her bed and headed downstairs.

She opened her door to Evan mid-knock.

"Whoa, sorry...um...wow, you look...beautiful." Evan lowered his arm, his gaze roaming over Cassidy.

Her pulse had already been pounding on her way to the door, but the fire she saw in his eyes sent it skyrocketing, and she swore her heart skipped. *He's the one.* The whispered words in her head had Cassidy blinking back tears. *Hold it together, Cass.*

"Shall we?" Evan held out his arm.

She floated over the threshold. Accepting his arm, she held on with both hands, then lifted her face and smiled so big her cheeks hurt. He surprised her by leaning down and capturing her lips in a soft, lingering kiss that overloaded her system.

The kiss was over too soon, but not before her ramped-up pulse throbbed between her thighs. Off-balance and at a loss for words, she walked beside him toward the limo parked at the curb.

The driver held open the car door, but Evan paused, then gently held her arm to keep her from getting inside. "Let's take a picture. I'll send it to you, and you can decide later if you want to post it on Instagram."

Cassidy nodded. She felt like she did that a lot with him. They posed, and he took a couple shots, then got in. The ride wasn't very long, but it was nice to have time to settle herself from the unexpected and thrilling kiss.

Flashbulbs greeted them as they exited the limo in front of the red carpet set up at the resort. The charity event was one of the biggest nights in Pineville and there were already local celebrities posing in front of The Children's Club logo along with major donor's names on the step and repeat backdrop.

The business side of her kicked in and she put her roller coaster emotions aside as she and Evan took their turn, deftly avoiding questions fired at them about a romance or Evan's upcoming new podcast.

When they entered the resort and walked down the wide hallway toward the event room, she spotted Rod standing at the check-in table. "Rod, I'd like to introduce Evan Slater my...date for the evening." Cassidy almost said boyfriend. She peeked at Evan to see if he noticed her stumbling over her words, but he'd taken Rod's hand in greeting.

"It's great to meet you, Evan. I'm a big fan of the Outlaw's and of yours. You're definitely missed and so is your batting average. Thanks for attending and supporting The Children's Club." Rod turned to Cassidy and gave her a hug. "I'll see you later."

She felt a shift in the air and wondered at Evan's silence as they circled the room, chatting with a few acquittances before finally finding their table. "Everything okay?" Cassidy asked.

Evan held her concerned gaze a beat before answering. "Is there anything I should know about Rod?"

Confused by his question, she frowned. "No. Can you be more specific?"

Evan looked handsome in his tuxedo, and the scowl he wore made him look dangerous. Handsome and dangerous was a heady combination she wasn't prepared for. Was he jealous of Rod?

"Sure. I get the vibe that Rod would have liked to be your date instead of me."

Cassidy's heart soared. Wow, no one had ever been jealous over her before. It was equal parts ego boost and turn on. She needed to reassure Evan there was no competition where he was concerned and Rod and she had simply grown close over the years with her support of the club, but that's where it ended.

"Well, I can't speak for Rod, but I've never seen him in that way and I'm pretty sure he only sees me as a friend. But it's kinda cute. That you're looking out for me. But you should know, I've recently met this guy who's more my type."

Evan picked up her hand and rubbed circles on her palm. The instant zap of electricity ran through her, increasing her confidence. Would her body react like this every time he touched her?

"Oh, yeah. Tell me about him? Does he have a job? Have you done a background check? You can't be too careful these days. Guys sliding into DMs have become a big problem. Or so I heard."

Cassidy giggled. "Actually, it's the ones who ghost you that you need to watch out for."

He lifted her hand and kissed the back of it, his lips lingering. More shivers. More need. When was the last time a man had turned her on with a simple kiss on her hand? Never, that's when. If she wasn't sure of her feelings for him before, her body was giving off every signal that Evan was special.

"Oh, yeah. I heard that somewhere."

Her cell chimed, interrupting their banter. Reluctantly, she pulled her hand from his to retrieve her cell. Checking the screen, she sighed. "It's time for me to introduce Rod."

The corner of his mouth lifted. "Promise you'll come back?"

Evan's husky tone wound its way through her, warming her from the inside out. "Count on it. It won't take long." Cassidy stood, surprised to see Kelsey and Maverick had joined their table.

Both were watching them intently and Kelsey had a huge grin on her face. "We'll make sure no one tries to steal him, Cass." She winked, then turned to Evan, who seemed a bit flustered.

Cassidy walked up to the front of the room. She didn't quite remember what she said, but the room filled with laughter. Rod joined her and began addressing the crowd of current and potential donors. The club's director had a way of weaving a story, and there was no doubt they'd reach their donation goal for the year.

Walking back to the table, she wondered at Evan's comment about Rod having a romantic interest in her. Hmm, she was positive he didn't, but it'd appeared he didn't have a date. Maybe she knew someone he'd like? She made a mental note to find out Rod's relationship status later.

She caught Evan's gaze on her the closer she drew to him. Dinner was being served, but he paid no attention to the waiter or to anyone else at the table. Another couple had sat down since she'd left, but she didn't recognize them. It didn't matter. The way his eyes blazed, it was as if they were the only two people in the room.

Whew, boy. It was going to be a long evening.

SEVEN

"Invite me in, Cass."

Evan had walked her to her door, his husky rasp curling her toes. The demand made her weep with relief. She'd worried the entire ride home, trying to come up with a casual way of inviting him in.

"Oh, but the driver."

"I told him there was a chance I'd be going in, and if I did, that was his clue to take off."

"Oh." *Stop saying that, Cass.* "Yes, I'd like you to come in."

Evan's smile lit his face, dazzling her. How she unlocked her door without dropping her keys or missing the lock as her hands shook eluded her. She felt his warm body behind her as they walked in. "I can make some coffee or would you rather have—"

Evan pushed the door closed and threw the deadbolt before she lifted her arm.

"You. I'll have you." Evan placed his hands gently on her hips and pulled her into him.

The raw desire in his voice heated her insides, her panties long since damp were now drenched.

She was all in and kicked her shoes off and wound her hands around his neck. He slid his hands down her hips, cupped her bottom, lifting her up. "Evan!" She let out a squeal, wrapping her legs around his waist.

"Which way?"

"Upstairs, second door on the left."

"Once we're upstairs, Cass, I'm not sure I'll be able to slow down. Tell me you want this. Us, naked in your bed." He put his forehead on hers and waited. Their rapid breaths mixing in the air between them.

Not making him wait another second, she lifted his face to hers and she whispered, "Yes."

Evan's lips slammed onto hers, devouring her as he carried her upstairs until he sat her on the bed. She watched in awe as he took in a shaky breath before stepping back. In a blink, his jacket went flying, followed by his tie.

He reached for his belt, and the movement knocked her from her stupor. She stood up, making sure there was just enough room between them to undress.

When his pants dropped and the evidence of his need for her was straining to be freed, she let out a moan at the perfection of the moment. She bent at the waist, grabbed the hem of her dress, then lifted it over her head.

They stood staring, eating each other up. Her breasts ached for his touch, her body demanding to be filled. Evan stepped into her and slowly dragged down the straps of her bra, trailing kisses along her collarbone, into the valley between her breasts, then cupped her flesh and grazed his thumbs over each hard nipple. Cassidy let out a small moan, then sighed.

"So beautiful." Evan captured a nipple, softly sucking, then flicking his tongue across each electrified tip.

Squirming against him, desperate to get closer, Cassidy ran her hands over his corded arms, then lower, brushing the back of her fingers against his rigid cock. "I need this, you inside me." She circled his erection and massaged him, base to tip.

Evan groaned her name. "Stop. Bed, now." He pushed her gently until her knees touched the edge of the bed.

Cassidy took his hand in hers, and he followed, bending a knee to keep from falling. He hovered over her, his arms bracketing either side of her head. His lips met hers in a frenzied kiss. He nudged her legs wider, breaking their kiss to trail his lips down her stomach, to the inner flesh of her thighs, paused a moment, then looked up at her.

"I've been wanting to do this all night." Evan's eyes flashed just before he dipped his head.

The first lick had Cass lifting her hips off the bed, the second tore a low moan from her. Heaven. Wicked heaven. Evan spread his tongue through her slit, wringing his name from her. He feathered his index finger over her clit, then filled her, zeroing in on her g-spot. When she moaned again, he worked her until tiny white lights burst behind her eyelids. "Yes!"

She rolled her hips, seeking more. His lips swirled around her clit, ramping her up higher. Her inner walls clamped on his finger as Evan hummed against her flesh. The increase of pressure on her sensitive bud had Cassidy lifting her hips higher, rocking them against his hand and mouth, chasing the orgasm till it exploded, releasing a thousand sharp pulses at once.

Evan continued to work her, his rhythmic touch prying

a scream from her. *Who was she right now?* More importantly, how was she going to keep him?

Winding down and gulping in deep breaths, she opened her eyes to find Evan easing back, dropping kisses on both her thighs. His hot gaze winding her up again.

"Hold that thought." He scrambled off the bed, picked up his slacks and was back over her before she could question what he meant.

Evan ripped open a condom and sheathed himself. She watched as he took himself in hand and slowly slid into her, pulling out and repeating the movement again and again.

"So wet for me." He dropped his forehead to hers, gliding in and out, then let loose an extended groan before increasing his speed.

She raised her knees and took him deep. Then she grabbed his ass and squeezed his cock. A tingle signaled the beginning of another orgasm.

Evan slammed into her, balls deep. He snaked a hand between them and rubbed her clit, sending her over the edge. "Yes, please." Her voice was raspy and unfamiliar to her ears.

His release quickly followed as he bellowed her name. Their bodies perfectly synced, riding out their orgasms. She hung on tight and rolled her hips, taking everything he gave before collapsing in a heap of happy, boneless satisfaction.

Evan kissed her neck, rolled to his side, keeping her tucked in close. Their heavy breathing filling the space between them. Words weren't necessary. A few moments later, he whispered in her ear, "I'll be right back."

She watched him walk into the bathroom, still in shock over the intensity of their lovemaking. She curled on her side and waited for him to return. Would he want to leave? Did she want him to leave?

Evan strode, or maybe he strutted. Either way, he appeared as satisfied as she felt. He took the washcloth he was holding and gently ran the warmed cotton over her, all the while softly kissing her bruised lips. He slid back into bed, gathered her in his arms, intertwining his legs with hers. Cradling her head, he brushed his fingers over her tangled hair.

Snuggling deep into his chest, Cass sighed. "I'd like you to stay." She held her breath. *Please say yes.*

"I'd like that." Evan covered them with her lightweight comforter, and in moments, they both nodded off.

A warm, hard body in her bed woke her before dawn. Cassidy stretched, her hip bumping into a very awake Evan. She scooted backwards, closer to the front of his body, and wiggled her hips.

He placed a hand on her waist and nuzzled her neck. "Hi."

"Hi back."

They laid still for so long she thought he'd fallen back to sleep.

His hand began moving back and forth between her hip and under her breast. "I have a confession to make. When I asked you to invite me in, I wasn't just referring to your house or your body. And by the way, thank you for that. You, us...it was amazing, Cass." He dropped a kiss behind her ear and lightly squeezed her breast, thrumming a thumb over her nipple.

His touch was driving her mad. She wiggled then turned to face him, swinging a leg over his waist and his now fully awake erection. "It was. Go on." She smiled as he lifted his hips and pressed into her core.

"You're making it kinda hard, literally. It's difficult to think with you straddling me." His hands rested on her hips, holding her still. "Keep that up and I'll be inside you again before I can finish another thought."

"Promises, promises. Okay, I'll be good." She leaned down and kissed him lightly, pressing her breasts into his chest. Almost every inch of their bodies touching the other.

Evan lifted a hand and cupped the side of her face. "I want in your heart, Cassidy Love. You're in mine and there's no way I'm letting you go."

Unexpected moisture pooled in her eyes. She laughed, then cried and laughed again, wiping Evan's face free of her tears. "You were in it that first day," she whispered.

Evan surprised her and flipped her under him, showering her body with kisses.

Taking his time, he placed open mouth kisses along her upper body until she couldn't stand it any longer. "Now. I need you, Evan."

"So demanding, Ms. Love." He chuckled; his lips pressed against the valley between her breasts. "But I like it. Feel free to make this demand anytime we're together. Let me get another condom."

His words offered her hope for something more with him than just tonight. When he crawled back into her bed, Cassidy opened herself, inviting him back into her body and her heart.

THE NEXT MORNING AT BREAKFAST, she checked her Insta as she drank coffee while watching Evan in nothing but his boxer briefs. He was making her scrambled eggs, and she was enjoying the view.

Scrolling through her feed she came across the selfie he'd taken of them last night.

When did he post this?

"Um, Evan?"

"Yeah?" He looked over his shoulder and grinned.

"When did you post this picture of us?" She couldn't help but check out his butt, his back, and his arms. He was quite the morning distraction.

"My eyes are up here, babe."

Laughter filled her kitchen. "Yeah, well, I think you like me looking." She held his gaze as she stood and walked over to him. She wrapped her arms around Evan's waist and snuggled into his back. He covered her hands and stirred the eggs with the other.

"I posted it last night."

"Yeah, but what time? Before or after we—"

"You mean, before or after you invited me in?"

She nodded against his back.

"Before."

Cassidy choked back a sob. Joy filled her. They'd all but said the "L" word. And as crazy as it was to believe, she felt it deep in her soul. It was something she certainly would have never thought possible before she met him. But there you go. When you know, you know.

Under the picture of them on his page was the word "My" followed by a red heart.

It made her heart thump madly for him, and it gave her courage.

"That was pretty confident of you. Must be a leftover from your playing days, huh?"

Evan set the spatula down, switched off the burner, then turned and gathered her tight against him. "Babe, you can call it confidence, kismet, fate or whatever. All I know is I love you and I wanted it out there for all to see."

His declaration should have freaked her out but when it

didn't, when it wrapped around her heart and her head agreed, she hooked a leg around his waist, placed both hands on his face tugging him down as close to her lips without actually touching. "I'm so very glad you ghosted me. I love you, Evan."

Lucky for them, love took no time at all.

EPILOGUE

Six months later

CASSIDY TOOK one more deep breath, then opened her eyes to see her father's smiling face.

"You'll be fine. I won't let you trip." Her father squeezed her hand and placed a kiss on her forehead. "Shall we?"

The music swelled, and the doors to the small church's inner sanctuary opened. It was the perfect setting to exchange their vows in front of their family and friends. She didn't need an extravagant ceremony and reception to mark the day or splash it all over her social media accounts. Her fans would understand and the ones that didn't, well, she wouldn't worry about that now. Today was their day.

With all the changes in her life since the day she and Evan met, the easiest one to make was to pull back on her daily posts. She'd been wanting to have her own restaurant and so she made it her mission to find a location in downtown Pineville.

Like everything else in her life lately, it happened

quickly and *Made with Love*, a small plate and to-go eatery, was set to open in two weeks. They would have gotten married that first month they were together if Evan had his way, but Cass convinced him that with his new podcast, which topped the charts soon after its debut and her new venture needed to get off the ground before they could even think of taking time for a honeymoon.

Plus, once everyone heard about their whirlwind romance, they needed to make time in their schedules to meet each other's family and friends. Evan got a kick out of retelling the story of how they met every chance he got, and once the local media heard about it, things had become crazy.

Cassidy focused on her bridesmaid's, then her maid of honor, Zoe, for a moment because she knew when her gaze fell onto her groom, the waterworks would begin. Typically, not overly emotional, the last couple days with the last-minute fittings and rehearsal last night had proven otherwise.

Now just steps away from Evan. She locked eyes with him, her heart and stomach both slowly rolled and settled, then her toes tingled and reminding her of what he'd whispered to her on the phone last night before they each went to bed, separately. The look she saw in his eyes now confirmed he was remembering.

Taking her soon to be husband's hand, she couldn't wait to fulfil the promise of tonight and all her nights with the man who'd unknowingly ghosted her then made up for it by giving her what she never knew she needed, but wanted for evermore—the love of an Outlaw.

USA TODAY BESTSELLING AUTHOR

L♥VE
at

Second
&
49TH

steamy

A RESCUED BY LOVE: LATER IN LIFE NOVELLA

DEBRA ELISE

ABOUT

Who knew sex got better at almost 50?

Not this widowed soon-to-be-grandma-nana-glamma, whatever.

Patrice Kincaid and Kade Holt are more than friends. Their lives have become intwined by her daughter and his son in marriage and now the upcoming birth of a grand baby.

But neither realized they shared one more thing--a secret crush on the other. And all it took to figure it out was a couple glasses of champagne.

Finding a solution to their ramped-up attraction proved all too easy. Work out the crush in bed--one month of sexy times before grandbaby Holt arrives--then go back to being just friends.

Will their secret, friends-with-benefits arrangement end in heartache, or will the curvy widow and the sexy grandpa take a second chance on happily-ever-after?

This 25k word novella first appeared in the A Season For Love Limited Contemporary Collection in early 2022.

ONE

PATRICE KINCAID WAS GOING to be a grandmother. In two months. She thought she was ready, but at forty-nine, staring down fifty, she was feeling anything but. She didn't consider herself wise or matronly, and she sure as heck didn't want to be called Grandma or Nana.

What she was—unsettled and horny. Yeah, she was horny. The word reminded her of teenage boys snickering during math class in tenth grade, but it fit. Her recent mega-pack battery purchase for her vibrator attested to that fact. Unbelievably, her libido had been resurrected.

Not sure what she could attribute it to since all she heard or overheard from women around her age was the demise of their or their partner's sex drives once they hit the big five-oh, some sooner.

Apparently, her hormones hadn't received the memo. Dreams had plagued her. Specific scenarios starring her longtime friend, Kade Holt. And since he was off-limits, she'd resorted to making up excuses to avoid spending more than a few minutes in his presence. Cowardly? Yeah, but she'd struggled all her life, keeping her facial expressions neutral.

Her dreams had begun right around the time their kids got married. His son Connor to her daughter Reese. And now Reese was pregnant, and she was going to be a... Nanny. Nope, don't like that name either.

Patrice shook her head to clear away thoughts of Kade before walking into her family room. Today was all about planning Reese's baby shower. Pasting a smile on her face, she handed her closest friend, Lois Campbell, a plate of cookies to share with Sophie Grant, an event planner, and friend along who with her assistant Evie Nolan who was also a friend of Reese's, her brother Royce's wife, Amber.

"Okay, let's talk party themes. Reese, have you finally decided on a design or colors for the nursery?" Patrice bit into a lemon shortbread cookie and sighed. She'd decided earlier, after picking up the order from the bakery, that she'd let herself indulge today—no guilt.

After turning forty, she'd taken up yoga to keep her curvy figure from succumbing to middle-aged spread and did her best at portion control with a monthly cheat day. Not as thin as she was in her twenties and thirties, but who was? Patrice felt comfortable in her body. And thanks to good genes, she and Reese were sometimes mistaken for sisters, which boosted her ego the closer she got to fifty.

The group discussed colors and whether Reese should go with a character theme for the nursery. Her daughter was thinking of waiting till after the baby was born to decide since she and Connor were thinking about waiting until the birth to find out if the baby was a boy or girl.

It was pretty much a given that if they had a boy, Connor would want to deck out the room in a baseball theme since he played for the Idaho Outlaws of the United States Baseball League.

Patrice loved Connor like a son. He'd grown up next door and was her son Royce's best friend. Connor's dad, Kade, had been her husband Stephen's best friend, but she had only seen him sporadically over the years since Stephen was killed in a car accident. It wasn't until Reese and Connor had reconnected a couple years ago that Patrice's feelings toward Kade had become more than friendly.

He was six feet of leanly muscled man. At the same age as her, forty-nine, he could easily pass for ten years younger. Kade's eyes were a dreamy blue. His dark blonde hair was liberally sprinkled with silver, and he had a dimpled chin she wanted to explore with her tongue. She shivered at the thought.

Now with their grandchild on the way, she saw him all the time. And it was becoming awkward, at least on her end. She'd always found Kade attractive, but recently the crush she'd put on low simmer had turned into something else.

Her body went on high alert whenever they were together for a family dinner or sitting next to each other when the Outlaws had a home game. She found herself daydreaming about him while at work. It was as if she was a schoolgirl again, although she didn't have to guess what sex was like this time. Instead, she wondered what it would be like with him.

If her recent dreams were any indication, it would be spectacular. And that was saying a lot since what she and Stephen had was okay in the beginning, then turning into an almost non-existent sex life with only the obligatory birthday and anniversary celebration.

She'd married Stephen during their sophomore year at college after discovering she was pregnant. Reese and twin brother Royce had been a handful, and they'd decided two kids were enough. Their marriage had been stable at best, lonely at its worst. It wasn't until she'd become a widow at thirty-five when Stephen had been killed in a car accident did her suspicions pan out—he'd been having an affair the last five years of their marriage.

She'd mourned his death, but more so for her kids. So many wasted years. For both of them.

In the years since, Patrice received plenty of interest from men. But she rarely dated, and when she did, she often stayed in a relationship long after the initial excitement wore off more for companionship and to have a plus one on speed dial.

She'd given up on finding someone who made her heart flutter, her stomach clench the minute he touched her or walked in the room. The last few years, she'd stopped dating altogether and put all her focus on her business and her kids.

But when Kade came back into her life, the realization of why her past relationships fell flat hit her. She chose boring and safe men. And compared to Kade's outgoing personality and the super-sized butterflies that attacked her each time he looked her way, solidified her choice to keep her time around him to a minimum.

They were practically family. She didn't want to chance ruining their friendship or making things awkward between them, especially with a grandchild on the way. So the only time she'd be getting down and dirty with Kade would be in her dreams.

"Mom?" Reese's voice held concern.

"Hmm? What'd I miss? Sorry, I was thinking about work." Patrice adjusted her blouse, then reached for her glass of wine, taking a long sip.

"I was hoping we could have the party here. Would that be okay? The backyard is the perfect setup for the guys to hang out. They can play corn hole or basketball since you still have the half-court from when Royce was obsessed with making the high school team."

Four pairs of eyes landed on her, waiting for a response. Patrice cleared her throat. "A co-ed baby shower? Sure, why not." *Did that mean Kade would be invited?* So much for keeping her distance.

KADE ARRIVED at The Club on Main, his daughter-in-law's restaurant and nightclub in neighboring Coeur d'Alene. The air was crisp, and the trees along the sidewalk still held their multi-colored leaves. He was meeting his son for lunch. The Outlaws had recently lost the USBL play-offs, but Connor was riding the high of soon becoming a father. The team was a talented ball club, and Kade was sure they'd be in the running again next season.

He spotted Connor as soon as he walked in. The hostess recognized him and flashed him a wide smile. She was young enough to be his daughter, but she'd made it known on his last visit she was available. He still hadn't figured out the best way to discourage her.

Kade nodded at her and kept moving. He wasn't dead. She was attractive, but he definitely preferred a woman closer to his age.

His interest lately had been locked on a woman he'd spent years keeping in the friend zone. They'd become close once again when their kids had married. In fact, the past two years had recently become a test he no longer wanted to pass. But he'd always avoided relationships having no interest in getting married again, not after the disastrous relationship with Connor's mom.

Patrice Kincaid had been on his mind lately—a lot. He needed to figure out a way to get her out of his system one way or the other. He just wasn't sure he was willing to put their friendship on the line.

"Hey, Dad. You need to dial down that smile of yours. Tricia has little hearts in her eyes every time you show up." Connor stood and leaned in for a hug.

Kade laughed. "I keep telling you, we're cursed with the Holt mojo. Besides, she knows she's too young for me." He took his seat and picked up the menu.

"*Riiight*. What about that lady you dated a few months back, Linsey, was it?" Connor flagged down a waiter and ordered two drafts.

"She was great, but she was still in love with her ex. I heard last week they got back together and are engaged." Kade rubbed his chin and looked around the restaurant. Reese had spent years improving the business and hiring local chefs. The place was always full, and when the Outlaws had a home game, it was impossible to get a table.

"Hmm. Maybe you should try one of those dating apps." Connor grinned.

"I can find my own dates, thanks. But we're not here to talk about my love life. How's Reese feeling? The doctor find any reason why she's so tired lately?"

Kade watched his son's expression closely. If he were trying to keep something from him, he'd know it. He'd been able to read Connor since he was about five and got caught in his first fib.

Connor held his gaze. "Not yet. I mean, fatigue kinda goes hand in hand with pregnancy. They did another blood test yesterday to check her iron and a few other things. The doc doesn't seem to be too worried, but he wants her to work only part time for now."

Satisfied that his son wasn't holding anything back, although Kade knew Connor was worried as any father-to-be would, Kade held up the beer the waiter just delivered. "Okay. But if there's anything I can do, you'll tell me. Now, here's to passing on the Holt mojo to the next generation."

Connor clinked his mug and chuckled. "What if it's a girl?"

"That's your problem." Kade grinned, set his glass down, and crossed his arms. "Now, let's order. I've got a client meeting after this."

The lunch progressed, with Connor a bit subdued. Probably at the thought of having a daughter. Kade couldn't blame him, although he didn't think raising a girl would be much different. At least not until boys started showing up at the door. And when that happened, he'd do his best to keep the teasing to a minimum. Man, he couldn't wait to be a grandpa.

After lunch, Kade had a few minutes and decided to work off his lunch with a walk down Main to check out the new sports equipment store. Maybe they'd have toddler-size baseball gloves. He'd held off buying anything until after the baby was born, but really, did it matter if they had a boy or girl? Baseball gloves were for everyone.

Whistling, he slid his hands inside his slack's pockets and waited for the light to change. A couple of young moms joined him, each with a stroller and one with a toddler in a fancy backpack carrier on her back. He took off his sunglasses and made a funny face at the child in the backpack. The little girl had ruby red cheeks and a pink hat covering her dark curls. She giggled and shyly waved at him.

Squealing tires and shouts laced with warning filled the

air. Kade whipped his head to the left. A dark shape filled his vision. He raised his arms, grabbed the woman closest to him, then latched onto her stroller, pulling them all backward. The car's front end jumped the curb grazed the light pole, narrowly missing their group.

The first mom stumbled and fell back on him. He caught her with one hand and thrust his right arm across the second mom's stroller, preventing it from running into the street. Cries rang out. Pounding footsteps headed their way.

The combined weight and momentum of his actions pushed him down. Kade lost his footing as time slowed. Faces flashed in his mind just as his head bounced on the pavement, and everything went black.

"Mister. Mister, please wake up." A female voice called out to him. For a moment, he thought he was still home, in bed. He heard shouts and sirens in the distance and came to with two women staring down at him, babies bawling in their arms.

"Oh, thank god. How many fingers do you see?" The woman with the toddler on her back held up three fingers.

"Um...ahem...three. Yeah, three." His voice sounded thick and faraway.

"Okay, ladies. Please step back. We'll check him out. Hey, Roger. Come get these women and their kids to the second ambulance and check them over."

Kade tried to sit up. He made it, barely, after bracing his arm on the pavement.

"Whoa. Take your time, sir. We need to do a few things before you stand, okay?"

"Yeah—yeah. Okay." Kade lifted a hand to the back of his head and drew it back. A small amount of blood laced his fingertips.

"It looks like a small cut. Can you tell me your name, sir?"

A paramedic began checking his eyes with a flashlight. He looked like a college student. Wavy black hair fell on the kid's forehead as he bent down into his bag and pulled out a stethoscope.

"Kade Holt. I live in Pineville. I just had lunch with my son. I need to call my son."

"You bet in just a second. First, we need to get you checked out, Mr. Holt. Make sure you don't have a concussion. Gotta make sure the town's newest hero is taken care of."

"Hero? Yeah, no. Anyone would have done what I did." Kade shook off the hero label from the Doogie Howser-looking paramedic and regretted the movement.

Kade sat still and let the paramedic do his job. He accepted endless thank-you's from the women after they were checked out and deemed well enough to go home without a visit to the hospital. He narrowly missed a trip as well after they determined he didn't have a concussion and covered the minor scrape on his head with a butterfly bandage.

Kade touched the back of his head. "It's my turn to thank you. I didn't catch your name."

The paramedic finished putting his equipment back in the ambulance, smiled, and held out his hand. "Rex Stafford, sir. And my partner, Austin James. We need to get back in rotation. Make sure to call your son and if you have any dizziness or headaches, definitely call your doctor, okay?" Rex gave Kade a quick salute and walked to the front of the vehicle. Kade assured him he would and looked around for the women and their kids. But they were gone, already picked up by friends or family, hopefully.

Rex and his partner had already taken off when Kade thought about offering them tickets to an Outlaw's game. Both men had been professional and a huge help to get the kids calmed down. They definitely deserved a trip to an Outlaws game.

Kade pulled out his cell and noted their names for later. Deciding against calling Connor since he felt fine to drive, he texted his client to let him know what happened and that he'd reschedule soon.

Once home, he sat on his sofa, put his feet up, and drank a gallon of water, all while puzzling over why the first face that had flashed in his head after the accident hadn't been Connor's.

It had been Patrice's.

TWO

"PATRICE, SIT DOWN. ENJOY THE PARTY." Lois wrapped an arm around her and guided them to the couch.

The "inside" baby shower games had finished. Most of the guests had wandered out to the back patio, where several rounds of corn hole had begun. The summer temps had held, the late September sun had drawn everyone outside to watch the men, and now a few of the wives tossed bean bags and trade good-natured smack talk.

Connor was holding court, and Reese, with her seven and half month baby belly, sat on the covered patio with her friends watching the games and heckled their husbands, boyfriends, and the one man Patrice had been avoiding since he walked through her door today. Kade Holt.

She'd heard about the accident and his heroic efforts from Reese, but she still hadn't drummed up the courage to approach him and find out how he was feeling. Now that she'd been thinking of him naked, she worried he'd be able to read it on her face somehow as she tried to focus on a conversation and not how she wanted his lips on hers.

"Patrice? Hey, what are you thinking about? You've been awfully quiet."

Lois Campbell was one of her closest friends. She worked for TS Scott, the owner of the Outlaws, was in her early fifties, divorced, and currently unattached. Maybe it was time she told her about the crush she had on Kade and figure out what she should do about it.

"Patrice? Hey!" Lois leaned over and put her hand to her forehead. "You feeling okay?

Laughing, she waved off her friend's theatrics and sighed. "I'm fine. I just have a ton of things on my mind." She shifted on the outdoor couch. "Is this better? You have my full attention."

Lois tucked a piece of her platinum blonde hair behind an ear and gave Patrice a look only a good friend could get away with. Lois turned and looked in the direction Patrice had just been staring and smirked. "You really want to know what I think? I think you need to get laid. And for that matter, I do too. But we're talking about you right now."

Patrice grabbed a throw pillow and hugged it to her chest. "You're not wrong. But I'm not really into one-night stands. And finding someone at my age—"

"Stop right there. You and I are close enough in age that I can say that's bull-pucky. And seeing the next generation finding their happily ever-after's, making babies, etc., has spurred me on. You and I need to stop waiting for a man to ask us out. And for that matter, we need to start having our girls' nights again. We need to get out there and find someone. We're far from assisted living or turning into snow-birds. We're attractive and we have a lot of life left to live, dammit. We should also have fun with a man who trips all our buttons. We've both shut ourselves off from relationships for too long."

Patrice busted out a laugh. "Bull-pucky? I've heard my sainted grandmother use more explicit language, Lo." Her good friend gave her a wink and settled deeper into the sofa.

Lois' words made her think about the many excuses she made over the years. Why she'd remained single for so long. Patrice had buried her grief and guilt at never having truly loved her husband. Then after his death, she had to work two jobs and learn coupon-clipping while raising her twins, Royce and Reese. She'd been too tired back then to put her all into a relationship.

"Let's make a pact, Patrice. From today forward, let's swear we'll put ourselves first. Over our jobs, our kids, our grown kids, by the way, and any outside forces demanding our time. And do what makes us happy, fulfilled, whatever. And take a chance on finding love again. Or at the very least, some really good sex."

Patrice wouldn't mind the sex. But love? It had not been a priority of hers. Her friends had thought she'd had the perfect life with Stephen. Getting pregnant at nineteen hadn't been one of her life goals, but once Reese and Royce were born, she'd instantly formed a new goal: best mom ever. And bless his soul, she'd come to terms a long time ago that she'd never loved her husband.

And now she was going to be a Granny, a Gigi, maybe a Nana, or a Glamma. Reese had sprung that last one on her when they'd gone breast pump shopping. Her daughter had been campaigning hard for Glamma ever since, and Patrice kind of liked it.

But she didn't feel old enough to be any of those. She didn't knit or crochet and sucked at scrapbooking. But she could plan parties, run her estate furniture business and volunteer better than when she'd been in her thirties when money had been tight and her sex life non-existent.

Laughter filled the air, and deep male voices rang out from the direction of an intense playoff to declare the winners of cornhole. Her son-in-law, Connor, and at least three traded smack talk on their way back into the house. "Okay, old man, but next time I'm going first. Then we'll see who has the better aim."

Patrice had set up yard games for the men to participate in while the ladies had *ooh'd* and *aah'd* over the baby gifts. But now that the games were over, it was time for cake. Then the grand gender reveal since Connor had talked Reese into finding out what they were having. She could honestly say it didn't matter if they had a boy or a girl. She just wanted a healthy baby to spoil then send home.

She watched as Lois stood, smoothed her A-line yellow skirt, and straightened her white linen blouse with a high starched collar. The look flattered her, and Patrice had always envied Lo's style. Her friend was always well put together in an age-defying way. She needed to up her game in the wardrobe department if she and Lois were going to be serious about finding men. Her clothes tended toward either waist-length linen jackets and matching skirts or practical and comfortable slacks and blouses when she was out scouting estate sales.

There was only a larger pool of eligible men within their age bracket. Reese had been badgering her lately to set up a profile on one of those online dating apps for "sexy silvers," and she'd put her off with excuse after excuse. Maybe she needed to rethink that offer.

"I'm going inside to get the cake. Can you make the announcement and have everyone gather over by Reese?" Patrice walked into the kitchen just as the reason she kept turning down her daughter's help to set up a profile just walked through the kitchen with Connor.

Pasting a smile on her face, "Hey there, we're ready for the reveal. I'm getting the cake and will be right out."

Kade paused and returned her smile, and her stomach flipped, then flopped. She felt warmth creep up her neck. Tongue-tied, she cleared her throat, "No...uh, I've got it. I'll be right out." She waved them both outside, then hustled over to the sink and filled a glass with water.

After a couple sips, she set the glass down and felt her cheeks. Yup, flushed. Damn. *Calm down, silly. He's the same Kade you've known for years.* And just as handsome and sexy as the day she'd met him. Get it together, Patrice.

She ran her hands through her hair and grabbed some lip gloss from the catch-all drawer next to the fridge. She looked around to make sure no one caught her freshening up. After a couple swipes of the raspberry gloss, she took out the sheet cake and walked through the sliders onto her back patio.

Scanning the area, she nodded at Reese, who was now sitting in the new rocker-glider Connor had assembled for her that morning. "Alright, everyone, let's have cake."

Since returning to Pineville several years ago, Reese had reconnected with a few friends and made some new ones. They were all here with their husbands and boyfriends. The group was pretty tight as most of them were either players for the Idaho Outlaws, a United States Baseball team, or connected in some fashion, including the owners to the team psychiatrist.

They were a diverse group, and Patrice loved spending time with them. She was lucky that her kids liked to hang out with her, plus they had no issues sharing their friends with her. Lois was her closest friend and the main owner's, TS Scott, secretary. The front office had done quite a bit of hiring lately, and maybe there would be someone that piqued Lois' interest. She'd have to quiz Noel, TS' wife, later.

"Connor, could you round up the men, so they each get some cake, please?" She smiled at her son-in-law and handed him two plates of cake. It had been somewhat of a surprise that he and Reese had reconnected, but now she couldn't think of anyone better for her daughter.

"Sure, Patrice. I'll get that lazy son of yours to help me out." Connor's blue eyes twinkled as he ducked and avoided an empty plastic cup as it sailed over his head.

"Don't think because you're having a kid with my sister that I won't mess you up, Connor." Royce reached out, grabbed his brother-in-law around the neck, and clapped him on the chest.

Royce's wife, Amber, stepped up and dragged her husband away. "C'mon, honey. He gets a pass for the day. You two can meet behind the schoolhouse tomorrow." She winked at Patrice and led him to their table next to Reese.

Connor followed the couple and stopped next to Reese. "Could I have everyone's attention?" He looked around the yard until everyone gathered had quieted. "Dad, Patrice, could you two stand over here? We'd like your help with this."

Patrice shared a surprised look with Kade. She stood on shaky legs and walked over to Connor and Reese, stopping next to Kade. They brushed arms. She froze at the contact and smiled up at him, then focused her gaze on her daughter. Reese cradled her stomach, excitement lighting up her face.

Connor reached into his back pocket, produced an envelope, and held it out. "Patrice, would you do the honors?"

Her hands shaking, she took it and quickly wiped a tear from her eye. "You sure you want me to be the first to know?"

Both Connor and Reese nodded their heads.

Taking in a deep breath, she ripped the edge off and pulled out a card. "It's a girl!"

Cheers and clapping erupted. Connor leaned down to help Reese out of the glider. They cried and kissed. Patrice held tight onto the card and grabbed Kade's arm. He wound it around her waist and hugged her. Sparks erupted everywhere he touched.

"Congratulations, Grandma." Kade grinned.

"Congratulations, Grandpa," Patrice whispered, tears rolling down her cheeks.

Connor wiped his eyes and cleared his throat. "Okay, Dad. Here's yours." He handed Kade an identical envelope.

Shocked silence lasted for all of two seconds before exclamations of "No way," "Twins?" And Reese's shout of, "Surprise!" filled the air.

Patrice swayed. Kade's arm tightened, and she sank into the comfort he offered. Dazed, she laugh-cried and looked up into Kade's teary eyes. "Go on."

Kade held Patrice's gaze, perhaps a moment longer than necessary, like they were an actual couple. Long enough to set her pulse pounding. Could he sense her reaction to him? He winked, then looked down at the envelope Connor had thrust into his hands. She noticed a slight shake as he tore into it. "It's a boy!"

Pink and blue confetti sprayed from well-hidden paper cannons, fluttering down on the ecstatic group. Hugs and kisses were offered all around. In shock, Patrice stayed rooted to her spot until Reese came up, and they embraced.

Laughing and crying, Reese managed to get out, "Surprise, Glamma! Can you believe I'm having twins?"

Oh, boy, were they going to have their hands full.

THREE

KADE MADE a final round in the backyard, picking up bits of confetti, stray paper plates, and plastic champagne flutes. He stepped onto the half-court and stood still, staring at the basketball hoop. Memories of playing with Connor and Royce flashed briefly but were swiftly replaced with him lifting first one toddler, then a second. Chubby hands wrapped around a ball straining to reach the rim.

Two babies. A boy and a girl. He'd been grappling with Connor becoming a father, not because Kade didn't think his son was ready, but he wasn't quite prepared to be a grandfather. He didn't feel or hell act old enough. He remembered his grandfather. Gnarled hands, a smoker's cough, and stooped over. His gait had always stood out to him whenever his grandparents had visited from Finland.

He'd definitely taken better care of himself than his grandfather and his dad. He ran and lifted weights regularly, and when he looked in the mirror every morning, he was happy with the image reflected. But did he see himself as a grandpa? Not yet.

His sex drive may not be what it once was, but it was there, and his morning wood was pretty consistent. Realizing how he looked and felt wasn't the measure of being a grandfather, it still took the wind out of his sails, thinking people would now only view him as one.

Kade was far from ready for a rocking chair, especially if his reaction to Patrice as of late was any indication. Cold showers had become the norm after spending any amount of time around her. He'd always been attracted to Patrice, but out of respect for Stephen before his death, then for his memory after Kade kept had kept his thoughts and his hands in check.

Her laugh was infectious, she had a quick wit, and they had spent a lot of time talking about everything from sports, her business, his business, and their shared worry over uncontrolled growth in Pineville.

On the flip side, his hands itched whenever they were together. She'd recently let her grow out, and he wanted to wrap his hands in it, back her up against a wall, and devour her wine-red lips till they both ran out of air.

Kade let out a low growl and walked back toward the house. He was just buzzed enough from the celebratory glasses of champagne to march into the kitchen, where Patrice put the serving dishes away and put his thoughts into action.

Why the hell not? They were adults. He'd caught her checking him out more than once. They had chemistry and were single. So what if their kids were married to each other. It proved that the men in his family had great taste in women. He snort-laughed at his pep talk and closed the garbage bag before he entered through the back door.

The sight that greeted him halted him in his tracks. Music blared from hidden speakers. Patrice's back was to him as she stood at the sink belting out the chorus to *Miss you Much* by Janet Jackson. Her hips swaying locked him in place. Blood pooled in his groin, his cock straining behind his zipper.

Patrice surprised him as she dipped down, then right back up, hips still swaying as she ran her hands through her hair. *Sweet Jesus.*

Kade set the bag down, leaned against the wall, folded his arms across his chest, and took her in. He couldn't remember seeing her this loose and happy. Perhaps never. She was always the busy bee organizer and rarely let her hair down as she did now. Or maybe she did only it when alone. He'd like to change that.

"Hey, Beautiful."

Patrice let out a squeak and whirled around, gripping the granite counter behind her. At some point, she'd pulled her pretty blouse from the waistband of her slacks with the top two buttons undone. The lace from her bra and the top of her breasts peeked out, ramping him up more.

Kade held out his hands. "Whoa. It's just me." He took in her shocked expression, flushed face, and wild eyes.

"Kade. I thought everyone had left. Wha...what are you still doing here?" She brushed her hair off her face and straightened her blouse.

His gaze followed her movements, resting on her nipples straining against the thin fabric. He groaned. He needed to figure out a way to get his hands on her.

"Yeah, um, I made a round in the back, picked up what I could see." He nodded his head at the bag at his feet. "I didn't realize everyone else had already gone."

They stood staring at each other, Patrice's breathing still fast, the front of his jeans getting tighter.

"That's... so...nice of you." She moved toward him at the

same time he picked up the garbage bag. He eyed an open bottle of champagne on the counter.

"I'll take it out to the garage. Give me a second, then you and I can toast to our grandchildren. We didn't have a chance earlier." Kade left the kitchen before she could say no. She was still standing in the same spot when he returned, breathing heavily.

He washed his hands at the sink and looked through her cabinets for champagne flutes, crystal not the plastic ones used earlier for the party. He grabbed two and the bottle and placed them on the island a foot away from where she stood, watching his every move.

"You really do look beautiful. No one would guess you were going to be a grandma soon." He grinned and poured them each a glass and handed her one.

"To Reese, Connor, and two healthy babies. And to us." He lifted his glass and touched the edge of hers.

Patrice hadn't made eye contact since after the first moment, she turned to find him holding the garbage bag. It should worry him, but he wasn't going to pass up this opportunity. They each took a sip of the warm liquid. Patrice twisted the stem between her fingers and shyly looked up at him. Her smile warmed him more than the champagne ever could.

"Why to us?" She set the glass down. Her movements slow, she half turned toward him, leaning her hip against the counter.

Kade set down his glass and stepped as close to Patrice as possible without touching her. Her face tipped back at his movement, their gazes locked, and he waited.

Waited for her to say something. Anything.

To step away from him. To show any indication that she

didn't understand or want what was happening between them. The instant crazy attraction. The need to touch, explore, and discover how hot it could be between them.

Her gaze dropped to his lips, and his breathing sped up to match hers.

"You had your chance," Kade whispered.

"For what?"

"To say no." His voice was thick and husky to his own ears. He waited another beat, then leaned in and captured her full lips in a kiss guaranteed to haunt his dreams for months to come.

―――――

ZAPS OF ELECTRICITY ran through Patrice as she held Kade's desire-filled gaze as his head came down and his lips caressed hers, soft, searching. She opened for him and let out a moan. He tasted tart and sweet from the wine, and she wanted her body wrapped around his and never wanted to let go. Kade Holt wanted her.

Frustration overtook her when Kade didn't deepen the kiss. Was he deliberately driving her mad? She wanted more. Harder. Deeper. She stopped thinking and acted. Patrice cupped his face, pulled him as close to her as she could, and let him in.

Kade let out a low groan, grasped her hips, and pulled her into his impressive erection. He quickly took control of their kiss. It was perfect. He was perfect. And she wanted to climb up and hang on for more.

Gasping for breath, they broke apart. Kade held her close with one hand and cradled her face with the other. He looked down between them and grinned.

She followed his gaze and found both her hands had tunneled under his shirt, stroking his abs. Patrice felt her face heat and pulled away.

She touched her swollen lips. "That was—"

"It was." Kade held her gaze. "It can be more. Do you want more?"

The kiss was everything she'd wanted in a kiss. He was everything she wanted in a man, and she needed to think, to cool down. Moving to the sink, she poured some water and gulped it down.

She felt his heat before he touched her. His hands wound around her waist, and he nuzzled her neck. Butterflies erupted in her belly, and she rubbed herself against his front. Oh, my. Could she follow through? Was she willing to sacrifice their friendship for...for what, one night of great sex?

Because she knew it would be great. No one who kissed like that was not-not great in bed.

And she wanted great. She wanted fireworks and multiple orgasms, and she wanted Kade Holt.

But.

And there was always a but.

They were going to be grandparents. Their kids were married, and what if this was just an itch that needed to be scratched. What if she wanted more, and he didn't? What if he wanted more?

"I can feel your brain worrying, Patrice."

Kade's breath tickled against her ear before he bit the lobe and sucked it into his mouth, soothing the sting.

"I think this attraction between us has always been there, and it's been building the last year. Maybe we just take it a day at a time, see where it goes. Maybe we just need to feast on each other, get it out of our system." Kade's right hand ran down her arm to her waist and hovered, waiting.

His raspy voice set off goosebumps along the nape of her neck, along her shoulders, and down her spine.

"It's a bit weird, don't you think? This. Us. Our kids are married. This could go all sorts of wrong, Kade." Patrice took in a slow breath and let it out. Then another. It didn't do anything to lessen her desire. Or her need for him to keep touching her, touching her where she desperately needed.

"It's only weird if we let it. But I'm not going to push you, Patrice. You mean too much to me." Kade took his hand away from her waist and stepped back.

Patrice immediately missed his heat and the promise of experiencing what it could be like between them. Taking a fortifying breath, she turned and faced him.

"How about we sleep on it?" He chuckled at her wide-eyed reaction. "Separately." Kade smiled, then ran a hand down his face.

"I'm going to be real with you. This thing I feel for you has always been there. But, it's been ramping up the more time we've spent together. And by your reaction just now, well yeah. I know it might be awkward around the kids, but Patrice...."

He took her hand and rubbed his thumb on the soft pad of her palm, and instant electricity ran up her arm, spread across her chest, and joined the butterflies still flapping madly in her stomach.

"Maybe all we need is a night together, work out this crazy connection, and—"

"You're crazy. If you think I'm going to sleep with you, then go back to just being friends. Especially with our grandbabies almost here. We're not kids anymore, Kade. If

I'm going to have one night with someone, it's not going to be with someone I know." Self-preservation had finally kicked in. However, she regretted the words as soon as she uttered them.

Kade's smile disappeared, his eyes darkened as he squinted. The muscles in his jaw became more prominent as he pursed his lips together.

She looked down at his hands gripping the edge of the granite countertop, his knuckles white. Was the thought of her with someone else the cause of his sudden mood change? It thrilled her to think he didn't want her to be with anyone but him.

"I know you haven't had a relationship in a while, Patrice. So, if it's just sex you want, I'm offering. No strings. To be honest, I'm not looking for any type of long-term commitment. I think if either one of us wanted to be in a relationship or even marriage, we'd have found that by now. Just think about it, okay?"

She met Kade's intense gaze and lost herself in the desire she found. Desire for her.

"I—I admit there's this undeniable attraction, and it's tempting to test it out, but how can you be so sure your idea would work? That it wouldn't mess up our friendship?" Was she really having this conversation in the middle of her kitchen with the guy who was always there for her in the early days after Stephen's death, after the discovery he had a mistress?

Hell, he'd been the star of her naughtiest dreams for years, so why was she hesitating?

Life was short.

They wanted each other.

She was almost fifty dammit, and she'd never done one wild thing in her whole life.

"Patrice? Just think about it, okay? I called a rideshare, and it's here. I'll call you tomorrow." Kade pulled her close, dropped a quick kiss on her lips, and left.

Cold and shivering from the loss of his heat, she touched her lips—bruised and still tingling—why the hell did she let him leave?

FOUR

PATRICE SPENT the following morning scrubbing her bathroom. Whenever she'd had a hard decision to make, she cleaned until her arms ached and an answer appeared. An hour later, she stepped from her sparkling clean shower, no closer to solving her Kade problem. She moved on to the kitchen and took out the mop.

She couldn't shake the desire in his eyes or the way his touch ignited a heated flush all over her body last night. One more glass of champagne, and she wasn't so sure that he wouldn't have been in her bed this morning, her body sweetly sore from something other than scrubbing floors.

An instant image of Kade's lips on her skin brought a tingle between her thighs. That man knew how to kiss, and she wondered how those soft lips would feel on other parts of her body. Her nipples hardened at the thought of him lavishing them with attention.

How long had it been since she had sex? Really good sex? So long she couldn't remember. But that didn't mean she should take Kade up on his offer. Not sure she could handle the complication of hooking up with her daughter's father-in-law no matter how much her body screamed: "do it!"

Her phone rang, and she jumped. Patrice covered her heart, set the mop up against the wall, and grabbed the phone, secretly hoping it was Kade.

It was Sophie.

Suppressing her disappointment, she answered. "Hey, there."

"Hi. So I need a favor. Grant wants me to go to dinner with a business acquaintance this Friday, but I don't want to be sitting there bored out of my mind. I checked him out on LinkedIn, and he's a solid eight and has a beard. Heck, he's probably a nine in person. And he's single. Please say you'll come with us?"

That was Sophie. Not one to beat around the bush. The timing was funny, considering her internal debate. Maybe she should test herself. See if someone else could create the same anticipation as Kade.

"That's what I love about you, Sophie. You don't waste time. A beard, huh? Not my usual thing."

Patrice debated. Reese would need her soon once the twins arrived, and then she wouldn't have time for anything more than a hookup, which she'd never done. But maybe friend-with-benefits?

"So, maybe it could be? Besides, it's not one of those bushy ones. It's nicely trimmed. What's that term for older hot guys...silver fox? He's one of those. C'mon, say you'll go with us? You're too young to be sitting home alone. It's not like you meet single guys at your shop, and you hardly ever go out. I've vetted this guy, so it's not like he's not some creepy dude hitting on you in a bar." Sophie chuckled.

"Like I go to bars." Patrice shot back. "How old is he?"

A low "yes" sounded over the line, and Patrice rolled her eyes.

"He's fifty-five, and he's fit. And he's a doctor. The team just hired him as their orthopedic surgeon. He owned a practice, but he was looking to sell it and work less, so if you two hit it off, he'll have time to date."

Whoa. Too fast. "I don't want a relationship right now, Sophie. He's not expecting you to set him up on a date, is he?"

Silence. Then Noah, Sophie, and Grant's two-year-old son's demand for attention filtered through the phone.

Patrice groaned. "So this is a set-up?"

"Well, kind of. But no pressure, okay. Grant's going to tell him that you and I already had plans together, so instead of breaking them, I'm bringing you to dinner. Please say yes. If nothing else, we all have a nice dinner. We're going to the new steakhouse on Lakeside."

What was one dinner? She had one more year till the big five-O, and she'd dated little in the last five years as her estate sale business took off. Plus, it would not only get Sophie off her back, but she'd also be able to use this "date" as an excuse with her kids the next time they complained she was alone.

Kade's handsome face flashed in her mind again. She closed her eyes. As tempting as he was last night, she didn't want to risk their friendship, right?

"What time on Friday."

KADE SPENT Sunday morning ignoring the devil on his shoulder, egging him on to drive over to Patrice's house, toss her over his shoulder and lock them in her bedroom.

Instead, he did more research on his latest client's stock portfolio. Working from home suited him, but work was always there. He snapped shut his laptop, deciding he needed a run to work off the sexual frustration he couldn't shake.

He wound his way through the city park, leaves crunched under his shoes as classic rock played on his wireless headphones. He spied a group of young moms with their kids at the fenced-off playground halfway through the run. Toddlers squealed while being pushed on the swings. He slowed his pace, noticing a woman lift her baby from a stroller, bringing the infant in for a snuggle.

He stopped and kept them in his peripheral as he walked over to a bench and adjusted the laces on his right shoe. The beauty of the scene caught him off guard. He never considered himself sentimental, but with grandparenthood looming, he found himself noticing kids and babies on TV commercials or, like today, out and about in the real world.

Kade stood as long as he dared, watching the mother smile and coo to her baby. He rubbed his chest and walked off. The woman had Reese's coloring, and it wasn't hard to imagine his daughter-in-law holding a baby. And there were two of them. After imagining what his grandchildren would look like, his second thought had been wanting to share with Patrice what he'd witnessed. Surprised at his sudden sentimentality, he wondered if other men about to become a grandfather also had these feelings.

Shaking his head, he turned from the sweet moment and retraced his route, heading home.

He worked out an idea as he ran. How did he approach Patrice without seeming desperate to get in her pants?

Increasing his speed, he made it back to his townhouse quicker than it took him to reach the park.

After Connor's mom had passed a couple of years after their divorce, his son had moved in with him after living in Chicago. Kade bought a house in the suburbs of Pineville next to Patrice and Stephen. Their kids were the same age, and Connor and Royce became best friends. And he quickly realized he was attracted to Patrice. But he pushed his feelings for her aside and dated casually, never finding anyone who tempted him to remarry.

Once Connor took off for college, it made more sense for him to move into town. Their home had been meant for a growing family. Not a single man who had the hots for his next-door neighbor.

Now he wished he hadn't wasted so much time keeping her in the friend zone. He stripped and showered in record time, then debated on texting her first or head over and surprise her with his idea of shopping for a double stroller. They would have something to do and talk about other than his offer. Plus, it would give them both a chance to banish any of the awkwardness of admitting they wanted to jump each other's bones twenty-plus years after becoming friends.

Kade grabbed his keys on the way out the door. Before he reached his car, his cell rang. Damn it. He looked at the screen briefly, intent on sending it to voicemail, but the caller was his newest client and long-time friend. He got in the car and answered the call on speaker. "Hey, Adam."

"Kade, am I catching you at a bad time?"

Never one to lie to his friends, Kade instead glossed over the truth. "Just on my way to do a couple of errands. What's up?" He pulled out of his garage and headed toward Patrice's house.

"I just wanted to run something by you. It's official, and I'm the Outlaws official ortho. Grant has invited me out to dinner with his wife this Friday to celebrate." Adam said.

"Congrats, man. I'm happy for you. Where are you going? You need a date?" Kade chuckled. He knew Adam had been approached for the position and was just waiting to accept after he finalized the sale of his orthopedic practice.

"You're not far off. Actually, that's part of the reason I'm calling. I wanted to check on something with you before I go. I just talked to Grant, and he says his wife invited one of her friends to go with us. Patrice Kincaid."

Kade checked traffic and pulled off the road and into a parking lot. *What the hell?* He picked up his cell, took it off speaker mode, and cradled it.

"Grant warned me it might be some kind of setup. That his wife claimed she already had plans with Patrice. I assured him it was fine. When you've been single as long as I have, I've gotten used to this kind of thing."

He'd been friends with Adam for a while now, and he understood the frustration of being a single man when most of your friends were married. He'd had his share of set-ups over the years.

"Isn't she your former neighbor and new in-law? I'm only asking because whether you realize it, every time I've heard you talking about her...well, it just always seemed like maybe you had a thing for her. I'm still going, but I wanted you to know beforehand."

Were his feelings about Patrice that transparent? "Yeah, well, the timing's just never been right, but I'm thinking it'll never be, and I've recently decided to do something about that." Kade's heart pounded at the thought of Patrice being out with someone else, even if it was just dinner.

"Good to know. Hell, I think we both need to find ourselves some better halves sooner rather than later. Oh, and don't worry. I'll do my best to be unappealing, and I'll even dial back on the charm. But it's gonna be hard."

"Damn, what a guy. Don't overdo it, though. I wouldn't want you to ruin your reputation as a ladies' man."

"Screw you, Holt." Adam barked out a laugh. "Anyway, let's get together soon."

Kade rubbed his face and held back a relieved sigh. "You bet. I appreciate you calling."

They ended the call, and Kade rethought his offer to Patrice. His reaction to Adam being set up with her knocked him off balance. It was foolish to offer up a night of sex to Patrice and expect it would be enough. The other day's near-miss accident further clarified he needed to go after what and who he really wanted in his life.

And with Adam calling him out on holding a torch for her after all these years, if he didn't realize that was the Universe further smacking him on the head, then he didn't deserve a chance with Patrice.

Decision made, Kade restarted his car and headed to Patrice's house.

FIVE

Hours after Sophie's phone call, Patrice was having second thoughts. Going to dinner knowing she was being set up with Adam, who deserved to meet someone interested in a real date, wasn't sitting well with her.

She hated dating, and she really hated misleading people. She knew how that felt. It sucked, and she just couldn't do it. Not until she figured out this thing between her and Kade.

Finishing her sandwich, she grabbed her cell to tell Sophie she couldn't make dinner this Friday after all. A knock on her front door made her jump. Smoothing her hair, she hustled to the front door, pausing in front of her foyer mirror to ensure she didn't have any lettuce stuck in her teeth.

A quick look through the side window showed Kade standing on her porch, hands in his pockets, looking straight ahead. His dark blue polo shirt hugged his shoulders and showed off his muscular arms. She stood back with a hand over her heart. It threatened to jump out of her chest.

Patrice pulled on the bottom of her torn t-shirt and

Capri length sweats, which had seen better days—ten years ago. Dang it. No one just shows up unannounced anymore. She nibbled on a fingernail and debated not answering.

"I know you're there, Patrice. I saw you peek out." Kade's voice held a note of laughter.

Damn. "I'm, uh. I've been cleaning, and I haven't showered yet. Now's not a good time." She crossed her fingers.

"I can wait. It's a nice day."

Patrice banged her head on the trim around the door. No way was she going to let him wait on her porch while she showered. What would the neighbors think? Throwing her shoulder back, *screw it*. "Don't say I didn't warn you." She unlocked the door and yanked it open.

Kade's blue eyes hit her first. His grin filled his handsome face.

"I like the ponytail. I'm not sure I've seen you wear your hair like that before." Kade's gaze traveled down her body, then flashed back to Patrice's face.

She felt a warm flush begin on her chest and bloom up her neck, then her face. "Um, yeah. Just when I clean. Well, you're here...so I guess you should come in." Patrice stepped back and waited.

He passed her closely. She inhaled his scent, a mix of man and something earthy. Covering her action by closing the door, Patrice took her time to turn and face him. "So, what are you doing out this way?"

Kade didn't answer right away. He rubbed the back of his neck, then looked around the front room. "I can't believe you're still living in this big house all by yourself. Have you thought about putting it on the market?"

Not the answer she was expecting. "Why, you in the real estate biz now?" Her tone was snippy even to her ears. Instant regret at the remark made her feel small and petty.

It wasn't his fault that she was waging an internal war within herself to keep her hands off him.

"Sorry, that's not the reason why I'm here. Just thinking of you cleaning this big house made me think why you're still living here. You're pretty busy with your business downtown. Why not sell this place and buy a condo?"

The fact she'd been thinking about that very thing for the past two years didn't matter. Not wanting to get into a back and forth with him about how big her house was, she tried to think of a reason to get him to leave without knowing it was because being this close to him befuddled her brain and made her skin feel tight and tingly. They stood there in a weird silent standoff. Him looking calm and unaffected, her sweaty and awkward. Had he dropped by to apologize? To tell her it was a mistake.

The thought filled her with disappointment. She'd replayed their kiss last night so many times after she went to bed, it'd left her frustrated and unable to sleep. Even now, just being this close to him had her body humming. As if on autopilot, her nipples hardened at the images of them together. She crossed her arms in an attempt to hide her reaction to him.

But not fast enough. Kade's gaze shifted to her chest. His eyes darkened to a deep blue. She sucked in a quick breath and shook her head in a lame attempt to banish the achy need triggered by his closeness and his heated gaze.

"Did you come here to pick a fight with me?"

Kade cleared his throat. "No, I...look, I'm sorry I said anything. I remember how hard it was to sell my house. I came by because I had this idea to get the kids a gift for the babies and wanted to bring you in on it, not get you pissed at me. But you are kinda cute when you're mad."

Nope. He didn't get to charm her out of this.

"That sounds fine. But you could have texted or called. Are you sure that's the only reason you're here?"

Rarely had Patrice seen Kade at a loss for words. The longer they stood less than a few feet apart, the higher the sexual tension rose. Denying it at this point would make her sound like a prude, but the opposite was true when it came to Kade Holt.

But why was he here? Then it hit her. He wanted her to make the first move, or rather, the second one. His move had been to kiss her stupid last night, leaving her wanting more.

And oh, did she want. Deep buried sexual need had gone unfulfilled from years of not receiving it in her marriage and choosing boyfriends who were, in a word, safe. Which also equaled dull and uninspired in the bedroom.

She wanted a physical connection, an immediate spark the moment they were in the same space. But how to tell him it could only be about the sex.

She wasn't looking to find love again, and she couldn't see herself in a long-term relationship, and she suspected Kade didn't want that either. So why not tear up the sheets with him? Work him out of her dreams.

He kept his gaze on hers as she worked through her thoughts. She wanted to tell him to follow her upstairs, but she desperately needed a shower.

"Okay, time to be honest. Me. Not you. That kiss last night was...*A-mazing*. But if we're going to do this, we need to set some ground rules first." Patrice licked her lips. She thought she heard him moan. The sound bolstered her confidence.

The only outward sign of interest at her statement was his lifted eyebrow, and damn, it made him hotter than ever.

"Okay, so one, we have sex, and that's it. No dating, no promises. If it's good, then great. If not, then at least we'll know, and we can move past it and still be friends. Two, we tell no one, and three—"

Kade stepped into her personal space and then some. "There's no three, and it's not if, but when we have sex, it'll be more than good, Patrice. Have no doubt I'm going to make you forget any other lover you've ever had."

He cupped her chin, lifted her face, and ran his thumb over her lower lip. "All it took for me was one kiss to know how good it's going to be for us. So, if we do this, once, hell, twice isn't going to be enough for me."

His mouth crushed hers. It was her turn to moan as he feathered his lips over hers, diving in between her lips, tangling his tongue with hers. If she thought the kiss last night was panty-melting, this one scorched her to her soul, heating her from the inside out.

Patrice held onto his shoulders, her fingers digging into his flesh, and met him stroke for stroke.

Kade broke the kiss and rested his forehead on hers. Each breathing heavy, he cradled her face in both his hands. His gaze was smoldering, and she felt branded everywhere it landed.

"Four weeks. And we only see each other. I decided a long time ago I'd never remarry, and I'm not looking for anything long term. I think you feel the same. We keep it simple, work each other out of our system, then go back to being just friends once the babies arrive. Deal?"

For a moment, she forgot about the babies, about Reese and Connor. After that kiss, she was lucky to remember her own birthday. Why couldn't she have met him in college instead of Stephen? Not once in their relationship had she felt this desperate to have a man inside her as she did right now.

Maybe that desperation meant she wanted more than

just great sex, but she wasn't going to look too deep into it. She'd take whatever time they had together, tuck it away and cherish the memories. So, four weeks, she could do four weeks. She worked well with deadlines. Besides, a month of sexy times was probably not enough time to tempt fate and create messy feelings, right?

Greedy for another kiss, she captured his lips and buried her fingers through his hair. This time, she was the one to end their kiss. Pulling back, she grinned, "Deal."

Kade returned her grin and gave her a light tap on her bottom. "Great. After you shower, I'm taking you shopping for strollers."

Patrice squinted her eyes and shook her head. "Wait, you want to go shopping? Now?" The look he was giving her did not read, "let's go shopping." His hot, predatory gaze made her shiver, and his baby blues read more, "let's get naked," then "let's go pick out strollers."

"Well, if you want the truth, I wanted you under me ten minutes ago." Kade's growly voice bounced off the walls.

If she hadn't been sure before, then his words locked in her decision. "Give me fifteen minutes, then meet me in my room." Patrice bounced on her toes, pressed a quick hard kiss on his lips, then beelined for the stairs.

SPEED SHOWERING WASN'T something she ever did. Amazing what the proper motivation could do for one's routine. Hair clipped up and out of her face; she poured a generous amount of her favorite body wash then lathered herself in lavender and sandalwood. She scrubbed her body in less than five minutes.

"Now I know the origin of that intoxicating scent you always wear." Kade's deep, sexy voice rang out.

Patrice let out a squeak, opened her eyes to find Kade stepping into her shower. His voice and his hard body had her heart pounding.

Her mouth went dry. At a loss for words, her gaze followed the drops of water falling off his chest. His pecs had a light dusting of silver hair. Mesmerized, she watched rivulets of water flow down to his abs. Yep, he still had them. It was hard to miss his reaction to her. Damn, the man was glorious, and he was all hers. For now.

"I couldn't wait." Kade took the loofah from her hands. "Turn around. I'll scrub your back."

Patrice nodded but didn't move. Couldn't. He gently turned her around until she faced the tiled shower wall. Kade began scrubbing her shoulders down her back, then rubbed the small of her back. Her body alternately relaxed under his efforts, then bloomed in goosebumps.

Kade kissed the sensitive flesh in the crook of her neck, and her knees wobbled. Her head fell back, and she released a soft moan. Then she wrapped a hand around the back of his head, needing contact.

Kade's hands ran along the sensitized flesh under her breasts, then covered them and softly squeezed. His thumbs ran circles over her nipples, pinching them in a delicious pleasure-pain rotation as warmth bloomed between her thighs.

She arched her back into his touch and sighed his name. "Kade."

"I love your body. Your curves. So many nights I've thought about doing this, hearing my name on your lips." He ground his erection against her bottom and dipped a hand down her stomach, palming her mound.

"Spread your legs for me." Kade's voice was thick and gritty.

Patrice happily complied and obeyed his command, widening her stance, opening herself to his wicked touch. He pushed a finger inside her, swirling over her clit. Pressure built as he added another finger. She whimpered her pleasure, leaning into him, unable to hold herself up as her body began to shake from his touch.

For the first time in forever, she felt alive, hungry for more. Her orgasm built as she rolled her hips, seeking, chasing its bliss. He had her on edge so quickly; she marveled at her body's response.

"I want to taste you, baby."

Kade's words inflamed her. His increased strokes broke her.

Patrice slapped a hand against the tile and rode out the wave. Sparks of white light flashed behind her eyelids. "Yes, Kade, yes!"

He grabbed her chin, tilted her face up to his, captured her lips, and plundered. Their tongues dueled. He pinched her swollen bud, and a second orgasm rocked her. The shock of the intensity nearly brought her to tears.

Seconds, then minutes passed as they stood under the cooling water's spray holding each other. But it didn't matter. She'd stand there with Kade all day. Her body shivered from the aftershocks, and when he removed his hand from between her thighs, she unashamedly whimpered. He turned off the shower and stepped out.

She followed him and was instantly swept up into Kade's arms. "Bed. Now." He snagged a bath towel off the hook and marched to her bed. He set her down and rubbed her arms, torso, and legs before doing the same to himself.

It gave her time to soak in him. Shyness gone, her gaze

greedily soaked up every inch of him. Time had been good to Kade. His leanly muscled body, thick hair, and dark blue eyes...the eyes looking at her now made her grin.

"I like your style, Mr. Holt." She reached up and wrapped an arm around his neck, drawing him down to the bed with her.

He braced his arms on either side of her head. "I'm just getting started." His mouth came down on hers, fusing their lips. His knee nudged her legs open, then his tongue dived deep, claiming her.

Patrice ran her down his back and onto his firm ass and moaned. Everywhere he touched ignited a new rush of warmth. He kissed her neck and down to her chest, cupping a breast and taking a pointed nipple into his mouth. Kade caressed her other breast, thumbing its peak. Her hips lifted off the bed. His cock rubbed against her folds, wrenching a groan from him.

Straining to get closer, Patrice felt him gently push her down. He moved swiftly between her thighs and nipped her sensitive flesh inches from her opening. His hot breath set off tingles, and she stilled, waiting.

He spread her folds, his tongue flicked her clit. Her body jolted. Pressing her arms into the bed, Patrice arched her back and surrendered to him. Riding his tongue, another orgasm rolled through her. This was an experience she'd dreamed of but had never received from a lover.

Kade masterfully prolonged her body's response and whispered encouragement when he replaced his tongue and lips with his fingers, wrenching an incredible third orgasm from her. As she rode out another wave, *was this really happening?* She heard the rip of foil. Opening her eyes, Kade's smiling face greeted her.

"Beautiful," he whispered.

She watched as he guided himself inside her. The fullness of him was almost too much at first, and he sensed that giving her time. It was sweet, but her body demanded he move. She gripped his biceps. "Now, please." She held him tight as he set a rhythm. Slow, then fast and hard. She wrapped her legs around his hips. *Oh, my god.* Her skin tingled and her ears buzzing; he reached that spot she'd only heard about but never experienced. Her heart shifted as his shout filled her ears. Her shouts joined his, and for a moment, she felt as if she was floating.

What in the hell had just happened to her?

SIX

Kade's schedule was crazy. A week after he and Patrice made their four-week deal, he was either working with clients or working her body up, wringing his name from her. He couldn't get enough of her reaction to him, and after last night's marathon, he wondered at his response to her.

Another red light. He smacked the steering wheel. The population of Pineville has been steadily increasing over the past few years. Some blamed it on the Outlaws coming to town, but unfortunately, the secret of their beautiful lakes, four-season weather, and boom in tech manufacturing jobs had leaked. It also increased his client load.

He shouldn't complain; however, all he wanted to do was be with Patrice. What had begun as a chance for uncomplicated sex between them had turned into a mass of confusing feelings he hadn't expected. At almost fifty, friends-with-benefits wasn't anything close to what it had been in his thirties and forties.

Traffic moved once more. He pushed thoughts of Patrice away and focused on his next appointment.

One of his best friends, Adam Riordan, had sold his practice and now worked exclusively for the Outlaws. They were meeting at The Club for lunch to discuss changes Adam wanted to make to his portfolio and, of course, enjoy the restaurant's famous lobster mac 'n cheese.

Kade scored a parking spot on the street. His gaze sought out the street corner where he'd helped prevent a tragedy. He'd tracked down the station where Tate and his partner worked and had sent a card to expect tickets to next year's game opener. He hoped they liked baseball.

The faces of the women and their kids, safe and unharmed, came to mind. What if Reese had been one of those moms? Or Patrice? The idea of not being around for his grandkids often worked into his thoughts as he went about his day. He rubbed his chest, turning toward the entrance, and walked into the packed restaurant.

Adam waved him over to a table in the back. "Thanks for fitting me in today, Kade." The doctor was in his early fifties but didn't look it other than a few streaks of silver in his dark brown hair.

Kade sat and shook his friend's hand. He'd wondered a few times if Patrice had gone to that dinner with Adam if she would have found him attractive. Probably. Adam was a great guy, and he was a definite catch for any lucky woman. Kade was just damn glad Adam also cared more about their friendship than getting laid.

"How's the new job going?" Kade took a sip from his water, eyes twinkling with humor.

"Best thing I ever did. And it's come with some unexpected perks." Adam grinned.

"Oh, yeah. Something better than free game tickets?" Kade asked. He was kind of jealous of his friend's ability to pivot to a new career. One that came with less stress and more time for fun.

"Time. When I had the practice, I always dealt with something or other, even when I hired people to take care of the business stuff. Now I can focus on my patients and golf. I also see why my ex was always on my back about it. But you can't go back, right? Although my boys aren't happy with me having all this time to bug them about giving me grandkids. I told them I expect at least two kids a piece within five years. You can imagine how that went over." Adam chuckled. "Which reminds me, you've got to be excited. Twins are due in another month, right?"

Kade's face split into a grin. The impending arrival of his grandchildren filled him with many new feelings. "Three weeks. Her doctor has said twins can come early, but so far, Reese has been doing great and has stopped working. She's determined to get those babies to full term. With the season over, Connor is with her all the time, driving her nuts. He won't even let her lift a milk carton."

Their waiter approached, took their orders, then before he left, he said, "You two are getting quite a bit of attention from two tables at the front. By the windows facing the street. I can make introductions if you're interested?"

In the not so recent past, Kade would have accepted the offer. "Spencer, right?"

"Yeah, good memory." The younger man said. "Reese said you never forget a face. How's she doing? Everyone's so excited for her and Connor."

Adam raised an eyebrow at Spencer's memory comment. Kade held back a retort and rubbed his jaw before answering. Maybe the kid wasn't referring to his age, so he'd give him the benefit of the doubt. "She's well. Resting, and Connor is taking good care of her."

"Awesome. So, you want me to hook you guys up with one of the women?"

"Which one's?" Adam asked.

"No," Kade responded simultaneously, and a tad too loud.

Adam slapped the waiter on the upper arm. "Thanks anyway, son. We can get our own dates."

"Uh, sure. I didn't mean anything. It's just both groups of women keep talking about the hot silver foxes and no wedding rings. They weren't being exactly quiet. So...well, anyway...." Spencer shrugged and grinned. "I'll get your order in right away."

Adam took another look toward the front of the restaurant, nodded, smiled, then turned to Kade. "What do you think, twenty-four, twenty-five?"

"If that. But he's a good kid." Kade took another sip of water. "So, what's been on your mind? Equities? If you tell me you want to try day trading or cryptocurrency, I'm going to double my management fee."

"Man, I know what you're doing. So, give. Why weren't you all over that?"

Kade crossed his arms. "I don't know what you're talking about. You're making me sound like a serial dater or something. Not that there's anything wrong with playing the field."

"Agreed. But you have to admit, women flock to you like bees to honey." Adam's gaze narrowed. He wasn't about to let the topic go. "Wait. You barely looked at those women. You holding out on me?"

Kade wasn't about to betray Patrice, but he needed to get his friend off his back. "No. I'm just focusing on the kids right now. I don't have a ton of time anyway. Business is good. Almost too good."

Adam's face lit up at Kade's news. "Too good? You thinking of paring back your client list?"

"No, just envious that you're playing more golf than me."

Their lunch arrived, and the cheesy aroma of the lobster mac and garlic rolls filled the air. Kade and Adam dug into the meal and, after a half dozen bites, Adam set his spoon down, then steepled his fingers above his plate.

"Look, I'm the last one to preach about women, relationships, life balance, or whatever the hell the latest fad is, but we're middle-aged, well-off, and single. Playing the field no longer holds any appeal for me. I think it's time to do something different. What do you know about Lois Campbell?"

Kade sat back. "Lois? Not much. I know she's Patrice's best friend. Divorced for a while. Her son is a local deputy prosecutor. She has a daughter too, but I'm not sure what she does. You thinking of asking her out? That might be a bit messy with her being TS' assistant and all."

Adam shrugged. "Not sure. There's something about her. And I get the distinct impression she doesn't like me. And you know me, I love a challenge. Forbidden fruit being a mighty temptress and all that."

"Huh, well, good luck with that." Kade needed to change the subject. He knew something about forbidden fruit, but he'd made a promise to Patrice to keep their deal secret.

"You know, Kade, I'm getting a similar vibe from you."

"About Lois?"

"No, about being fed up playing the field. So, tell me, you and Patrice finally hook up?"

Yeah, that's precisely what they were doing, but hearing it on his friend's lips generated low-level rage. Was it because of their agreement of secrecy, or did he not want

Adam putting her in the same category as the women from his past?

Appetite gone, Kade pushed his plate away. "Patrice is my daughter-in-law's mother. She's a good friend and anything between us, or not, isn't up for discussion."

Adam paused mid-bite. "Man, you got it bad for her. Don't you?" He set down his fork and held up his hands. "It's okay to admit it, Kade. I've seen it in your eyes before, and I see it now. And you want to hit me right now because I noticed Patrice is different from all the other women. She's special, right?"

Kade shook his head. "Look, I appreciate the concern or interest or whatever this is. But life is good right now. What you're picking up on is...happiness, contentment, I'm not sure." Pulling out his wallet, he took out his business credit card and flagged down Spencer.

"If you're on the lookout for something serious, I'm happy for you. I hope you find someone special. That's just not me." Kade took the bill folder, added his card, handed it back to the waiter, and noticed the look on Adam's face.

Yeah, he overreacted. Damn it. "Look, I'm sorry. That was uncalled for. I'm just tired and worried about Reese and Connor, I guess. So, what do you say we get back to your questions on adding to your portfolio? I've got some great ideas."

Adam shook his head. "Don't worry about it. I was curious, so I asked."

Kade released the breath he was holding. Like him, Adam had had a nasty divorce. Unlike him, Kade's ex had passed away years ago, leaving him a single parent. But they both had sworn off serious relationships. His friend's change in tone shook him up a bit.

"Women like her don't just show up. How many years

have you wanted to cross that line? If you haven't already, you need to let her know and never let go."

Kade couldn't believe his ears. He never discussed personal stuff with anyone. He was okay with friends-with-benefits. And until just now, he thought Adam was too.

With Patrice, he never thought he'd give in to his years-long attraction to her, but now that he had, a flood of feelings were battling within him that he didn't want to deal with.

Kade wasn't about to open up and share his feelings. That wasn't how he operated. Keep it simple. Find a woman, have fun, have great sex, and move on.

"What's gotten into you? If anyone should be against all that sappy second-chance at love crap society tries to force-feed to us, it should be you. Hell, Adam, I know what your settlement amount was. You telling me you want to go through that again in another ten or twenty years?"

"No. Because I'm not the same man I was. I learned a hard lesson, no doubt. But I've come to realize I want someone in my life. I don't care if it sounds cliché. And I'm not going to settle for the next woman I take out, either. I've got three sons I didn't set a good example for, and I want them to see their old man in a healthy relationship. They've all expressed no interest in marriage, let alone love, and I want to help change that."

"And where has this sudden enlightenment come from?"

"Kade, I never took you for a guy who wasn't willing to change. Take a chance. You know what doesn't work, so if it's not Patrice, then open yourself up to someone else."

How did this conversation get so far off track? Kade was comfortable talking numbers, not feelings. "Shit, this is the trouble with having a doctor as a friend."

Spencer appeared at the exact right time, handing Kade the bill. He signed it, pulled cash from his wallet for a tip, then stood.

"And why's that?"

"Because when you decide to do something, you don't just jump in headfirst. You educate yourself on the subject, then share it with your friends. It's your most annoying flaw. Well, this is one area where I'm happy to remain exactly where I'm at—single."

"*Hmm*," Adam said.

"Hmm, what?"

"I'll tell you what. I think I hit a nerve. But don't worry, I have no intention of preaching to you about opening yourself up to finding love again. I know it's not easy, but I've come to the realization it'll be worth it. For me at least." Adam's tone was so matter of fact, it took Kade a moment to realize he was allowing his confused feelings for Patrice to spill out as unjustified anger toward his friend when all Adam was offering was empathy.

"I have another meeting. I appreciate the concern, Adam. I do. And I'm sorry for lashing out. But I'm good. I'll email you later today with some options for you, then follow up with a call tomorrow to finalize any additions or changes you want to make." He stuck out a hand as a peace offering.

Adam grabbed it, then pulled him in for a half hug. "No need to apologize. And you're right about me. Just want all my friends happy. Speaking of which, you're still getting several interested looks. Go work your charm. I'm going to finish up lunch, then head back to the stadium to oversee the remodel for my exam rooms. The off-season is busy already with a couple of players needing minor surgery."

Kade avoided the tables Spencer had mentioned earlier

as he left the restaurant. He was pretty sure he recognized one of the women he'd had a brief fling with last year.

On the drive to his next meeting, all he could think about was seeing Patrice later tonight. They were having dinner with Reese and Connor, then after they were going to help out with the nursery. He found himself worrying about how long they would have to stay before he could drag her away.

Now, thanks to Adam calling him out over his response to hooking up with her, he questioned whether his feelings were beginning to shift from lust to...Nope. He wasn't even going to think about the L-word.

Because it wasn't going to happen. Ever. Hopefully.

———

DINNER OVER, Patrice scanned the living room. Her attempts at being causal around Kade when around other people had improved, hopefully.

She caught his attention. He lifted an eyebrow at her and grinned. A warm flush shot through her, prompting her to edge closer to the stairs and further away from Reese. Her daughter could read her moods like a book. She'd never thought of it as a negative until now.

Kade cleared his throat. "Son, you and Reese relax for a bit, and we'll go start organizing the nursery and getting things ready to assemble the second crib. Shouldn't take more than thirty minutes or so." Avoiding eye contact with Connor, he stood and held out a hand toward Patrice.

"You ready?" He placed his hand on her waist, then immediately dropped it.

She shivered at the brief contact and averted her face away from her daughter. Would the sparks she felt at his merest touch ever end? She hoped not. She just hoped she was able to hide her body's response.

Patrice went up the stairs, acutely aware that Kade was close behind her. Another full-body flush enveloped her. "Do you think they suspect anything?"

They walked into the nearly finished nursery; boxes strewn about. Delivery packages stacked on the changing table threatened to topple over. She sighed. "It's going to take us more than thirty minutes, Kade."

Determined to keep Reese from worrying about everything that needed to be done before the twins arrived, Patrice took the top-most package and tore into it. Newborn onesies in neutral colors with matching mittens to prevent those pesky scratches spilled out. Memories filled her of Royce and Reese as newborns and the constant outfit changes and early morning feedings. She let out another sigh and sniffled.

"You okay?"

The concern in Kade's voice made her turn. She watched him push the door to within an inch or so of closing all the way.

"Need to be able to hear them in case they sneak up." Chuckling, he captured Patrice's gaze and held it.

Soaking in his playfulness, she allowed her gaze to roam over Kade's lanky six-foot frame. At almost fifty, he kept in shape with running and golf. Her fingers itched to touch him. Three-day-old scruff covered his face. Her gaze traveled from his blue eyes dancing with mischief to the unmistakable bulge behind his zipper.

He caught her checking him out. His nostrils flared, and his eyes did that sexy squint as he walked toward her.

"Come here." He pulled her in close and rubbed his hands up and down her arms.

"Relax. They're focused on other things right now." He dipped his head and brushed his warm lips behind her ear.

With each touch, he set her skin on fire. Shivers traveled down her spine. She had to steal herself from getting lost in him. They agreed this thing would not last forever, but every time they touched, it was as if her soul sighed and exclaimed, "there you are." She had to be strong—stronger.

"Relax, huh? You think it's that simple? Name one time anyone actually relaxed when told to do so?" Patrice eased away from Kade and wrapped her arms around herself to ward off the instant chill she felt after leaving his warmth.

"You're so cute when you're nervous."

"Nervous? Me? More like perpetually turned on whenever we're together, and it's beginning to become a problem." She grabbed another package, ripped it open, and stacked the baby outfits with the others to be washed.

Keeping her back to him, she took in a couple slow breaths to calm her need to jump him and beg for more kisses.

He was silent so long Patrice turned to see if he'd left the room. He stood less than a foot away with a questioning expression on his handsome face. "Yeah, I know exactly what you mean."

"And why do I feel like I'm a teenager again, constant butterflies churning in my stomach and debating on buying a box of condoms?"

Kade barked out a raspy laugh. "I've got condoms covered. You just worry about making time for me, and I'll take care of everything else." He stepped behind Patrice, placed his hands over her crossed arms, squeezed, then pressed his front to the small of her back.

She gasped at his hardness. His hands began to wander up her sides, touching her flesh in feather-light strokes. All thoughts of baby clothes and organization vanished. This man was dangerous.

"Hey, Dad. Here's another package Reese forgot about."

Connor's voice drifted in from the hallway. They both jumped apart. Patrice's hands went automatically to her hair, then quickly smoothed her blouse. She pretended extreme interest in the pack of onesies she'd tossed in the crib.

Kade dropped to a knee and began tearing into the box holding the second crib they were supposed to be prepping. He kept his back to the door.

Poor guy. Having a kid interrupt your clinch was embarrassing, but it seemed more so when it was an adult child, especially when hiding your body's response was imperative.

She let out a low snort and walked over to the door just as Connor arrived. "I'll take that. Now go back to Reese. You're going to appreciate your alone time after the babies come home and they're up every half hour wanting to be fed. Often at alternate times."

Connor's face lit up. "Thanks, Patrice." He looked over her shoulder at his father. "You got that okay, Dad?"

Patrice looked down and almost lost her cool at Kade's expression.

"Sure. Give me another fifteen minutes, and then we can bang this thing out in no time."

Oh no, he didn't. Laughter threatened to explode out of her as Connor left.

Kade gave her a wink. "I guess we better hurry. You get the packages unwrapped, and I'll—"

"You said package." Patrice laughed louder than she had in forever. Covering her mouth, her eyes widened as Kade stood and stepped toward her until she bumped into the crib behind her.

"Naughty-naughty girl. You know what happens to naughty girls, don't you?" Still laughing, she only nodded. Words were not possible at the moment.

"They get spanked." Kade circled her wrists and brought them down between their bodies.

She sobered up immediately.

"You want to be spanked, Patrice?" Kade didn't wait for her to answer. "Later." He whispered and moved back.

"Right now, we need to stay as far away from each other as we can; otherwise, there will be no doubt left in Connor's mind what we've been up to."

Patrice gasped. "Do you think he suspects anything?"

Kade didn't even pause. "Knowing him, he's more likely to wonder why I haven't made a move on you by now."

SEVEN

IT WAS ALMOST the end of the third week of their deal, and Kade knew he wanted an extension of their agreement. Four weeks wouldn't be enough. The one roadblock in his way had been bringing Patrice to his condo. Connor would drop in at random times now that it was the off-season, and Kade couldn't bring himself to putting an end to his son's habit.

Sneaking around, at first, had added to the excitement, but he was over it, and the worry he had the first week of losing interest in Patrice as he did with all the women before her never materialized.

He was hooked, and he couldn't get her out of his head. Kade pictured her face during meetings with clients, on the golf course, and on the nights they didn't spend together, which were few. He'd been daydreaming like a damn four-teen-year-old over his first crush.

Kade checked his watch for at least the dozenth time since he left his house this morning. He'd been counting down the minutes until he could see her tonight. He was on his way to another client meeting. Maybe he'd pick up some takeout and talk her into having dinner with him before they ripped each other's clothes off. He grinned at the image his thoughts created—*The image of Patrice opening her door, and in seconds, he'd slam it behind himself, grabbed her by the waist, and captured her naughty smile in a breath-stealing kiss*—

A horn beeped behind him. He let out a curse looked up to see the light that had turned green while he became lost in his head. God, he had it bad for her. And her curves. And the sweet noises she made when he was buried deep inside her.

Dammit. *Get a grip, Kade.* He stepped on the gas and tried to push all thoughts of Patrice to the back of his mind. He didn't think arriving with an obvious hard-on would create a good impression on his new client.

Once he arrived, he parked and stayed in the car, taking several deep breaths, forcing himself to visualize the spread-sheet he'd created earlier in the day with the different investment options his client requested. It took five minutes longer than he wanted, and he walked into the meeting late. He was never late for appointments.

A shift had occurred in his thinking since the close call downtown. And he couldn't stop imaging Patrice in his life. Not as a friend, but *in his life*. Whenever he envisioned himself playing with the grandkids, she was there. Having dinner with friends, she was there. At Connor and Reese's place, she was there.

And then, when he imaged them at her house, it had become their home—years from now.

He gathered his briefcase and, once inside, sped through the meeting. Secured a commitment from the client to move ahead. He left within thirty minutes.

Back in his car, he scanned his calendar. The next

meeting wasn't until three, and it would be virtual. Eleven-thirty now, and he was hungry. For Patrice. He wasn't going to make it till later to be with her. He dialed her number.

She picked up after the second ring. "Hello there."

The sound of her voice sent warmth to his groin, and he was hard again, the second time in less than an hour. For her. "What are you doing for lunch?" Kade practically groaned the question. Jesus, if just her voice could do this to him, how was he ever going to stop being her lover?

"Kade, you alright? You sound...different." Concern laced her voice.

"Different, huh? Yeah, I guess that's a good word for it. I can't get you out of my head. Can't work and forget sleep. All I can think about is how you taste, how you feel underneath me."

Silence greeted his declaration. Screw it. He was done holding back his feelings. He knew she hadn't hung up on him, although he wouldn't blame her if she did. Heavy breathing flowed through the speaker, and it wound him up even tighter.

"Meet me at your house. Now." Kade grinned at the demand in his voice and the quick intake of air he heard from Patrice.

"Listen, I have customers in the shop. I just can't—Kade, what's gotten into you?" Patrice's voice trembled.

Kade picked up an undertone of desire in her voice, even as she scolded him. And he knew he had her interest. He didn't care that it was the middle of the day, and they both had businesses to run. He needed her. Now.

"I'll be at your place in fifteen." He ended the call.

Man, he'd lost his mind. Spontaneity wasn't in his wheelhouse, but today he was making it a new thing. He had one week left, and he wasn't going to waste any of it being conventional.

PATRICE'S HAND shook as she pulled her cell away from her ear and stared at her phone. Did he just order her home so they could have sex?

"Mrs. Linden is looking at the black chesterfield. Should I handle the negotiation, or do you want to?" Her assistant asked.

It took Patrice a moment to focus on what Sheila had said.

Sex in the middle of a workday? That man was crazy. But...maybe not. She'd been thinking of him more than she should. She'd also wondered how long either one of them could keep up the every-other-day frequency they'd been maintaining for the past three weeks.

She thought she'd be more worn out, instead she found herself energized. She'd also worried he'd get tired of her, but surprise, surprise he hadn't, and the more they had each other, the better the sex had become.

"Patrice?"

"Right, yes. You go ahead. I uh...I forgot. That was a potential new client who finally decided to sell her grand-mother's Louis Majorelle armoire. I need to leave. Just in case, can you lock up if I'm not back by five?" Patrice scooped up her handbag, tossed in her cell, and headed toward the back door.

She left Sheila staring after her, possibly wondering if she'd lost her mind. And maybe she had. But she wasn't going to miss this opportunity to be more than a bit wild.

Traffic mid-day in Pineville had increased the last

couple years, and she hit every light on Main. She still made pretty good time. Winding through her neighborhood, she passed Kade's empty SUV a block from her house. Anticipation wrapped around her, and goosebumps erupted on her arms and neck.

Patrice popped open the garage and scanned the front porch. No Kade. Maybe he'd gone around back? But she couldn't see him climbing over her fence. Scrambling out of her car, she forgot her handbag, hesitated, then decided to leave it.

She stepped into the kitchen. Where was he?

A flash of movement caught her eye, and she headed for her sliding doors. Stretched out on her favorite Adirondack chair was Kade. She drank him in, noticing the rigidity of his body. The fingers on his left hand drummed the armrest. She flipped the latch, pushing open the door.

He jumped from the chair and made it to her in three long strides. His eyes flashing with need. She stared, hypnotized, as a hand shot out to cup her neck, pulling her into his hard chest.

The kiss was swift and hard and just what she needed. Kade walked her backward into the room, paused to pull the door close, and locked it.

Kade placed his hands on either side of her face, his gaze full of daring and need for acceptance. "I don't think I can go slow, and I sure as hell can't wait to get upstairs. Tell me you want this as much as I do."

The sheer animal need in his eyes, for her, created a matching hunger she didn't want to deny. Pressing her body into his erection, sparking an ache between her thighs. Every nerve ending was calling out to be touched and pleasured. There was no way she was missing out on this moment.

The yes that passed her lips sounded foreign to her own ears. Drunk on passion, its husky tone was instantly swallowed by Kade's open-mouthed kiss. The first touch of his tongue on hers sent a shudder cascading through her. Her panties soaked, she wiggled closer.

Kade pushed her lightweight suit jacket from her shoulders and pulled her blouse from the waistband of her matching dark blue skirt. Frenzied need for skin-to-skin contact had her hands fumbling on his dress shirt.

"Let me. Take your skirt off and hop up on the counter." Kade nudged her toward the kitchen island, unbuttoning his shirt, then whipped it off his body.

Patrice shimmied out of her skirt and peeled off her hose and panties. Kade's hands returned to her, plucking at the pearl buttons of her blouse. Her skin flushed at the frenzied touch of his fingers. Finished, Kade grinned, lifted her at the waist, and gently set her down on the cold granite.

"Spread your legs, Patrice. I need to taste you."

Her legs trembled at his words. She leaned back on the counter and opened herself to him. Cool air hit her, contrasting with the heat of her pussy. Her pulse pounded where she wanted his touch. She let out a whimper as he ran a fingertip between her folds.

"So wet." Kade pressed into her flesh, their eyes still locked.

She lifted her hips, "Yes." He stroked her deep in reward, and she moaned his name. He flicked his tongue on her swollen clit. The contact had her close to orgasm. It had been building since he touched her at the door, but she wanted more. Rotating her hips, desperate for him, "Again," she moaned.

"So demanding. I'm not going anywhere, baby." Kade licked her again and pumped his finger. He swirled his tongue over her sensitive nub, then spread her lips, exposing her flesh as he feasted.

Pinpricks of light swam behind her closed eyelids, her womb spasmed. The intensity of the orgasm slammed into her, her breath caught, and she held it as spasm after spasm hit her. Kade slowed but didn't stop, pressing his thumb over her clit, prolonging the orgasm. *Yes.* She wanted to shout to the stars how this man made her feel—opening her eyes to see Kade's face above her as he continued to touch and soothe her swollen flesh.

"God, you are so gorgeous, Patrice. How am I ever going to walk away from this?" Kade leaned into her, captured her lips, and consumed her.

There wasn't time to reflect on what he'd just said. Kade pulled back, grabbed a condom from his pocket before unbuckling his belt. She watched in wonder at the swiftness of his movements as he freed his cock, rolled the protection down, grabbed her hips, pulling her flush against him.

She let out a startled squeak. The pressure of his cock against her clit wrenched another moan from her.

Kade cupped her bottom. "Hold on." He picked her up, turned, took two steps, and pressed her back into the wall. He reached down between them and guided his cock into her. She was more than ready for him. She wrapped her arms around his neck, holding on tight.

"Can't wait." He ground out and pounded into her; the second orgasm caught her by surprise. She clamped down on his hips as he found his completion. Their heavy breathing filled the room, along with the musky scent of their lovemaking. She cupped his face and feathered her lips across his. Aftershocks rocking her, she lightly sucked his bottom lip and sighed.

This. Was. Perfect.

Patrice didn't want to let him go. Not just in this moment, but the next and the next until there were no more moments. And she didn't dare let out the one word that would ruin all the moments to come.

Instead, she laughed at herself and the absurd idea of ever being able to have, then end without heartache, a friends-with-benefits arrangement with Kade Holt.

EIGHT

"Mom? Did something happen between you and Connor's dad?"

Patrice bit her lower lip. It had been three days since their "lunch." Kade had been over again just last night, but neither one of them discussed the obvious intensity of that moment. She felt hurt, but she also knew she had no right to push him, to find out if he felt as confused as she did. Or was it just another hook-up during their four weeks together?

She glanced at her daughter's questioning look. Patrice hated keeping secrets. And this one was a doozy. But was she ready to open up to her daughter about her time with Kade? Nope, not ready. "What makes you think there's something between us?"

Reese shifted and rubbed her belly. "Why did you answer my question with a question?"

Gazing at her beyond-uncomfortable daughter, who at nine months pregnant was committed to keeping those babies right where they needed to be, even if that meant letting go of the day-to-day running of her business.

"I'm not interested in a relationship. You know that, hon. My life is full. Besides, no man is going to compare to my grandbabies when they arrive." Patrice stood and helped Reese adjust a pillow behind her back. "I'm going to go fix you some lunch. What sounds good?"

Reese let out a long sigh and rested her head on the back of the couch. "It's just that I've noticed Kade looking at you...kinda differently than before, and Connor thought the other night he saw...well, anyway. I know you don't need a guy to be happy. I've heard that line from you more times than I can count. But don't you miss, you know?"

Her daughter's face flushed pink. Patrice paused in the entryway to Reese's kitchen, debating whether to ignore the question. And what did Connor think he saw? Darn it, Kade had told her they were in the clear, but what if he was wrong?

Her heart began to race, and she wiped her palms on her thighs. It felt as if their roles had reversed, and Patrice was now the daughter having to make sure her mom didn't find out she'd had sex.

"Sex. You're talking about sex, right? Sure. And maybe one day, who knows? It's not like I've been celibate since your dad died. I've just been...busy with everything the last few years."

Reese rolled her eyes. "Mom, I know you. You're not the friends-with-benefits type. But I'm just worried about you being alone. The right guy is out there for you. I just know it."

Patrice was bursting to tell her the truth. She would. Later. Much later. Maybe when the twins turned five.

"I'm not going to tell you not to worry about me, but really there's nothing to worry about. And yes, Kade and I have been talking more, but we want to make sure we're supporting you and Connor. Plus, we're making sure we don't buy the same things for the twins. Nothing more."

Patrice dared a peek at her daughter. Was Reese buying the shovel full she'd just delivered?

The last thing she wanted was to add more stress to Reese's long list of things she needed to focus on before the twins arrived. And her and Kade hooking up would definitely cause worry or, god forbid, get her thinking that what they had was serious.

They all had been deflecting anything that came even close to raising Reese's blood pressure, but perhaps she needed more to focus on besides the babies?

Patrice realized that she hadn't been doing a very good job sharing what was going on in her life. They'd always been close and shared almost everything, but since she and Kade had gotten together, that had pretty much come to a stop.

"Okay, that makes sense—I guess." Reese picked up her phone, tapped it a few times, and held it up for her to see. "So, since we're on the topic, I heard about this app for people in their 30s, 40s, and 50s."

"Reese, c'mon. I don't need an app to find a date or a hookup or whatever." Patrice shifted and looked out the front window. Anywhere but at her daughter's hopeful face.

"Mom, it's not a hookup app. It's more of a speed dating site. You and Lois should check it out. They have local events too. I'm not saying either of you is desperate or anything. But you two are in your prime. You both should be dating, having fun, and...*ahem*, sex."

Well, she wasn't wrong. But there was no way she could date anyone else. At least until her time with Kade was over.

"You seem to have put a lot of thought into this." Patrice had to get out of this conversation. "I appreciate your concern, but now's not the time. Maybe in a few months...."

"Mom, I get it. But the babies won't be here for at least another couple of weeks. Just try it, please? You don't have to do it alone. That's why I mentioned Lois. I'm going to send this to her right now."

"Reese, wait!" Patrice bolted toward Reese, but her daughter was too quick.

A devilish smile appeared on her daughter's face. "Mom, it's not that big a deal. It's not like there's anyone in your life right now, right?."

Dammit, she knew.

Which meant Connor had seen Kade kissing her in the nursery the other night.

Squaring her shoulders, Patrice stood. "I'm sure Lois will get a good laugh out of it, but she won't be interested, either." She turned back toward the kitchen. "Turkey on rye sound good?"

———

"WHAT DO YOU MEAN, you signed us up?" Patrice threw her key fob onto the kitchen counter. She'd left Reese's after making sure her daughter finished lunch and settled in for a nap.

"I looked into it, and I think it's perfect for us. There's one tonight at O'Malley's."

Lois' breezy voice did little to reassure her that it was a good idea.

Patrice tried and failed to come up with a good enough reason to turn her down. At least one that wouldn't raise suspicion. One more week to go. That's all she needed, but then the twins would be here, and she wasn't about to give up her free time for a random guy. Not after experiencing Kade's kisses. He'd been over last night, and her muscles still tingled from their two rounds of lovema—sex.

"You there, Patrice?"

Sighing, she tucked a piece of hair behind her ear. "Yeah. You just caught me off guard. Why don't you come over? We'll have dinner and talk about it."

"Wish I could. I'm meeting Sam at six, so I can meet you there. His workload has finally slowed some, and he's able to take his dear ol' mama out for dinner." Lois chuckled.

Her friend had two adult children. Neither were married nor close to being in a serious relationship, and Lois was on a mission to change that. It was the perfect way for Patrice to wiggle out from the speed dating thing with her.

"You know, Lois. You should get Sam and Heather signed up. With their schedules, that app is the perfect solution. And then you and Heather could do it together." Patrice crossed her fingers.

"Oh no, you don't. You're not getting out of this. You and I are going. Besides, no one wants to do this with their mother in the room. Pick out something sexy, and I'll see you Friday at seven. Gotta go, the boss is calling."

After Lois hung up, Patrice wondered if she could fake a head cold. She had two days to come up with a plausible reason to back out. The way things had been going with Kade, they'd been getting together at her place every couple of days, which meant he'd probably call or text her to set something up for tomorrow, so technically Friday could work. But could she handle the sudden feeling this would be sneaking around? Speed dates weren't actual dates, right?

Maybe she needed to dial it back with him? When they'd made their agreement, she never thought they'd be together so often. And then there was the one thing she thought friends-with-benefits never did. Kade would stay after. Not all night, but he would stay for a while, holding her. Her ex never did that, and they'd been married.

Kade would tell her about his day, ask about hers, or they'd discuss random things. And sometimes, like last night, they'd get all worked up for each other again, and it would be after midnight before he left for his place.

But he'd never once asked to spend the night.

Patrice found herself wanting him to.

They were getting too close to acting as if they were an actual couple. She was getting used to having him in her bed. That was so not a good thing. She'd made a mistake once of making a man the center point of her world. Patrice couldn't do that again. She knew if she didn't do something soon to put distance between herself and Kade, then her heart would never recover.

Maybe she should go with Lois on Friday? She'd tell him she and Lois were going out on Friday to have some girl time. She wouldn't participate in the speed dating thing, but she'd encourage Lois to do it, and she'd watch from the sidelines. And if it didn't look too scary, and Lois had some success with it, then maybe after the twins were born, she'd give it a try.

NINE

Hey Dad wanted U 2 know. Patrice is going out with Lois on some speed dating thing at O'Malley's. Starts at 7 pm.

KADE RE-READ the text from his son for the fourth time. *What the Hell?*

He tossed his cell onto the overstuffed loveseat in his home office and ran both hands through his hair, then down his face. He leaned his elbows on his thighs and rested his chin on his steepled fingers as he stared at his dual monitors.

It was a good thing he hadn't read the text from Connor when it had chimed thirty minutes ago. The market had closed ten minutes ago, and he'd just finished making adjustments to several of his client's portfolios. *What the Hell?*

Dammit, she agreed to four weeks, and according to his calendar, they still had four more days. Had he missed something? When he left her last night, she'd clung to him for one last kiss before he dressed and went home, which he didn't mind admitting puffed up his ego.

Considering he was pushing fifty, an age when most men had already dealt with some performance issues, he felt damn lucky to be still able to have an active sex life. And sex with Patrice was hands down the best he'd had. But what if she didn't feel the same? Was this her way of looking for an off-ramp?

More importantly, did he want to find someone else when four weeks were up?

Kade stood up from his office chair and pushed his conflicting feelings away. He was getting too close to admitting he had real feelings for Patrice. Feelings that were leading him closer to wanting a commitment from her.

He paced his kitchen. He took out the garbage. He stomped back into his office, grabbed his cell, and read the text one more time, then replied to Connor:

Why R U telling me this?

Ten long minutes later, phone still in hand, three dots appeared on the screen:

So you won't let her get away.

Kade let out a snort, then laughed. Tension he'd been holding since he got Connor's first text left his body, and he took in a deep breath and let out a sigh.

He wasn't sure if he was hurt or pissed, but he knew he wasn't relieved at the news Patrice was already looking to replace him. Well, he still had four more days, and he intended to fulfill his end of their deal.

Sure, he could call her, find out if it was true, but he had a better idea.

He sent Adam a text to meet him at O'Malley's.

Three hours later, he pulled into the parking lot noticed Adam had just pulled in, so he waited at the entrance.

"Tell me again why we're here?" Adam looked around O'Malley's and followed Kade to the end of the bar.

Kade signaled the bartender and ordered two house drafts. "Patrice is going to be here with Lois any minute, and I need to talk to her about something." He set a twenty on the bar, took his glass, and handed one to Adam. Keeping his back to the main door, he drained half the beer, set it down, and turned to his friend. "Let's say that Patrice and I have been seeing each other the last few weeks, and I may want to keep seeing her."

Adam took a second sip of his beer. The news didn't seem to surprise his friend. "Are you looking for my approval, or do you want me to talk you out of whatever it is you're planning on doing when she gets here?"

Before Kade could answer, a voice came over the PA system, "Alright, ladies and gentlemen, welcome to O'Malley's first-ever speed dating event. We'll get started in fifteen. If you haven't signed in, there's still time. Jenna, over there at the check-in table, will be happy to get you all signed up. Ladies, if you already have your assigned seat number, now's the time to find it and settle in. A bell will sound at seven exactly, and your first date will take his seat across from you."

Kade tuned out the rest of the directions, focusing on the entrance. After the announcement was over, the volume in the bar rose with excitement.

Adam's eyebrows lifted as they both watched Patrice and Lois enter the pub and make their way over to the afore-mentioned Jenna. "Oh, hell no. Kade, what is going on?"

"Hold on. I didn't sign us up for this thing. Look, I know I told you that nothing was going on between Patrice

Kincaid and me...." Kade turned to keep his back to Patrice. His plan centered on the element of surprise, and he still had ten minutes to figure out how he was going to approach her.

"Well, color me unsurprised. But if you two have got something going, why is she here?" Adam took another sip of his beer.

"Exactly. That's why we're here."

"No, that's why you're here. Why'd you drag me into this?"

Kade rubbed the back of his neck. Nerves began to work their way through his body. Shit, he had it bad for her if he was willing to make a fool out of himself and in a popular bar, no less. "Moral support."

"You asking or telling me?" Adam's tone was heavy with sarcasm.

"Both. I was hoping you could deal with Lois if she decides to interfere. I know, I know this seems high school-ish, but man, if there ever was a time I needed back up, it's now. Just keep an eye on Lois, and if it looks like she's going to interfere or anything, use your charm."

Adam let out a harsh laugh. "Charm? Yeah, I don't think Lois Campbell is interested in my 'charm.' I've been butting heads with her lately over the remodel in my office at the stadium. For some reason she took an instant dislike to me, and I haven't been able to figure out why."

Kade dared a quick look and noticed Lois take a seat, but Patrice was still speaking to the event coordinator. He returned his gaze to Adam. "I'll owe you one. All you have to do is stand here, drink your favorite beer, and try not to attract any women."

Adam remained silent. "No promises on keeping the ladies away, but I'll do my best with Lois. Who knows, maybe she's less of a tyrant outside of work." He lifted his glass and touched the side of Kade's. "Good luck with whatever it is you're planning."

The bell rang, and men came out of the woodwork, pulling out chairs across from about ten women, including Lois. Kade noticed his friend's shoulders go back and his eyes squint as he locked his gaze on Patrice's best friend.

Kade didn't have time to wonder what was going on between those two. He was more concerned about where Patrice had gone. Why hadn't she taken a seat? He scanned the area behind the section of the pub designated for speed dating and saw her sitting at a two-top, sipping a glass of wine. Her gaze was locked on Lois. Perfect, she wouldn't notice him heading her way. But before he could make it to her table, a man stopped at her side and began speaking to her.

His fists curled at the sight of another man showing interest in Patrice. He quickened his stride, weaving between tables until he was two steps away. He overheard the guy telling Patrice she was pretty. And he lost his cool.

"So, girl's night, huh?" Kade didn't try to hide the anger in his voice.

"Kade, I uh...." Patrice's eye widened. "What are you doing here?"

Kade's heart pounded in his ears. Keeping his focus on Patrice, he gritted out, "I'd like to speak with my *friend*, if you don't mind." He pulled out the chair across from her and sat without waiting for the other man to respond. Patrice's would-be date took the hint and left.

Patrice leaned forward and crossed her arms on the table. "Well, that was rude. Why are you here, Kade?"

Holding her gaze, he noticed her eyes had darkened, appearing almost black, her lips pursed in a straight line. He hadn't expected her to be angry. Embarrassed maybe. Or guilty of being caught in a lie but not pissed off.

"I heard through the grapevine that you were going to be here tonight—speed dating. But I thought that couldn't be right. We made a deal. And I still have four days." As soon as the words left his mouth, Kade knew he wanted to take them back. Patrice pulled back from the table, hurt and tears filled her eyes. *Dammit.*

Another bell sounded, and more scraping sounds filled the room as men moved on to their next date. Patrice's gaze flicked to where Lois sat, and Kade turned to see her friend smiling at a gentleman who looked to be in his early sixties. Movement at the bar caught his eye. It was Adam walking toward Lois' table, but halfway to it, he stopped and turned back. Interesting.

When Kade turned his attention back to Patrice, she put her jacket on. She was looking anywhere except at him.

"I'm not sure how to deal with this side of you, Kade. I don't know what you think is going on between us, but I don't owe you any explanations. But I know how this looks. I'm here to support Lois. Period. If you can't handle that, then you can forget four more days." She pushed back her chair and stood.

Dammit, he'd screwed up. Was this what jealously felt like? He wasn't going to use it as an excuse. No way. But he needed to get his head out of his ass and fix this. Now.

"Patrice, sweetheart. I'm sorry I should have called you instead of showing up like this. It's just...." *What? What exactly could explain this dumb-ass move?* That he was scared of losing her. Of losing what they'd had in three short weeks. Was he ready to admit to her he wanted more?

"Can we go somewhere else and talk? Your place? Or maybe—"

His cell phone rang. It was Connor's ringtone. At the same time, Patrice's cell went off.

"It's Connor."

"It's Reese."

They shared a look full of concern and excitement.

"It's just a coincidence, I'm sure," Kade answered the call. "Hey, Connor."

Patrice turned from him and answered her phone. He kept his eyes on her as he listened to his son tell him to get to the hospital. He reached out and placed a hand on Patrice's shoulder. She whirled at his touch, tears in her eyes.

"It's time, Kade. Our grandbabies...." Her face glowed with excitement.

"Yeah." His heart pounded with anticipation. "I guess we should leave. Connor thinks it'll still be a few hours, but this isn't how I wanted tonight to go. Please believe me, Patrice, I want to make things right. It wasn't my intention to be such an ass."

She shook her beautiful head and tucked her cell away into her purse. "That doesn't matter now. I'm going to tell Lois I'm leaving. Then I'm heading to the hospital. I guess... I...I'll see you there." Patrice walked the long way around the table, avoiding any contact with him.

Jesus Holt, how the hell are you going to clean up this mess and convince her you aren't some jealous loser?

TEN

PATRICE WOKE to a gentle shake on her shoulder and the sound of her name. *Kade*.

Not sure how long she'd been asleep, panic set in that she'd missed everything. The argument at the pub flashed into her mind. Oh, yeah. Crap. She had to pretend that hadn't happened, for now. Glancing at her watch, it read 4:22 a.m. She stretched and met Kade's concerned gaze.

"Connor says we can go in now." He smiled and offered her a hand.

"They're here?" Happiness filled her. She took his hand, warmth spreading through her at the contact. She ignored the zap of awareness and walked with him down the hallway to Reese's room.

"Yeah. I'm surprised you didn't hear her shouting." Kade stopped at the open door and took her other hand in his. "The babies are doing great. The doctor wanted some extra time to have them checked out before we could go in. Ready to meet our grandbabies, Patrice?"

She couldn't believe she'd slept through the birth. The last time she checked, it had been two a.m., and they'd been taking turns going in to visit before Reese had decided she just wanted Connor in the room. She was more than good with her daughter's choice since she wasn't sure she'd be able to keep it together during the birth.

Nodding, she turned and walked in to see Reese gazing at her babies in twin bassinet's next to the hospital bed. Tears flowed. Hugs and kisses were exchanged. And through it all, Kade was by her side. Handing her tissues, rubbing her back, and taking her picture with the twins.

"Well, Glamma. How does it feel?"

She looked up to see Kade's gaze locked on her and the twins, and for a moment, she allowed herself to soak in the love she saw in his eyes. Did the emotions she saw pouring out of him include her? He wiped a tear away, crouched down next to her, and placed a hand on their grandson.

"Welcome to the world, Hudson Kade and Lacey Lynn Holt."

PATRICE WAS SO tired she didn't argue when Kade insisted he drive her home from the hospital. Reese was beyond happy and tired. Connor couldn't stop smiling, and the twins continued to sleep through all the attention and cuddles.

"I'd like to come in. Explain why I showed up at O'Malley's." Kade continued to stare straight ahead.

She chanced a glance at his profile. It didn't matter why he'd shown up. She'd already made up her mind that things needed to end, and in a way, him doing what he did, for whatever reason, made it easier to end things now.

"Kade, I can't do this anymore. My heart can't.... What I mean is...as much as I want it, any more time in your arms is going to ruin me for anyone else. Hell, it probably already has." She had to keep this light.

"I know we went into this thinking we'd be fine on the other side, but it's not fair to either one of us or our kids, our beautiful grandbabies. My god, Kade, we are so lucky to have our family. But we need to move on. We need to stop."

The look he gave her made her heart shift. If she gave in to that look...no, she knew if things didn't end now, her heart was in danger of shattering.

"Friends-with-benefits isn't working for me. I know I can be alone for the rest of my life, be happy, continue to run my business, travel, spoil Lacey and Hudson until Reese puts me in time-out." Holding back tears, she blew out a sigh than a nervous laugh. Knowing she couldn't make him say the words she wanted to hear, she knew she could live without him, but the love she had for him would carry on whether Kade returned it or not.

She let out a sob as she realized she had just admitted to herself that she loved him. He sat silently, looking out the front window of his SUV. She thought he would protest. Wanted him to protest, beg her to change her mind. Patrice wanted him to declare his love for her, that he couldn't live without her.

The silence finally got to her. She let out a laugh and wiped her eyes. "Thank you for the ride home," she whispered.

"Patrice, I—"

"You don't have to say anything, Kade. That's the beauty of friendship, right? I will always be your friend, but being together like we have...it's just time to end the...fun." *Stop talking Patrice.*

Kade's face showed little emotion. He'd listened, and that was all she'd wanted. To get her feelings out without breaking down. Wishing for him to feel different was futile. She'd spent her marriage with unfulfilled wishes and false hope that love could re-bloom between her and Stephen.

She wasn't going to spend any more time spinning her wheels and losing herself to another man who couldn't return her love. Desperate to get inside so she could have a good cry, she opened her purse, fumbling for her keys.

Kade stilled her hand with his and tugged her close until his forehead touched hers. She inhaled his scent, then pursed her lips. Holding back another sob and a plea to beg him to sweep her up and take her to bed, she instead did the hardest thing she'd ever done in her life.

She cupped his face, "Goodnight, Kade." Placing a soft kiss on his full, warm lips, she used what little will she had left and got out of the car. She wasn't sure how she made it to her front door, but she managed to unlock it and closed it without looking back.

Locking the door, she stood in her entryway, frozen. Emptiness seized her heart, and tears clouded her gaze. How was she ever going to get over him?

KADE COULDN'T REMEMBER how long he'd sat in the car in front of Patrice's house before driving home on autopilot. His sheets were twisted after a night of turning his body and mind over and over, figuring out where the hell he went wrong.

He'd been with women where it had been all too easy to walk away. Didn't say a lot about him, but he'd never led anyone on or wanted any more than a brief encounter to settle his body's most basic needs.

Kade's heart squeezed tight at the thought of never

touching Patrice again. Watching her face light up when she laughed at his lame jokes, spending hours discussing favorite books, movies, or how excited they were to become grandparents—a platonic friendship wasn't going to cut it for him.

Today was Saturday. No work, no commitments other than to get his head out of his ass and figure out what he was going to do. Connor had texted him to say Reese and the babies would stay one more night in the hospital. Kade offered to pick up lunch from The Club and bring Reese her favorite meal.

All the employees were excited to see him, and he forgot his troubles while showing off the pictures of the twins. Until he came across the photos of Patrice with the babies. His heart flipped into overdrive, knowing he'd see her again at some point later today. Just because they'd ended things, that wouldn't keep her from those babies and her daughter.

He grabbed the food and made the short drive to the hospital. Everyone but Connor was sleeping. He set the container down and peered into the bassinets. Both Hudson and Lacey's lips were puckered in perfect bows, their heads covered in Outlaw logo beanies. He itched to pick them up and hold them, but knew there would be plenty of time for that soon.

Connor followed him into the hallway. "Hey, you talk to Patrice today?"

Kade jerked at the mention of her name. "No. I would have thought she would have been here at first light."

They both chuckled.

"Oh, yeah. But after the two of them had another good cry over Hudson and Lacey, I noticed Patrice had dark circles under her eyes. And then it hit me that her eyes were already red and puffy before she and Reese began blubbering over the babies." Connor paused and sighed. "I kinda thought you two would show up here together, you know?"

Kade rubbed his neck and ignored the bait.

"Okay, I get it. None of my business. So, anyway, Reese asked her what was up, but Patrice kept deflecting. She left about an hour ago." Connor stared, waiting for Kade to respond.

But Kade wasn't ready to spill. Yet.

"Dad, give me something here. I mean, I didn't tell Reese about giving you a heads up about the whole speed dating thing, so maybe you could put me out of my misery here?"

Hearing that Patrice looked as tired as he felt gave him a spark of hope in a twisted way. Maybe it meant she spent her night like he had: tossing and turning and wondering what if?

It had been nothing short of a revelation how deep his feelings went for Patrice. However, he needed to be honest with himself—it scared the shit out of him, too. After Connor's mom, he locked down his heart. Sharing his body for a short time? No problem. But sharing himself, to be vulnerable with another woman, was he ready to take another chance?

His heart screamed yes, while his head reminded him of how badly it had ended.

Connor's hand on his shoulder brought him back to the moment.

"Dad, I'm gonna guess it didn't go well. So take it from a guy who screwed up big time with Reese, then got a second chance. Tell Patrice how you feel. You two have been all starry-eyed for a month. Reese and I are pretty sure something's going with you two, and we couldn't be happier, so if you guys are worried about us, don't be." Connor's hand squeezed Kade's shoulder, then pulled him in for a hug.

"How'd you get to be so damn smart?"

"Good genes, I guess." Connor's blue eyes filled with tears. "I just want my dad to be happy. If Patrice does that, you need to go work it out with her."

On cue, one of the babies began crying. Reese's soothing voice carried out to them, and they both turned and watched as she plucked Lacey out of her bassinet, cuddling her close. Hudson chimed in with a low whimper.

Kade patted his son on the back. "Go get him, son... Dad. I'm good. Thanks for the advice." He stood in the hall marveling at the family his son had created.

Time was not on anyone's side. The kids would be walking, talking, and so on before anyone was ready. And he couldn't think of watching all of that happen with anyone but Patrice because he knew now there was no going back to being just friends.

ELEVEN

"Patrice, open the door!" Kade pulled out his cell and began typing. He'd been on her porch for five minutes. *Dammit, Patrice, just talk to me.*

How the hell had he lived all these years and not realized that when you found someone you wanted to share the most mundane topics with, who lit that inner flame of need every time they were together, that *that* was what made life worth living?

Man, he sounded like a sap. But would he rather be alone or be a sap with a woman who couldn't have been more tailored made for him than she was?

Patrice finally opened her door, glaring daggers at him. "Come on in Kade. You're scaring my neighbors."

Her hair looked as if someone's hands had been run through it and her cheek sported a crease, probably from her pillowcase. His chest tightened: she'd never looked more beautiful to him than she did right now.

"Yeah, sorry. I didn't even think you'd be napping. Tough night?" Kade stepped over the threshold, inhaling the scent she wore. The memory of its flavor on his tongue from the last time they were together went straight to his cock. His hands curled. He needed to keep his hands off of her until he said what he needed to say.

"Please, don't. I said all I wanted to say last night and—"

"Sit with me on the couch, Patrice. I promise I won't take too long." Kade opened his arms toward her, inches from touching. "Please?"

Patrice crossed her arms and lifted her chin. "Who told you about the speed dating? Lois? Reese?"

"Connor. He texted me, and I saw red. Hell, I've never had a jealous moment in my life until yesterday. It was a stupid caveman move, demanding the remaining days of our deal like some love-sick fool. I'm so sorry, Patrice. I'd really like a chance to make it up to you." Kade strode over to Patrice, took her face into his hands, and whispered, "Please?"

She closed her eyes at his touch. "Kade, I don't know what to say."

"You don't need to say anything. I'm almost done with the sappy stuff."

Patrice released a sigh. "Okay. Let's sit. I can't wait to hear what you consider sappy." She pulled away from him and sat down. "But no more touching. I can't think when you touch me."

Her whispered confession sparked hope, allowing him to breathe a bit easier. "Okay, no touching. At least until I'm finished, then no promises."

"When you walked into the house without a backward glance, it was a gut punch—more painful even than the disaster of my first marriage. I made a stupid promise to myself that I wouldn't let another woman get close enough to hurt me."

Taking a long, deep breath, he continued.

"And I didn't, not until I met you. And the thing is, I never once thought about being hurt by you because I was too busy discovering how funny, caring, brilliant, and incredibly mind-blowing sexy you are when you let me touch you. Patrice, all these years as friends, I stayed away on purpose. You probably had no idea how attracted I was to you. And then, after Stephen's accident, you had so much on your plate with the kids, and I was stupid to think I still didn't need anyone permanent in my life."

"Kade, I—" Patrice's eyes rounded, her mouth dropped open, then she quickly shut it.

"Let me finish. I wasted a lot of years, and then Reese and Connor found each other again, and suddenly we're back in each other's lives. My attraction to you grew, but I still held back. And then I was stupid enough to make that deal so that I could get my hands on you while building in an automatic out. I thought...I could protect myself from being hurt. And then, last night, I hurt both of us."

Kade's voice was raw from emotion. He hadn't thought about what came after his declaration, but he hadn't expected to see tears streaming down Patrice's face. If he thought he was scared before, it was nothing compared to this moment. "On that first night together, I knew, and it scared the shit out of me. I knew there was no going back for me. I'd fallen.

He promised he wouldn't touch her, but it was ripping him apart to see her so sad. He cupped her face and wiped away her tears using the pads of his thumbs. "Don't cry, sweetheart. Tell me what you're thinking?"

Patrice closed her eyes. He held his breath. The gravity of the moment shook him. He got it now. What it meant to be genuinely vulnerable as someone else held your heart in their hand.

"I love you." The whispered words fell from his lips. He couldn't hold back. No matter how she felt about him, he wanted her to know.

He placed a soft kiss on her trembling lips. "I can't believe it's taken me this long to tell you. From the first moment I laid eyes on you. And yes, I know it sounds corny. Even then, I knew how special you were, still are. But you belonged to someone else. And even after he died, I kept you out of reach. Convinced myself that being your friend was enough...until three weeks, four days, and twelve hours ago."

Patrice laughed, "This is crazy." Her tears splashed onto Kade's fingers. "I mean like crazy fast, what—"

Kade knew what she was feeling, and it was heady and new, and he wanted to show her just how much he loved her. He lowered his head again in a kiss meant to claim and show her how rare their connection was.

"I don't need any more time," Kade whispered between kisses. "I don't want to hide *us* anymore. I want a second chance at life, at love with you. I want forever, Patrice."

"I want that too. I love you." Patrice's declaration was filled with laughter, joy, love.

Another breathless kiss. More tears and laughter. Kade removed his jacket, then lifted her legs, stretching them out on the couch. He covered her body with his and nibbled her neck. "Thank you for letting me in."

He traced his tongue around her ear and absorbed her body's shudders from his touch.

"Thank you for agreeing to that crazy deal." He blew in her ear and grinned when she wriggled her hips under him, pressing herself into his hard cock.

"And most of all, thank you for helping me realize how empty my life would be if I went on pretending. That being your friend would ever be enough. Patrice, I love you so much."

Patrice touched his lips with her fingertips before he could kiss her. "You are a sap; I had no idea. I like it. Now, Kade Holt take me to bed. I believe we still have a couple of days left on our deal. Then we can surprise the kids with our news." She hooked a leg around his hip, locking him in place.

Kade groaned. "Keep that up, and we're not going to make it to the bedroom." He ran his hand over her hip to her waist, resting it on the side of her breast. Man, he loved her curves. "So, what news are we sharing?"

Patrice's face bloomed into a slow, sexy smile. "That their parents have decided that friends-with-benefits was great and all, but they, meaning we, have decided on a May wedding. Here. In the backyard."

Kade waited a beat for panic to seize him, but it never came. "Do we have to wait until May?"

"For the wedding, yes. For everything else? No. Our forever starts now." Patrice pulled him in for another kiss, wrapped her arms around him, wrapping him up in love.

EPILOGUE

Six months later

THE GRANDBABIES STOLE THE DAY. Chubby legs, rosy pinchable cheeks. A frilly pink dress for Lacey and a mini white tux for Hudson. The twins happily crawled on the large playmat Kade had set up in their backyard. Safe and secure, they were surrounded by a clear plastic playpen while the grown-ups danced under the twinkle lights strung from the basketball hoop to the large oak tree on the opposite side of the patio.

Patrice was happy. Beyond happy, actually. The weather was perfect; the ceremony was simple but sweet, and she only cried twice. Their closest friends and family witnessed the late spring wedding, and thanks to Sophie and Evie, she hadn't had to do anything but pick her dress and flowers, and they designed, organized, and pulled off the intimate gathering perfectly.

She held onto her husband as he led them slowly around the dance floor set up on Royce's old basketball court. Her son had surprised her with a few tears as he gave her away. Then, both her kids surprised her at how accepting they'd been when she'd told them she was marrying Kade.

However, she held back from sharing the real story. There was no need to embarrass them, since she was sure her kids thought that sex wasn't something she was still having at almost fifty. Well, maybe Reese had a clue.

The song ended, and Kade stopped them in the middle of the yard, placing a hand under her chin. "Is it time yet? Can we kick everyone out?"

"Another hour, at least. I know. I want you too." She kissed him on the cheek, afraid if she touched his lips, there would be no doubt what the newlyweds would rather be doing.

"Okay. One hour. I need something cold to keep myself from carrying you into the house. How about some champagne?" Kade lifted their joined hands and kissed her fingers.

This man was killing her. His need for her continued to amaze her. All those warnings of sex after fifty fading away made her chuckle. Thankfully, not with them. She let out a sigh and smiled. "Perfect. I'll go check in with Lois. She brought her son as her date, hoping to introduce Sam to a couple of Reese's single friends, but I don't think it went as planned."

Patrice watched her husband walk over to the bar where Connor and Royce and a few of the Outlaw players, who'd become more like family, had stationed themselves. They'd planned the ceremony around Connor and the team's schedule, making sure it was on a Saturday they played at home.

She found Lois in the middle of the playpen. Lacey and

Hudson were nodding off. "Looks like you drew baby duty, huh?" Her friend looked up and smiled.

"Happily. I volunteered when Reese mentioned she wanted to drag Connor onto the dance floor. Speaking of which, seeing you two together dancing, lost in each other... I'm so happy for you both, Patrice."

She looked back at Kade. Yup, she was lucky, and she knew it. Lois deserved that same happiness. But after a couple dates that went nowhere after the speed dating event months ago, Lois decided she wasn't going to try it again. "You know, Kade has a few friends. Single friends."

Lois rolled her eyes. "It's your wedding day, Patrice. Don't worry about me. If it's meant to be, I'll find someone. If not...." She shrugged her shoulders. "Hey, have you seen Sam? He's been avoiding me since I introduced him to Evie. Well tried to introduce. Evie was talking with Sophie and Grant after the cake was served, and he walked away from the table when he saw her sitting there."

Patrice had met Sam several times but didn't know him all that well. He was a deputy prosecutor and seemed rather intense, career-driven. She worried Lois was setting herself up for disappointment in finding him a wife. She'd probably have better luck finding someone for Heather to date, as her daughter at least showed interest in having a family—one day.

"Do you want me to try? Maybe not with Evie, but I'm pretty sure there are at least a few other single women here." Patrice turned and scanned the tables set up around the backyard. It was getting late, and several people had already left, but who she was thinking of, Kara Wyatt, was her daughter-in-law, Amber's sister.

"No. But thank you. I think if I try any harder, then I'll be in for another lecture on how important his job is, and that he doesn't have time for a real relationship, blah, blah, blah."

Patrice held back a chuckle. She knew how Lois felt. After all, she'd despaired of Reese and Royce of ever finding love, but now she had two grandbabies, and Royce had surprised everyone by eloping with Amber last year. It was only a matter of time before they had baby news, she hoped.

A warm, muscled arm wrapped around her waist; without looking to see who it was, she cleared her throat. "Sorry, buddy, I'm taken."

"Oh, yeah. Well, I hear he's a lucky guy." Kade pulled her tight against him, then leaned down and nuzzled Patrice's neck.

"What are you two discussing over here?" He handed a glass of champagne to his wife and bent down and gently rubbed both their heads. Each twin smiled.

Lois sighed. "Sam and his lack of a girlfriend."

Kade straightened and chuckled. "I'm not touching that one. But that brings up something I've been meaning to ask you."

Patrice and Lois looked quizzically at the other before turning back to Kade.

"You jumping into the match-making game now that you're happily married?" Lois let out a laugh, stood, and gracefully stepped over the edge of the playpen.

"As a matter of fact, no. But I was hoping you could tell me why Adam Riordan can't stop staring at you?" Kade nodded his chin in the direction his friend stood speaking with TS Scott and Grant Conrad, the owners of the Idaho Outlaws.

Patrice, surprised at Kade's observance of his friend's interest, gave Lois a sympathetic look. "You don't have to answer that, Lo." She turned to Kade. "What do you know?"

Kade's right side lifted in a smile. "Nothing. Just curious."

Lois remained silent, but Patrice sensed her friend was holding out on her when it came to the handsome surgeon, but she wasn't going to put her on the spot—yet. She'd wait until they got back from their honeymoon in Costa Rica.

"Lois, you don't have to answer that. Could you help me? I need to find Sophie and let her know Kade and I are ready to leave."

Patrice and Kade shared a smile and watched Lois make her way to Sophie, expertly avoiding Adam as he stood next to Sophie's husband, Grant.

"What are you up to, Mr. Holt?"

"Why would you think I was up to anything, Mrs. Holt?"

Patrice narrowed her eyes. "*Mm-hmm.*"

Kade dropped a kiss on his wife's pouty lips. "Don't worry. I'm just stirring the pot. Seeing what floats to the surface. I asked Adam the same question earlier and got a similar response."

"You naughty boy."

"Just wait. The night is young." Kade wiggled his eyebrows. He took Patrice's glass, set it down with his on the nearest table, and pulled her in tight. The next kiss he placed on his wife's full lips left little doubt to her or their guests that the honeymoon had just begun.

L♡VE at VE

First

&

35TH

A RESCUED BY LOVE: LATER IN LIFE NOVELLA

DEBRA ELISE

ABOUT

Evie Nolan is surrounded by couples—engaged, newly married, baby-expecting couples. As a party planner, it's great for business—not so much for her personal life. Hook-ups, setups, and swiping right gives her hives, but the clock waits for no woman. If Evie wants a family of her own, and she does, maybe she should have started last decade.

Sam Campbell is on the verge of a mid-life crisis and he's only 35. His mom is on his case for grandchildren, his new boss wants his beard gone and the woman, who's been hiding in the shadows, is the only one he wants to jump start his long-neglected sex life with, but she wants nothing to do with him.

They've been circling each other for years and now well-meaning friends plot against them, setting them up for a long weekend at a lake cabin. When Sam decides he's done ignoring their sparks, will Evie be able to resist his irritating yet sneaky smirk that morphs into a seductive smile along with those oh- so-wide shoulders?

No, no, she can't. But will her heart let her walk away when the fun is over?

ONE

"I'M NOT INTERESTED." Evie Nolan said firmly.

She loved her business partner and friend, but she'd had it with all the happiness surrounding her. The babies, the honeymoon pictures and all the sex talk.

"Please, listen carefully and pass it along to...to, everyone: no more blind dates, casual set-ups or invitations to join dating apps." Sighing, she hoped she hadn't come off too bitchy. She was simply *over* it.

"But Evie." Sophie Conrad rubbed her round belly and frowned. "We just want you to—"

"Have what you all have. I get it. But love can't be forced, it can't be planned. Lord knows as ecstatic as I am for you and Amber and Reese having babies, and Patrice getting her second chance at love, I am not a project for any of you."

Evie picked up the iPad they used to design floor plans for their events, tapped the screen and handed it to Sophie. "Now, I'd really like your input on the Hines-Smith engagement party this Saturday."

"Evie, we don't see you as a project. It's just, I feel awful about what happened last time."

Last time was three months ago when Evie caved and agreed to be set up by Sophie's husband, Grant, a co-owner of the Idaho Outlaws baseball team. He'd thought the veteran player Sophie had mentioned might be compatible with Evie.

And truth was Evie had a crush on the player for a while. The Outlaws' outfielder was super-hot, so she took a chance and agreed to the date.

"Soph, it wasn't your fault. I'm a big girl, well past thirty, and I handled it. And now I know what it's like to be confronted by someone's ex-girlfriend, in public, with photographers lurking."

Unfortunately, her friends hadn't known about the ex-girlfriend.

Yeah, Evie was still finding bits of pasta in her car thanks to the jealous ex flipping David's plate. A full plate, mind you. And did it land on David, the intended target? No. The ex-girlfriend had lousy aim, and the food ended up all over her top then slid into Evie's lap.

At least David had offered to pay for her dry cleaning. But the silk blouse had been ruined, one of her favorites, and the next day she burned it in her wood-burning fire-place and swore that was her last set up.

She decided that would be the last time she let her hormones overrule her good sense. After arriving at the restaurant, she'd quickly found they had nothing in common and he was still hung up on his former girlfriend. Pictures of David and his ex in a lip-lock had been plastered all over social media the very next day. Never again was she going to be the rebound girl.

So, no. Evie Nolan was done with friends setting her

up. Unfortunately, that left few options to meet someone new since she worked so much. There was always the old-fashioned way and she could go to a bar: nope. Or, like her grandparents, use a matchmaker. That wasn't going to happen either.

Sophie was still staring at her with puppy-dog eyes as she held the iPad in her hands without looking at the screen.

"C'mon, you know I can't take it when you do that." Evie had to bite her lip to keep from laughing. She would not be talked into another date, even if he was *perfect* for her. She didn't want perfect. Instead, she wanted someone she could have a good argument with, then make up, spread out on the dining room table or at the very least somewhere unexpected.

Evie wanted someone who'd could challenge her stubborn ways. Hello Capricorn, but also someone who was comfortable doing absolutely nothing besides recharging for the next workday. She wanted someone who couldn't keep his hands off her when she cooked or walked past him in a room.

She wanted someone who could curl her toes and make her insides flutter with a look—a look meant only for her—and bonus if he knew his way around an orgasm, preferably multiple. Seeing all her friends settling down into wedded bliss made her realize she should have been more open to finding "the one" long before now.

And long before her friends started having babies, making her admit she really did want a family after years of thinking it wasn't for her. But she still refused to be set up again. She'd find her own guy, thank you very much.

Evie waited Sophie out. She was not giving in. Besides, work was crazy and in a couple months Sophie would be on maternity leave with baby number two and work would become triple crazy.

She'd spent enough years on go-nowhere relationships and had come to terms with the conclusion that love in all its messy, heart-pounding wonderness may happen for her if she stopped trying so hard and let it happen.

Evie hadn't always looked at love that way, that it could just happen. Like instantly. But when you're on a cliff and the only lifeline is love, the only thing that's missing in your life, then the thought of love at first sight seemed less...silly. There were nights lying in bed unable to sleep where she couldn't help but wonder had it already happened? Had she messed things up?

Because there was one man she couldn't stop thinking of, no matter how hard she tried.

He was not her type.

He was too tall, too handsome, and too damn alpha for her taste.

Or maybe it was his perma-smirk and fancy three-piece suits that put her off. She could never see Sam Campbell as someone who'd spend a lazy Sunday in sweats and a t-shirt, napping, reading, or hanging out in bed with her. And yet, when she fantasied about someone, Sam's imperfectly perfectly sculpted face always appeared.

An arrogant face that no matter how hard she tried, she couldn't banish it.

Yeah, he was so not the one. Simply her hormones wishing for one night together—maybe.

"Okay, message received. You win."

Sophie's declaration of defeat snapped Evie from her wayward spin into "it's-never-gonna-happen-ville."

"Let's lock in this floor plan, put in the order for the tables, chairs, etcetera, etcetera and call it a day because this baby needs to eat." Sophie scrolled through app and signed off on Evie's design.

"Thanks. I know everyone wants to see me with a guy of my own. I do too, but from now on I'm done using my friends and apps as a dating service. If he's out there, he'll show up. Because, my friend, I'm not settling."

———

IT WAS ALMOST six p.m. when his cellphone began ringing. Sam Campbell ignored it. He needed to finish reviewing his notes for tomorrow's opening arguments. He was working on an attempted murder case that had taken over a year and a half to bring to trial. When he'd been assigned to it as deputy prosecutor, he thought he had a slam dunk. They had an informant, and a wiretap recording of the defendant arranging the murder for hire. But the man refused to take a plea deal, so here he was spending another night working on this damn case.

The local media had turned it into a circus. A cheating husband, a well-known and prominent business owner in Pineville, had gone looking in the wrong place for someone to kill his wife after she found out about his affair, well affairs.

She'd threatened to take the kids and half his business holdings. Luckily for the wife, the husband hired an ex-con who couldn't shoot straight and was willing to sell him out.

Unfortunately, the case had so many reschedules in the last year, he'd had to cancel numerous personal plans and vacation time. And dammit, he needed a vacation.

And he needed to get laid.

His position with the prosecutor's office left little time for a private life. In the beginning it hadn't bothered him, but lately he'd noticed the number of friends who could meet him for a beer or act as his wingman had been dwindling. Marriage, kids, sleep all became more important to his buddies.

Then there was his new boss, who'd taken an instant dislike to him and his facial hair. The man thought a clean-shaven appearance equaled trustworthiness in the eyes of a jury. Sam had managed to keep it by changing the subject each time it'd come up, but he wasn't sure how much longer he could hold off the older man. He needed a win in this case.

His cell started up again. If it was the judge's office or the court letting him know the defense had weaseled another delay, he was going to...well he didn't want to speculate, but the breakable objects in his office would definitely be in jeopardy. No way in hell he was answering the phone.

Blessed silence reigned for only a minute when it started up again. Sam threw down his pen, ran his hands through his hair, noting it was past time for a haircut and debated.

The phone went silent again for exactly thirty seconds. He counted before it rang once more.

"Dammit." Sam stood, retrieved the cell from his discarded suit pocket, and looked at the screen. It was his mom. Thank God it wasn't the judge.

"Hi, Mom. Everything okay?"

"No. My son is ignoring my calls and messages. Do I have any legal recourse counselor?" Lois Campbell's voice sounded as stern as when he was a kid and got caught in a fib or with cookie crumbs on his face, swearing it was his sister who'd swiped the last two cookies from the cookie jar.

"I object. We had dinner just last month. Didn't we?" Sam stretched his back and sat back down. His mother's sigh made him wince. Okay, so two months ago. And she was right. He hadn't returned her calls.

"Mom, I promise once this case is over, I'll call you every day and you'll see me at dinner so often you'll start complaining I'm around too much."

A loud snort erupted, then his mother chuckled. "Don't make promises you can't keep. And I know how busy you are, but once in a while it's also nice to know that you're still breathing. But that's not the only reason I called. Noel and TS are hosting a party at their place. It's the All-Star break and they're having the players and their families over plus friends, some of whom are female and single, and I want you to come. It's going to be a laid-back beach day and barbeque. You work so hard—"

"Mom, the trial begins tomorrow and will last at least through next week. As much as I'd love to play hooky, there's just no way. When the trial is done, I plan on getting some time off and I'll take you and Heather out for dinner. A celebration dinner, hopefully."

"I'm sure your sister would be happy to celebrate, and I know you'll put that no-good bastard away for a long time. What a poor excuse for a man."

Sam smiled at his mom's colorful description of the defendant, and he did indeed plan to put the bastard away for a very long time. "Thanks for the vote of confidence. So, what have you been up to lately? Anything I should know about? Did you go back to that speed dating event at O'Malley's?" His mom had gone to one a while back with her friend Patrice, who'd recently married after years of widowhood.

"Really, can you see me going through that nonsense? No, I'm perfectly happy the way my life is. I'm not looking for a man at this point in my life, Sam. Besides, at my age, love is overrated."

He hadn't realized how cynical his mom had become about dating and men. Divorced for a long time, she'd dated sporadically over the years. Although he or his sister hadn't expected her to get remarried, not after what their father put her through, but she deserved to be wined and dined; have some fun. Maybe it was time for his mom to focus on her love life and not his or his sister's?

And he refused to think what type of fun his mother could have, nothing like the fun he'd been missing the last few months.

"So, who are you planning on setting me up with this time?" Sam closed the file he'd been reading and saved the document on his laptop he'd been typing with notes for tomorrow's court date. Might as well head home and finish his notes after grabbing something to eat.

"Oh, no one specific. All I want is to see you relax, have a bit of fun." Lois' voice held a hint of sadness.

He knew she wanted to see her kids happily coupled up and providing her grandchildren, but he would not find a woman to settle down with just for his mom. He didn't plan on settling for anyone, period. Besides, he'd yet to find anyone that would make him change his thoughts on marriage. The closest he'd come had ended before it could begin shortly after he was promoted to deputy prosecutor. He'd never been able to figure out what it was about Evie Nolan, but she managed to piss him off and turn him on all at the same time. It just hadn't been in the cards for them.

Marriage for him was way down on his to-do list. The dye had been cast early by his father souring him on marriage. Sam was determined to avoid making the same mistakes as his father.

"I know you do, Mom. But right now, I need to focus on this case. I'll call you next week, and hopefully it'll be over, and I'll take you out to dinner." He hated disappointing her, but this job just allowed little personal time.

"Okay. But if you change your mind, just know you're welcome. I'm sure TS and Grant would love to catch up." His mom ended the call with a wistful sigh.

Sam put his phone away, gathered his things and headed home, wondering if the woman his mom wanted him to see was the same woman who'd been appearing in his dreams lately?

TWO

"Evie, you're gonna be thirty-five in a month. You say you want a family, yet you spend your weekends orchestrating other women's engagement parties or wedding receptions. When are you going to give a guy a chance beyond the first date?"

"First, it's called my job, *Thea*. And second, ouch." Evie pulled her wet hair away from her face, wrapped a scrunchie around it, laid back on the lounger and let out a loud sigh. She knew her Thea meant well, and she never shied away from telling it like it was.

They'd just finished spending time in the pool even though it was technically a beach party, but that area had been claimed by the children of the many guests. In mid-July, the northwest weather had warmed into the high eighties, making the lake water the big draw over the infinity pool where the kids were constantly being told to "stop running" or "no splashing".

"Sorry, Ev. You know I love you, and I know I'm one to talk, but you've got to get back out there."

Evie let her gaze roam the large estate of their friend Noel and her husband TS, one of the owners of the Idaho Outlaws baseball team. The area was filled with players and their families since it was the All-Star break. And plenty of single players. But not one of them gave her the butterflies most women used as their main barometer of attraction. In fact, she'd only felt them twice in her life.

The first had been for her high school boyfriend and the second time almost three years ago.

Yeah, Thea had hit a nerve, a big one. But Evie didn't want to argue.

It was time to let the truth win and stop making excuses about why she was still single.

Love.

Being in love with someone.

It scared the ever-living poo out of her. She'd seen what her parents had gone through but buried beneath all the lies and arguments she'd witnessed, the heart of a true romantic beat steadily if warily.

Evie looked over at Thea sitting on the twin lounger next to her and gave her friend a small smile. "I love you too. What if I never find the one? Or worse, what if I already met him and I screwed it up so bad I don't get a second chance?"

Thea's eyes widened. "Oh, my god, Ev, who are you talking about?"

Evie let her eyes close. Dammit, she said too much. When she opened them instead of seeing only Thea, a tall figure appeared, crossing behind her friend. Her gaze followed the man who somehow always seemed to show up when she tried not to think about him.

"Evie, come on, give it up. Who's the guy you screwed

things up with?" Thea leaned forward. A deep frown marred her features, but her copper haired friend still managed to look beautiful.

"Uh, no one. Just thinking, 'what if' you know?" Evie shaded her eyes and watched Sam leave the pool deck. He wore an unbuttoned short-sleeve shirt, and she couldn't look away. The open shirt showcased his defined chest and abs as the material billowed behind him as he jogged down the steps to the horseshoe pit on the beach below.

Darn it. Why'd he have to be so good looking? And why did he take pleasure in pushing all the wrong buttons whenever they spoke?

"Yeah, I'm not buying it, but whatever. We need to get you out of your rut before your birthday. And what better time when there's a ton of eligible men hanging out in one spot?"

Evie let out a short laugh. Easier said than done. It wasn't like she hadn't been trying, well, expect with David and that was a disaster. But now wasn't the time to begin a relationship when Sophie would be on maternity leave in a month.

"Look, I'm not saying you have to find 'The One' today, but you need to shake things up a bit. Pick a guy, have a conversation, or better yet, kiss the hell out of him and see where it takes you." Thea settled back in the lounger, then pointed her margarita glass at Evie. "I dare you."

Evie threw up her hands. "And what's that going to get me?"

"A start." Thea smiled and sipped her drink. "I mean, it's not like you're pining away for someone, right?"

Was she pining or simply lusting? Evie wasn't shy when it came to men or sex, but was that only because she never gave them an opportunity beyond a couple of dates?

"Hey, ladies. What has you two looking so serious?" Sophie stood at the end of the loungers, her two-year-old Noah on her hip.

"Men." Thea and Evie replied.

"Now there's a subject that calls for more alcohol."

"Amen. I'll go get us another round." Evie stood up, tickled Noah and made her escape.

"Coward."

Thea's laugh followed her as she walked to the upper level of the outdoor deck. She passed by several people she knew but didn't stop to chat. She'd catch up with them later. Too much was on her mind to make small talk.

She smiled at the bartender Noel had hired for the party. "Hi, Slade. How are you?"

Slade Johansson worked full time at O'Malley's Pub, co-owned by Maverick Jansen and Luke Garibaldi, two of the Idaho Outlaws' star players. They were both playing in the All-Star game today, but their wives had stayed home since each had toddlers, plus Lara, Luke's wife, had just announced she was expecting their second.

"Not bad. You having a good time, Evie?" Slade began making more margaritas without asking her what she wanted.

She pushed aside the thought of yet another of her friends being pregnant and focused on the handsome man in front of her. Slade was a couple years younger than her, and as far as she knew, single. Taking in his thick hair, which brushed the collar of his Hawaiian shirt and his striking features, Evie thought he was cute. But she'd never felt that spark of attraction.

Not like she did whenever Sam was...nope, not going there.

"How can I not be having a good time?" Evie took the two glasses Slade handed her and turned to go.

"Hey, can I ask you a quick question?"

Evie turned back and gave him a friendly smile, praying he wasn't going to ask her out. Today she just wanted to relax with friends and not worry about being hit on. She straightened her shoulders and debated on the best way to let him down gently.

"Your friend Thea, is she single?" Slade's face lit with hope.

Wow, talk about an ego deflater. She laughed at herself. "Oh, um. Thea? No. I mean yes. Yes, she is single." Evie bit her lip and practically ran from the cute bartender, who had no interest in her.

"Thanks." Slade grinned and turned to a couple she didn't know and took their drink order.

She continued to chuckle to herself as she walked back to the pool. She handed Thea her drink and said, "Well, at least one of us may end up with a date after all."

"Darn, that was fast." Thea looked in the direction Evie had been. "Who'd you find?"

"Not me. You." Evie took a big gulp of her margarita. "The bartender. Slade? He asked me if you're single."

"No, he didn't." Thea shifted back toward the pool and pulled her wrap tighter around herself.

"Don't do that. You look great." Evie hated that her friend didn't believe someone would find her attractive. Thea was a super confident person: tall, curvy, and gorgeous, so her reaction was curious.

"You did not just tell me that Slade Johansson wanted to know if I'm single."

"Okay, I didn't." Evie waited a beat. "But he did."

"Dammit. I mean, he's hot and yeah, I'd love to go out

with him, but I'm looking for someone who doesn't draw barflies like bees to honey, you know." Thea finger combed her drying hair and let out a long breath.

"Yeah, I know." Evie whispered.

Evie knew exactly what her friend felt. Slade gave off definite bad boy vibes, and yeah, who didn't like a bad boy. But when you reached a certain stage in your life and were ready to find a life partner, a girl wanted a guy who was done being the playboy.

And didn't that fact make her thoughts return to Sam and what had happened years ago when they'd first met? She'd just begun working with Sophie and through her had met a new group of people. And a guy she thought might be the one for her. Until he wasn't.

Boisterous laughing rang out from the horseshoe pit. She did her best to not look. That lasted for two seconds. The group of men who'd been playing were headed back up the steps from the beach. Each one was more handsome than the next. All of them taken except the last one bringing up the rear.

Her gaze locked on Sam. His dark hair was tousled by the light wind and his smile dazzling captivated her. He patted Grant, Sophie's husband, on the back as they passed the pool deck. She couldn't bring herself to look away. She'd never seen him so loose and happy. On the handful of occasions they interacted, he'd either tease her with a smirk on his face or they were caught up on opposite sides of a debate neither seemed inclined to compromise on.

She continued watching him and noticed he was sporting a new beard, adding to his attractiveness. It hinted at an evolving rebel side as he settled into his position with the prosecutor's office.

Before she could tear her gaze away, he caught her

checking him out. The smoldering look the usually well-dressed and buttoned-up lawyer gave her ignited a fresh wave of fluttering in her abdomen.

Stupid butterflies.

THREE

SAM GRABBED another beer and sat next to the fire pit with Rod Davis, an old friend he'd recently reconnected with. Rod was currently running the Children's Club, an after-school and summer program for disadvantage youth. He'd been a star football player at Eastern Washington State, where he was destined for the NFL when an injury ended his dream. But he'd finished college, earning a bachelor's in child psychology before moving pack home to Pineville.

Sam half listened to the surrounding conversation, instead focusing on the small group of women sitting across the patio at the table. He couldn't take his eyes off the lone blonde who appeared to be doing her best at avoiding him. Sam's face broke into a small smile when her gaze darted to where he sat, then just as quickly returned to her friends.

Her movement made him wonder what Evie thought of him. In fact, he'd puzzled over her—them. Why two attractive, single people continued to ignore each other when the chemistry between them was so obvious?

If he had to label them, he'd say they were friends of friends, but in the beginning they'd bumped heads, wound up on opposite sides of an argument neither one cared to resolve. And because of it, she continued to intrigue him, despite the underlying animosity.

But damn if she didn't stir a flame within him, something unmatched compared to the women he'd date when he had time to date. His workload at the prosecutors' office had been crazy the past year. In fact, today was the first night in a very long time.

Movement to his left had him automatically shifting, giving them more room as they took the seat next to him. Draining his beer, he kept his gaze on Evie.

"You know I shouldn't have to attend a friend's party just to see my own son." Lois Campbell's soft reprimand was meant only for Sam's ears.

Sam jolted at the words and stared into his mother's face, dropping a kiss on her forehead, and wrapping an arm around her shoulders, hugging her to him. "I agree. Point him out and I'll have a chat with the ingrate."

Rod laughed at Sam's lame joke. "Hi, Mrs. Campbell. It's nice to see you."

"Rod, good to see you, too. Have you taken your mother out for dinner lately?"

His friend had been around Sam's mom enough to know this was an old joke between mother and son. Sam didn't need to step in and save Rod from answering because he knew what the answer would be.

"She lives in Texas. I take her out to dinner every chance I get when she's in town or I'm there visiting." Rod winked at Lois, then excused himself.

"You're a good son, Rod. Give your mom my best the next time you talk to her and tell her what a lucky woman she is to have such a considerate son."

Sam thought he heard Rod mumble, "you're on your

own man, sorry" as he walked over to the bar to grab another beer.

"Mom, was that really necessary? I try to make it home for dinner at least once a month, right?"

Lois chuckled, patted his arm, and sighed. "What, I can't tease you now? Anyway, congratulations. And I'm glad you could make it today."

"Thank you. I was surprised more than anyone the defendant took the plea bargain, thank fu...um, thankfully and so here I am. Playing horseshoes, drinking beer, and relaxing for the first time in forever. Aren't you proud of me?" Sam looked at his mother's upturned face. Her beautiful features belied her age. Lois could and often did pass for ten years younger. She'd been coloring her hair platinum blonde for as long as he could remember. She swore no one would ever see her with gray hair.

Looking around the people gathered outside, he spotted the new orthopedic doctor, Adam Riordan the Outlaws had hired this season. He'd heard his mom bring up his name a lot lately, but not in the nicest of ways. He wondered if there was something going on there he needed to know about. Maybe it was time to turn the tables on her a bit to see how she enjoyed being questioned about her personal life.

"Mom, isn't that Adam over there? I still haven't met him, may—"

Hi mom steamrolled right over his words. "You know I'm always proud. Often miffed and frustrated by your schedule, but that's an argument I know I'll never win. So, tell me. Which one of the pretty girls over there were you just staring at?"

Sam rolled his eyes and groaned. Leave it to his mom to never let an opportunity pass her by. He placed his empty beer bottle on the ground under his seat and stood, offering his mother a hand. "I hear there's pie and ice cream. The least I can do is have dessert with my favorite girl, the prettiest one here."

"Samuel Campbell, drop the flattery. I'll find out who you had your eye on. There aren't that many single women here tonight." Hands on hips, Lois admonished.

He'd stared down plenty of felons. His mother didn't stand a chance at cracking him, and she knew it. But that didn't mean she wasn't sneaky or would figure it out on her own.

Sighing in defeat, she took his hand and said, "Lead the way."

"I DARE YOU." Thea snickered.

"Really? You know I don't fall for dares." Evie shot back.

"You haven't been in the pool since this afternoon. Not since most of the available guys showed up. Besides, the sun is setting. Everyone else is busy with dessert or has left already. C'mon. You bought the new suit specifically for today. You look great in it, Ev."

Evie wasn't worried about anyone seeing her in the tankini. She was worried that one man would see her and be underwhelmed. It irritated her that she gave *him* space in her head and worried about what he would think of her.

Screw it. She was comfortable with her body and had never worried about her cellulite or less than model thin body. She wasn't giving in to Thea's dare. Not really. She'd get back in the pool because she wanted to, and besides, the party would be ending soon.

She tossed aside her matching blue cover up and marched up to the edge of the pool and dove in. Evie loved the feel of the warm water gliding over her. She swam to the bottom, touched the tiles, and made a wish. It was a silly tradition she and her brother did when they were little thinking they'd receive their hearts' desire if only they could make it to the bottom of the pool at the local YMCA.

Kicking up from the depths of the infinity pool, she broke the surface, greeted by whistles, and Thea cheering her on. Wiping her eyes, then running her hands over her hair, she smoothed the long strands away from her face. Swimming toward the underwater steps, her gaze landed on tanned feet attached to long, muscular legs. Not sure who they belonged to, she continued toward them, ignoring her friends and what was undoubtedly a few players jumping into the pool, creating waves and droplets of water to spray her as she reached the first step.

"So, you do have a fun side. I never would have guessed." Sam stood at the edge of the pool, smirk in place, his shirt still open, and his chiseled abs on still on spectacular display.

Instant heat filled her. Her belly did a flip-flop, and she felt her nipples pucker. Fighting to keep her jaw from dropping at his intense stare as it roamed her body, she refused to show him how he affected her.

Ignoring his outstretched hand, she lifted her chin and used the safety railing to assist her out of the pool. As much as she tried, she couldn't tear her gaze away from his dark brown eyes. For a moment she thought she saw need, desire for her in his stare. Shaking her head, *"Don't kid yourself, Ev. He's looking for a sparring partner. He could have any woman here. Why would he pick you?"*

Back straight, head high, Evie walked toward her

lounger. "I have many sides, Sam. Only a special few get to see them all." Scooping her cover up, she closed her eyes. What made her say such a stupid thing? It almost sounded as if she was flirting with him, and that was the last thing she intended. Seeking a quick exit, she jammed her arms into her wrap, sent a glare at the still smirking Thea and made her way into the house for a piece of cake.

Don't look back, Ev. There's no way he's still staring at you. Did she listen to her inner voice? No, no, she didn't. So, at the last possible second, she turned and sought him out. *Damn her curiosity.*

Sam stood where she'd left him, his gaze locked on her. Evie's body vibrated from the intense stare. A warning shiver traveled down her spine and for a moment she couldn't look away, frozen in the possibility that Sam wanted her. Which was ridiculous.

Complete opposites. They couldn't have a civil conversation to save their lives. For almost three years, every encounter ended in an argument. Pick a topic. He had an opposing viewpoint and didn't hesitate to let her know it. Running in the same social circle had been awkward, but she'd avoided him, mostly.

But now that she'd seen him out of his typical business suit, his hard body on display in those damn swim trunks allowing her to imagine what the rest of him looked like? Damn her traitorous body. It was screaming for her to go back out there and see if there was just one thing they could agree on.

"Evie. Hey, what's up with the frowny face? Come get yourself a piece of this cake before the guys polish it off."

Focusing on the two women in front of her, Evie shook off the overwhelming arousal from a look that probably meant nothing to Sam and plastered a smile on her face for her friends, Sophie, and Noel. Both women had a child secured to their hip. A twinge of envy tugged at her heart.

Sophie's son Noah threw his chubby arms in the air and leaned toward her. "Effie, Effie!" She stepped close and took the toddler in her arms and hugged him close. He snuggled into her, wrapped his arms around her neck, and giggled.

"What's all the commotion in here?" Grant walked into the great room where Noel had set up tables for the food and drink, picked up a plate, and dug into a piece of cake.

Evie sighed. Noah's cuddles soothed her rattled nerves, but she still wanted cake. "Hey, that was mine," she mock scolded Grant.

"Then why aren't you eating it instead of hanging out with my son?" Grant shared a piece with Noah, who proceeded to smear the icing on his cheek, missing his mouth. Letting out a yawn, he rubbed his eye and plopped his head on her shoulder.

Laughing, Evie wiped the boy's face and kissed his forehead. "Someone's ready for bed, I think."

"Here, let me have him." Grant set down his plate, then grabbed Noah. "I'll get his things together, Soph, and meet you in the car." He placed a kiss on his wife's upturned face.

Sighing, Evie cut herself a slice of cake, took a bite, and moaned. "This is so good. From Just Desserts, right? Holly is the cake queen."

Sophie nodded. "Is there any other? I just wish she could have stopped by, but one of her employees quit and until she finds someone new, she's working weekends."

"Hmm, I might know someone. I'll give her a call." Evie finished the last bite and debated a second piece. Maybe she could ask for it to go? "Hey Noel, do you mind if I wrap up a piece?"

Noel handed her a small container. "Holly included

these boxes with the order. Take two. One less for me to eat tomorrow."

"Cake to go? Where do I sign up?" Sam's baritone filled the room.

Evie closed her eyes. Dammit, her wish didn't work. Pretending she didn't hear him behind her, she finished putting the cake in the go box and walked into the kitchen. "I'm going to wash up, then head out and find Thea."

She thought she heard Sam mumble something as she made her quick escape, but Noel and Sophie were laughing, so she wasn't sure.

A few minutes later, Sophie joined her. "So that was interesting." Sophie crossed her arms over her very pregnant belly and stared.

Evie had never discussed her issues with Sam with anyone, but it wasn't hard to tell that the two of them never really got along. "I'm not sure what you mean." Avoiding eye contact, she dried her hands and headed toward the patio door.

"Not so fast. The tension in there was sky high. Did something happen between you and Sam?"

"Nothing specific. I'm sure you've noticed we just don't get along in general." Evie inched closer to the exit.

Sophie said nothing, just tilted her head and let out a "*hm*," as if unconvinced. "Okay, if you say so. Before you go, I had a thought. Once I'm on maternity leave, you're going to have a ton of work on your shoulders. Why don't you take this next week and hang out at our new lake cabin? Grant had the pantry stocked, and the furniture was all set up. All you'll need to do is bring some groceries. It's just going to sit there until after the baby comes."

The idea was tempting. "A whole week? Are you sure? I mean, I know you can handle it, but should you? The baby is due in less than a month and you really should think about going to half days." Evie had toured the cabin with Sophie months ago when it was being renovated. It was located on a small cove off Lake Coeur d'Alene that had yet to be overrun by developers and was the perfect hideaway. But could she really leave Sophie so close to her due date?

"You've more than earned a vacation, Ev. Go. Relax and come back rejuvenated and ready to take over for me, please?"

An entire week to herself? Nothing but sunbathing and reading to fill her days? How could she say no?

FOUR

Sam knew how to read a room, even with the prickly Evie pretending he hadn't spoken directly to her. What was it about her that made him keep trying to engage her in conversation? Setting aside her beauty and how she looked in her bathing suit, *hot*, he had long ago chosen the women he dated by more than their physical appearance. But Evie Nolan pressed all his buttons while ramping up fantasies.

Noel shrugged her shoulders as they all watched Evie's escape.

"Something I said?" Sam asked, tearing his gaze away from Evie's hips before he got caught.

"Maybe, but to be fair, you two have never quite gelled." Sophie offered him a sympathetic smile and followed Evie into the kitchen.

"She's not wrong, Sam. What is it with you two, anyway? Did you date then have a bad break-up, or...?"

"It kinda feels like it, but no. We just end up rubbing each other the wrong way?"

Sam watched Noel as she bit her lip. Her shoulders shook, and he knew what was coming.

"Don't say it."

"What?" Noel shifted her sleeping son to her other shoulder. "Let's go find TS. He's better at this than I am."

Sam followed her to the front of Grant and Sophie's home, wondering what Noel meant and why he couldn't stop thinking about Evie.

"Mom. I thought you'd left already." Sam wrapped an arm around his mom's shoulders.

"That's my fault, Sam." TS grinned. "It seems I can't get through a day without her. We were discussing travel plans, and she mentioned you unexpectedly have a week off. Congrats on the plea deal."

"Thanks. I'm not ashamed to say it was pretty unexpected, but it's very welcomed. And to be honest, I'm ready for a break."

His mom let out a cough and everyone laughed. Seems his work schedule had been discussed among the Outlaw family more than he realized. "Okay, okay. You're getting your wish, mom. Now I just need to decide what to do, where to go. I can't remember the last time I had this much time free."

Sophie walked into the foyer, rubbing her back. "So, this is where the party moved to. What'd I miss?"

"Sam's latest trial. The defendant pled out, so now he's got some time on his hands and we're going to help him decide how to spend it." Grant spoke as he gently rocked Noah. He then reached out his free arm toward his wife, tucking her into his side.

Sam watched the couple as they shared a look. Had a woman ever looked at him that way? He knew he'd never looked at someone the way Grant was at Sophie. Their moment of unspoken communication screamed contentment and love. And it caught him off guard and threw him into a panic.

He'd never witnessed his parents hug each other or share a tender moment. Let alone in front of other people. In the brief time it took for Grant and Sophie to share the love-filled moment, Sam knew he needed that in his life. Talk about having an "aha" moment.

"Lois, remind me again where did Patrice and Kade go on their honeymoon? Maybe Sam—"

"Yeah, no. I'm not spending a week at a couple's resort. I'll come up with something. Maybe I'll just sleep all week. I'm good." Sam decided he needed to leave before all the women in the room mapped out the next seven days of his life. "Thank you for including me. I'll head out. Mom, I'll walk you to your car."

Sophie let out a muffled shout, "No! I mean, Lois, I have some cake for you to take home. It's in the kitchen."

"Cake?" Lois responded with a quizzical look on her face.

"Yes, you know. You asked for an extra piece. There's plenty left." Sophie patted her husband's arm. "I won't be long, I promise." She walked over to Lois, grabbed her arm, and pulled her toward the kitchen.

"That must be some cake." TS chuckled.

"You have no idea." Noel answered before following her friends.

THE NEXT MORNING Evie held herself back from eating cake for breakfast. She had a lot to do before she left for the cabin. She'd save it for her reward after she settled in. It was only a half hour drive from her house, so she had plenty of time and she'd stop at the grocery store on her way. She wasn't sure about the internet service, so she downloaded a bunch of new books just in case it wasn't up and running yet. In fact, she hoped it wasn't. It'd be nice to disconnect and not be compelled to check in with Sophie or her friends constantly.

She debated on what to pack. Toiletries, of course, but since she'd be on her own, did she really need anything besides some comfy shorts, tops and a couple of bathing suits? Not really. And maybe she really didn't need a bathing suit. The closest neighbors were hidden by dense trees on either side of the cabin.

No one to answer to but herself. No bridezillas, or socialites calling every fifteen minutes, wanting to change something. But no one to share her time with, either. Letting the sober thought sink in, Evie wasn't sure how to go about finding "the one." Yes, she'd be turning thirty-five in a month, but was she ready? Ready to open herself up and find someone to laugh with, cry over and love? She was making herself crazy with all this back and forth over what she wanted in her personal life.

Maybe this break was coming at the exact right time for her.

On the drive to the cabin, as hard as she tried to focus on her time off, her single status kept popping into her head. Her professional life was about to ramp up for the foreseeable future, so her best bet there would be to cross her fingers and hope she ran into a single guy at a wedding or engagement party for one of their clients. The thought of it left her feeling desperate.

And if she really wanted a family before she turned forty, she needed to make it her number one priority. Also, was it asking too much to want someone who wanted her for her and not because their clock was ticking too, or caving into the pressure to hurry up already and get married? *Ugh.*

The longer she worried over it, the more she wanted to run screaming in the opposite direction. Because really did she think just because she was finally, maybe, ready for her own prince charming to swoop off her feet and get her pregnant before her eggs closed shop that it was going to just happen?

Sighing, she turned onto the private road leading down to the cabin. Ponderosa pines lined the recently paved entrance. The blue-green lake came into view in between varying in size, thick branches. Evie gripped the steering wheel; a mix of excitement and relief overcame her. Yeah, she really needed this break.

The mid-day sun bounced light off the dark green metal roof as she maneuvered her car down the sloped driveway. Fumbling for the garage door remote on the passenger seat, she hit the button, parked the car, and hit the remote again. A sense of peace enveloped her as the door came down, sealing her in and away from distractions.

She was serious when she told Sophie she was done with setups, so what was her next move? Maybe a good old-fashioned matchmaker? Couldn't be worse than an app, right?

Well, she had almost an entire week to do some serious soul searching and figure it out.

———————

A TYPICAL MORNING found Sam already at work by eight a.m., sometimes earlier. Not today. His body didn't know what to make of still being in bed at seven, even with the late night he'd had. Stretching, he threw off his sheets, padded to the bathroom, and turned on the shower. Standing under the spray, a memory hit him.

A certain curvy blonde who continued to throw him off balance. Yesterday she wore a bathing suit that had him constantly adjusting himself as she lounged by the pool. And lord help him when she emerged from the water. Hair slicked back, her modest bathing top did nothing to hide her puckered nipples, leaving him tongue-tied. Just thinking about that moment made him hard.

From the beginning, Evie had been a puzzle he couldn't quite solve. He'd spent more time arguing with her than he did most of his jury cases. Something about her made him want to prove himself worthy of her attention and respect. Sam couldn't help himself from baiting her whenever they were together. Why he didn't just sleep with her in the beginning and get her out of his system was unlike him. It had worked well for him with most every woman he had an interest in—until her.

Soaping up, Sam attempted to banish her from his thoughts, but he couldn't shake the vision of her, ignoring his outstretched hand as she emerged like a goddess from the pool. He'd had the irrational desire to make her put her coverup back on so no one else would see her. What the hell was that? And when she walked away from him, it took every ounce of his control not to storm after her and carry her off like a caveman to somewhere private.

Deep down, he knew why he hadn't made a play for her from the start. A part of him worried she'd laugh in his face and then he wouldn't have a reason to spar with her verbally. But after yesterday?

Sam spent the night tossing and turning, imagining her under him, on top of him, whispering his name as he filled her until finally taking himself in hand, pretending it was her. He came shouting her name and dammit, now just thinking about her, had him hard all over again. He jammed the handle to cold and soaked his head until his heart rate settled.

Shaking his head, and for the second time in two days, he thought to himself, he really need to get laid.

Dressed and coffee'd up, Sam scrolled through his phone. He had few options for a booty-call since most of the women he'd met in the last year were now in relationships. Unfortunately, they no longer held his interest. And what did that say about him? He hadn't been with a woman in months. Not since Evie had begun popping up more frequently everywhere he went.

Friends' barbeques, baby showers, you name it; she was always there. And when she wasn't, he compared the women he was typically interested in to, well, her.

His mother's assigned ringtone blared from his cell, snapping him back into the moment. "Hi, Mom."

"Sam, you're up."

Letting out a chuckle, Sam finished his coffee. "Don't sound so disappointed. I can hang up if you'd like and you can call back and leave me a voicemail."

A snort sounded over the line. "Well, at least the voice-mail doesn't give me an immediate no whenever I ask to see if you're available."

Yeah, there was that. Guilt at his chosen career's heavy toll on his private life had been weighing heavily on his mind as of late. He did his best to make time for his mom, as did his sister, Heather. Their mom had been single and on her own for a long time and Sam often wished she'd find someone who'd treat her like the queen she was, but she gave him as much push back on that subject as he did to her when she asked him about his dating life.

To broach the subject with her, especially when she was patiently waiting for grandkids, was definitely a slippery slope. "Touché. Let me start again. Good morning, Mother. What can I do for you on this fine day?"

"Stop being a smartass, Samuel." Lois scoffed.

"Yeah, but you love me either way."

"It's a duty I take seriously. And you're going to be glad I called you today because I have the solution to your current problem."

"Oh, yeah? Which one?"

"Where to go on your time off."

"It may be a little late to book a place unless it's close. But I'm good. I'm going to catch up on my reading. And before you ask, fiction. I'll be reading the latest thriller by L.T Ryan. No boring case studies for this vacation, boy."

His mom giggled in response. He loved her laugh. She needed someone in her life to laugh with. "By the way, before I forget, I met that doctor last night you told me about. He's actually—"

"Don't go there. Besides, I called to talk about you and how you can spend a few days away. So, here's the deal. Sophie and Grant bought a fixer-upper lake cabin, but since she's due within the next month, they've decided not to use it this summer. It's available, it's close, and you'll feel like you've actually had a getaway."

Sam didn't answer right away. Typically, anything his mom recommended had an imbedded ulterior motive. Like a friend's single daughter would be at the party or dinner or whatever and she'd act surprised. He was getting good at sniffing out a set-up. But this time, it was a straightforward offer.

"Is the renovation done? Is there wi-fi? How about running water?"

"You really think I'm going to send you anywhere without electricity and a proper bed? I'm still recovering from the great camping disaster of nineteen-ninety-seven."

Sam closed his eyes. He walked right into that one. "Mom, you promised."

Lois' sigh held a faint note of laughter. "Yes. I did. My bad. So, what do you think? It's fully finished, has furniture, appliances and Sophie said the pantry is fully stocked. It's ready to go. You just need to bring beer, snacks and steaks, and you'll be set."

A few days at a lake cabin with guaranteed wi-fi, no meetings to attend, no gatherings where *she* might be there.

Just solitude.

There really wasn't any reason to say no.

FIVE

EVIE FLICKED the bug away from her face. After the third time, its persistence really pissed her off. She cracked her left eye open. A shadow blocked the late afternoon sun. She'd picked this spot on the deck specifically for the angle and guarantee of direct sunlight. The annoying bug seemed to have disappeared. In its place was something, no, someone much larger.

And taller.

And familiar.

A chill traveled down her spine. She was out here alone. And she was topless.

"What are you doing here?" Evie's words came out loud and squeaky. Her arms smashed over her breasts as she searched for something to cover herself.

The shadow morphed into a man and handed her a towel. She maneuvered her left arm to cover both breasts and snagged the cloth to her chest. There was no getting out of this position with her dignity intact. But she had to try. "The least you could do is turn around." Her breathing quickened from her exertion and from the man still staring at her.

"Here, let me help you up." Sam leaned down and offered a hand.

Evie eyed his very masculine, very large hand with its long fingers she'd more than once had a dream over. If there was ever a contest for the sexiest hands, then Sam Campbell would take top honors. She'd never thought a man's hand could be such a turn on until she met Sam.

"Evie?" Sam's eyes locked with hers.

"Just turn around. I can get myself up." Evie huffed out. She swung her legs to the side of the lounger, wrapping herself with the sun warmed towel the best could. Struggling to get her breathing under control, she bit her tongue when what she really wanted to do was scream in frustration. Not because she couldn't stand, but in that split second after she opened her eyes and realized it was Sam and not a bug playing with her hair, Evie wished he'd woken her with a kiss. How messed up was that? After years of bickering, attempting to one-up him or avoid him altogether, he was also the one that set a team of butterflies loose in her belly.

Most of the time she had trouble catching her breath when he first walked into her space, forcing her to ignore her body's reaction and creating a detached attitude when he engaged her in another round of back and forth. It had been such a constant thing between them that the stark desire she saw in his gaze now threw her off.

Was Sam attracted to her?

"Don't be silly. Come here." Sam took her free arm and waited.

His touch sent off a wave of longing. Tilting her head toward him, she froze. She'd seen him as an adversary for so long, she never noticed he had laugh lines or that his eyes were more hazel than brown. And he was still looking at her with a raw need she'd only read about. Had never expected to be on the receiving end of such naked desire.

"I...uh, thanks. What are you doing here?" Evie broke eye contact, then using her legs to lift herself up, she cleared her throat and took in a deep, cleansing breath. What was supposed to be an effort to relax her racing heart backfired as she took in Sam's unique scent. Spicy and all male.

Still holding her arm, Sam smiled. "I was going to ask you the same thing."

"Really? Was that before or after you noticed I was sunbathing topless and didn't look away?"

Something dangerous flashed in his eyes. "When I find beauty in nature, I take my time and admire. But you're right, I could have turned away." He let his hand fall to his side and took a step back.

His words turned her insides all gooey, igniting thoughts of him touching her instead of simply looking. What would she have done if he had touched her, or caressed her exposed flesh, or kiss her? Was she brave enough to drop the towel and find out? Hell no.

Wait a minute, she just realized he said "could" instead of "should". So, did that mean he shot down the idea of giving her privacy and instead looked his fill before waking her? The thought thrilled her, then sent her into a panic. This side of Sam was new to her. He wasn't acting like the know-it-all she'd become accustomed.

Evie instantly reverted to shields up status, a sharp reprimand on the tip of her tongue when he held up his hands in surrender.

"I know what you're going to say before you say it. So let me save you the trouble. I'm sorry I saw your breasts.

However, to be fair, I wasn't expecting to see anything or anyone when I arrived. What I expected was an empty cabin for me to use over the next few days." Sam rubbed his chin and turned his gaze to the dock below where tethered to one of the pilings was a pair of jet skis she had debated about trying before deciding on the topless sunbathing.

He ran a hand through his hair and let out a long sigh. "My plan was for some fun on the lake and to catch up on my reading, relax for the first time in I don't know how long, but now..."

So was hers. Well, minus the jet skis. Her plan was swimming and maybe try out one of the paddle boards. She wasn't about to give up and go home just because he looked tired and in need of a vacation more than anyone she knew.

"How come you're here?"

"Sophie convinced me to take the week off. The baby's due in a month and then I'm taking over while she's on maternity leave. And you? How'd you even know they had a lake cabin, and it wasn't being used this week?"

Sam returned his gaze to Evie and barked out a laugh. "One word. Okay, two. My mother. I should have known this was too good to be true. I'm getting the feeling we've been setup, Evie."

It took her a moment to understand fully what he meant, so caught up in him saying her name. Pretty certain she'd never heard him say it so intimately in all the years they'd know each other, and now today, it created a flutter in her belly. It had been a long time since someone had rendered her speechless. How could she get him to say her name again? Just one more time so she could test out her theory.

"Evie?"

Oh, yeah. There it is again. Damn butterflies. Plus,

what was she going to do now that he'd seen her naked? Well, half naked and now the mere the sound of her name on his full, kissable lips made her panties wet.

Wait, he said set-up? Shaking her head to clear the sensual fog he probably unknowingly put her in, she had to agree and would put good money on that possibility. "How'd your mom know about this place?" Tugging her towel tighter, she shifted a step back. She needed some breathing room, otherwise she might do something mortifying and lean toward him.

"Oh, I think we both know the answer to that." Sam's gaze traveled down to her hands clutching the towel before snapping his darkening gaze back to hers.

The silence grew between them until she couldn't take it anymore. "Stop looking at me like that."

"Like what?"

Was she imagining what she saw in his gaze? Was it wishful thinking or her own sexual frustration?

"Like you might want to kiss me." Her voice came out in a whisper, "or something." Mortified, she felt her face flame, and she needed to get inside. Get dressed and get him out of here.

"Hm, or something." Sam stepped closer and leaned his six-foot-two solid frame into her space and tucked a loose strand of hair behind her ear.

She sucked in a breath at his touch, her eyes fluttered closed, and she waited. And waited. She sensed him taking a step back from her. Although the July air was hot, she immediately felt cold for his withdrawal.

"Well, I'm not leaving." Evie lifted her chin. "It may sound childish, but I was here first."

Shaking his head slowly, Sam released a short laugh. "For once, I'm too tired to argue with you. And you're right.

You shouldn't leave. However, I'm not going anywhere either. It's a big cabin. We could share the space. We're grown-ups. We can work this out." He swept his arm toward the cabin. "There's at least be a couple of bedrooms if not more. What do you say, Ev? I brought steaks and beer. I'd be willing to trade for some guaranteed down time."

Trade? What did he think she had to trade? But more importantly, could she be around this relaxed version of Sam? She'd fought her attraction to him for years because she convinced herself he had a terrible personality. But what if she'd been fooling herself all along and now being together, seeing each other every day in swimsuits and, lord help her less, made her say and do things guaranteed to embarrass herself if he didn't see her in the same way?

Was he thinking she'd be a convenient bed partner since they'd been set-up? Then what? They already could barely stand each other.

"Trade? All you've ever traded with me is snark and condescending remarks. Besides, I have a rule about not sharing lake cabins with men I don't know." *Would he just leave already?*

"Well, it's a good thing you know me then. I admit the last few years have been...interesting between us. Maybe it's time we trade something...more enjoyable?"

Evie's jaw dropped at his remark. *Were they really having this conversation right now?* No matter how many times she'd imagined things could be different between them, she wasn't prepared for sexy banter. Her ability to give as good as she got disappeared. Instead, all she could think of was his hard body and how he looked yesterday.

"And finally, I'm far from a stranger."

His words filtered through her, hitting all her pulse points. The sound of his voice had always stirred her senses, but it, combined with the innuendo behind his words, made her resolve weaken. How was she going to continue to keep her shields up with him? Evie was old enough to know when a man was flirting with her, and the invitation in his gaze left no doubt what he was offering.

Not sure she trusted herself to speak, she rolled her shoulders side-stepped the hot, tempting man Sophie made sure to put in her way and walked away with as much dignity as she could muster.

"No need for trading. As you said, it's a big cabin." She didn't wait for his reply. Was she crazy? Had she given herself permission to explore whatever had just happened between them? Because if she were honest with herself, there was no way she was walking away from the dare she heard in his voice and the desire in his eyes.

SIX

WHILE EVIE HID in the room on the opposite side of the cabin, Sam explored the secluded home. He'd carried in his weekender bag and supplies, put the beer and steaks in the refrigerator and checked out the pantry. Finding it fully stocked, he opened the door in the kitchen. It led to the garage where Evie's car was parked. It made him wonder. If she had parked out in the driveway, would he have turned tail and left straight away after seeing her already here?

He'd the shock of his life when he stepped outside and found her sunbathing topless on the back deck. His immediate reaction to her bare curves was to turn his back. Why he didn't fess up when she called him out and, more importantly, why he'd returned his gaze to her sleeping form was unlike him. He considered himself a gentleman, except apparently when he was around Evie.

She'd always tested him, both intellectually and physically. There were times when they'd been in a heated discussion that his focus had been locked on her full lips, wanting to cradle her face and drag her against him. Then when he realized he'd lost his train of thought, it was everything he could do to will himself back to the topic they were debating before she realized how she affected him.

And just now, he'd been tempted to touch her warm flesh, caressing her full breasts and wake her with a kiss instead of brushing a curl off her face.

He knew staying would test his will to keep his hands off her. And something in her gaze had him thinking she was just as interested in this turn of events as he was.

Yes, he'd always found her attractive, but she was always seemed more interested in sparring with him, debating local politics that sometimes he would purposely play devil's advocate so he could see her all riled up. Now that they were alone and none of their friends could see them, he would not let Evie hide from him.

He might not have a lot of time to convince her that a fling was just what they needed, but he had patience enough to let her see a different side to him.

SOMEHOW, they avoided each other until just before sundown. But there was no way she was going to miss the sunset. Evie closed her tablet, then freshened up in the en suite bathroom. She grabbed a lightweight coverup and walked barefoot through the cabin, noting none of the inside lights had been turned on. Had Sam left? Was she that lucky?

The wall facing the lake was made up mostly of windows. If she wanted to, she could stay inside and have a spectacular view of the sunset from the couch. But this was her vacation too, and no way was she going to sit inside to avoid running into Sam. She was over her embarrassment from earlier, mostly. Thinking he must have used the paddle board or kayak since the cabin was so quiet, Evie stepped out onto the deck, assured she had a bit more time before he showed up before the sun fully set.

"Hello."

Evie sucked in a breath and clutched her chest. "Don't do that!" Heart pounding, she closed her eyes, taking a minute to calm herself.

"You always jump when people say hello to you?"

She cracked one eye open just enough to see Sam spread out on the lounger she was in earlier, a glass of wine in his hand and the other cupped behind his head. He was wearing nothing but a pair of cutoff sweats, his hair wet and slicked back and his glorious body on full display.

"Evie?"

Sam's quiet voice shook her. So much for enjoying the sunset by herself. Her brain just went offline at the amount of toned skin she wanted to touch. Lick and kiss. What would he do if she did just that? Could she be so bold? Probably not. Not unless she knew for sure he wouldn't rebuff her.

"Yeah, I'm fine. Um, just didn't expect you out here." Debating on whether to sit in the chair next to him or put some distance between them, she eyed the bottle of wine. "I forgot my drink; I'll be right back."

"I brought a glass out for you, too. Will you join me?"

Bad idea flashed in her mind. She glanced at the label. Dammit, it was a Cabernet Sauvignon, her favorite. And knowing Sam, it wasn't a ten-dollar bottle, or even a twenty. She had learned over the years he had excellent taste in wine from the many events they'd both attended.

"Sure. Thank you. Did you go out on the paddle board or the kayak?" Determined to keep their conversations neutral, she really didn't want to fall into their typical debates. This was her only vacation this year, and she was determined to relax. Even with the hottest man she knew, sitting mere feet to her right.

He poured her a glass, handed it to her, and smiled. Man, he had the best smile.

"To us."

"Us?" The thought of them being an "us" sent a zing to her heart and unleashed a horde of butterflies in her stomach.

"Sure. Two overworked, thirty-something's enjoying a quiet evening watching the sun sink and the fireflies...fly." Sam touched his glass to hers and sipped.

Caught up in the moment, she zeroed in on his lips as he drank, then pressed them together. A drop of wine clung to the lower one, and she wondered what he would do if she leaned over...*Dammit, Evie. Don't go there.* She averted her gaze, quickly took a sip before leaning back in her chair. "You know, there are no fireflies this far north. In fact—"

"Evie. Just enjoy the wine. No debating, okay?"

"You're right, this is nice, thank you."

"No need to thank me twice and you're welcome."

What was her problem? She'd never felt this nervous around Sam before. She'd also never been alone with Sam before. And he'd never seen her half naked before. At the memory of him seeing her, she felt her nipples tighten.

"I had a thought earlier. We know each other only through our friends, but we don't really know each other on a personal level. I was hoping to change that. I mean, we're sharing the cabin and all. What do you say to a round of twenty questions?"

He was right. After years of only seeing one another a few times a year and a good portion spent sparring over their viewpoints, what she knew of Sam personally could fill a shot glass. But twenty questions seemed like something you'd do on a first date. And getting to know Sam on a personal level could be dangerous, especially if all he was looking for was a fling.

"Oh, I don't know. I kind of like how things are and I was hoping to enjoy the sunset. Do you have a burning need to know my favorite color or movie?" That was a chicken shit answer, and she knew it.

"Why do I get the feeling you've been keeping me at arm's length all this time? You have no trouble discussing world events or local politics with me, but anything personal has you running the other way." Sam's voice sounded raspy, intimate, and it twisted her insides.

The cloudless sky turned a soft pink as the sun dipped below the horizon, giving her the perfect excuse to change the subject. "You know it's funny how when we're in the city that enjoying the sunset is almost an afterthought, but out here it's an event." She kept her gaze skyward, afraid to turn and look at him. He was trying to connect with her, and she wasn't sure she could handle it.

They sat in silence sipping the excellent wine, watching the stars appear as the last rays from the sun crawled back toward the horizon. At first it was uncomfortable, but soon Evie relaxed. "Isn't it beautiful?"

"Very." Sam said.

At his answer, she felt a tingle along her right side. The side closest to him. She turned her head and found him looking at her instead of the sky. A flush of heat ran from the tip of her toes to the top of her head. "I meant the sunset, the sky." She whispered; their gazes still locked.

"That too." Sam smiled.

Reaching toward her. For a moment, she thought he was going to touch her hand or crazier than crazy, maybe kiss her. Instead, he picked up the wine bottle and refilled their glasses. The moment over, she swallowed the lump that had formed in her throat and took a sip of wine, sinking lower in the lounge chair.

Time slowed, and the sky darkened to the point she felt safe sneaking peeks at Sam. His profile was backlit by the light below on the swimming dock. She marveled at his chiseled jawline, his nose, and cheekbones. His hair had long ago dried, her fingers itching to smooth back the lock that had fallen on his forehead. Sam shifted, and she twisted her gaze to the lake.

Time to call it a night. Her heartbeat still not quite settled from his presence, she set her glass on the small table between their chairs. "Thank you for the wine. And the company."

"Goodnight, Evie."

Rising, she could feel his gaze on her, but when she turned to look back at him, he was looking off into the distance. She'd made it halfway to her room when she remembered her wrap. Did she dare go back? Something was pulling her back out to that deck. To Sam. Not going along with his request to get to know each other better was nagging at her. And something else. Something a bit more primal.

She pivoted back the way she'd come and ran smack into hard muscle. "*Oomph!*"

Sam's arms came out to steady her and, like a deer caught in the headlights, she froze at his touch. Head tilted up, all she could do was stare at his face, at his lips and wondered what he would do if she just stood on her tiptoes and—

"You forgot your sweater." Sam blurted.

What? Oh, yeah. "Um, thanks. I was just coming back

to get it." She tried to raise her arm, but his hands were still on her, and he didn't seem inclined to let her go. Still watching him, she licked her lips and waited.

Sam let out a low groan, mumbled something that sounded like, "What the hell?" And kissed her. Not a chaste goodnight kiss, but a hard, commanding plundering of her lips. And she kissed him back. She put all three plus years of pent-up desire for this man into her kiss, opening her mouth, giving him full access. His tongue swept between her lips, tangling with hers.

The only thought she had was *more*. More kisses, more of Sam as they stood in the middle of the dark cabin. He loosened his grip, bringing both his hands to her face. His large hands cradled her face. His long fingers delved into her hair.

The kiss deepened, then slowed. Time stood still as they fed from each other. Untapped desire flowed between them, and it was perfect.

When breathing became a necessity, they broke apart. She watched him take a step back from her with a confused look on his face. He looked everywhere but at her, running a hand over his face.

"That was...unexpected," he said.

"Unexpected?"

"In a good way. The very best way. But...hell. I don't regret it. Maybe it's best if we sleep on it. Not with each other, I mean. Separately." He rubbed his face again and took another step back. "Good night, Evie." He leaned forward, kissed my cheek, then walked to the other side of the cabin to his room.

Standing where he left me, the sound of his door closing broke the spell he'd put me under with that devastating kiss.

What just happened?

SEVEN

THE SOUNDS of chirping woke her. Birds were awesome. This morning not so much. Her night had been spent tossing and turning. That kiss. That damn kiss had her hot and bothered all night. Sitting upright, hair in her eyes, she let out a frustrated sigh. Why? Why kiss her as if they were long-lost lovers, then turn and leave her ready to give him anything he asked?

Men were so confusing. No wonder she did her best to keep from falling into the same trap her parents had. She knew she had hang-ups when it came to relationships. Anytime she sensed a boyfriend becoming too serious, she managed to self-sabotage. Every time. On the outside, she played off her long list of failed relationships as no big deal to her friends' concerns. She'd tell them she was holding out for the perfect guy, when deep down she knew he didn't exist.

But what could you do when most of the world revolved around getting married, having kids, finding your soul mate, and living happily ever after? She only had so much time left if she wanted to dive into the deep end of that pool, but the idea of handing her heart over to someone else still gave her hives.

A soft knock sounded on her door.

"There's fresh coffee. I'm headed out on the lake."

Her eyes locked onto the doorknob. Would he open it? A minute ticked by. Something held her back from answering. When she thought he'd finally left, she heard throat clearing.

"Um, okay. I'll see you later in the afternoon." Sam's footsteps faded. The sound of the sliding door hit her. She flopped backward on the bed and let out a long raspberry. It was for herself more than Sam.

She was such a coward.

She should have thanked him, at the very least. Instead, she sat there safe under the covers instead of manning up, er *womanning* up, and facing what had shaken her to her core. The reason she didn't sleep a wink last night was because it had hit her. Sam was the one.

A few hours later, she was back out on the deck with her tablet, this time fully covered in her favorite tankini. She had trouble concentrating on her book. Her mind kept going back to last night and the realization of her true feelings for Sam.

Letting out a long sigh after re-reading the same paragraph three times, she went back inside to mix up a pitcher of peach lemonade, then added some vodka. If she couldn't be in the tropics, then the tropical drinks had to come to her.

Even though she promised herself she wouldn't, she snuck a peek at her phone. No texts from friends since she put the word out she was hibernating for the week at Sophie and Grant's lake house. But there was one from her brother, Cole. He wanted to know what her plans were for Thanksgiving.

They were close. Well, as close as two siblings could be who lived on the opposite ends of the country. Plus add in the time he was deployed, time spent together had been rare since she graduated from college.

He said he was getting time off this year for the holiday and wanted to see her. They hadn't seen each other since she'd traveled back east to stay with him several years ago when he'd been injured in the war and was going through physical therapy. Cole was the strongest man she knew, and after losing part of his leg to an IED, he worked hard to adapt and walk again. He was her hero.

She returned his text and told him she'd make time. He hadn't been to her new house. She now had a guest room where he could stay. Excited at seeing her brother later in the year, she missed the sound of the back door sliding open.

"Good news?"

Sam's husky voice made her jump. She fumbled and almost dropped her phone.

"Sorry. I thought you would've heard me come in."

Heart racing, again, Evie looked across the informal dining area on the other side of the open kitchen, and found a wet and smiling Sam. Oh, what his smile did to her. Her stomach dropped, a pool of warmth settled even lower, and her nipples tightened. His lean, muscular form was on full display. He acted as if nothing had happened between them last night.

Looking at him, you'd never guess he was an attorney, spending his days behind a desk or a courtroom because Sam Campbell could easily be on the cover of a men's fitness magazine.

"Evie? Everything okay?"

"Hm? Oh, yeah. It was my brother. I mean, I just read a

text from him. He's coming for Thanksgiving. We haven't seen each other in years. So, yes, it was definitely good news."

Sam nodded. "Great."

Yeah, great. She bit her lip and stared. I mean, how could she not? The longer they stood there staring without speaking, the more awkward it became. Should she bring up the kiss or just act like having her socks knocked off was an everyday occurrence?

"Well..."

"Um..."

Both laughed. "You first." Sam offered.

"How come you're back so soon? I thought you'd be out on the water most of the day?" Still a coward, damn it.

Sam waved an arm toward the lake. "An idiot on a jet ski buzzed me and the wake dumped me. Which would have been fine except there was a floating log I couldn't avoid, and it took out a chunk off the tip of the paddle board, so here I am."

Evie rushed over to Sam, scanning him for injuries. "Are you hurt?" She placed a hand on his sun warmed arm. A zap of electricity traveled through her hand at the contact, setting her nerve endings singing throughout her body. Doing her best to ignore her reaction, she walked around him, looking for any cuts or scrapes.

"No. I'm good, just pissed. I think I'm just going to hang out here today. Maybe do some swimming off the dock then reading this new thriller I brought with me. What about you? I saw a book next to your chair outside. You going back out?"

Well, she was. But now she wasn't so sure. Could she concentrate with Sam feet away in the water? Thinking about their kiss. Watching him with his swim trunks molded to his hard body? Maybe it was time to stay inside or offer to fix them lunch.

"I hadn't thought about it. I came in to make lemonade, but it's almost lunchtime. How about I fix us something to eat, and you can get some laps in? I'll call you when everything's ready?"

"Okay, that sounds awesome. But first about last night... I wanted to talk to you earlier, but you were still sleeping and—"

Evie suddenly wanted to be anywhere but there. She wasn't sure she could handle whatever letdown was coming from Sam. Maybe he wasn't that into her? No problem. She was a big girl. She'd been through more embarrassing situations.

"Sam, it's okay. It happened. We had a couple glasses of wine...so, no need to apologize. I get it."

His lips thinned out and his eyebrows came together as he frowned. "I, no. I don't think you do. At least for the kiss, I didn't want to apologize. The kiss was...not something I regret. But I shouldn't have walked away. But it was the only thing I could think of to keep from throwing you over my shoulders and taking you to bed. Look, I know we've had this adversarial thing between us for years, but I'd want—"

A loud knock interrupted Sam. It came from the sliding doors behind him and had him quickly spinning around. A man in uniform was standing on the deck, peering in at them. She watched as he strode away from her.

But that wasn't as half as shocking as what Sam just admitted to her. *He wanted to carry her off to bed?* So many questions raced through her head as she watched Sam converse with the much shorter man who looked to be a county marine officer. When it was obvious they wouldn't be done anytime soon, she began preparing some lunch.

Evie had just finished arranging food on the dining table when Sam came back inside.

"Hi. I need to go with the officer and show him where I think I went in the lake so they can locate the waterlogged piece of wood I hit. I'm going to go get a shirt and join him." He saw the food and grimaced. "Sorry. I'm not sure how long I'll be. But when I get back, we'll finish our conversation, okay?"

She nodded, not sure she could keep the disappointment out of her voice.

On his way to his room, Sam had stopped near her. So near she could see the frustration in his eyes and how his gaze swept over her, landing briefly on her breasts, then to her face zeroing on her lips. One corner of his mouth lifted at her increased breathing. He leaned down, kissed her quick and hard before taking off to his bedroom, leaving her slightly dazed. She shook off a sense of déjà vu and began removing the food from the table.

With so much on her mind, her appetite gone, Evie decided what she needed was a good nap.

EIGHT

Evie stretched and rolled to her side, glancing at her cell to see what time it was. A few minutes after six p.m. A scent of grilling meat tickled her nose, which was immediately followed by her stomach growling. She hadn't meant to sleep so long, but after little sleep and no lunch her body needed it.

Wiping the sleep from her eyes, Evie sat up and listened. No sounds came from inside the cabin. Sam must be outside. Was he fixing the steak he'd promised her? Another growl from her stomach sent her to her feet. She changed into a matching short set made of soft jersey, then grabbed her sweater and thrust her arms into the soft material and headed back outside.

The sun shone high and bright, reflecting on the still lake water. Sam had his back to her as she exited through the glass door. He'd changed from earlier and wore a white linen shirt and a pair of khaki shorts that hugged his backside nicely.

Evie cleared her throat and waited for him to notice her. It didn't take long. He turned and the smile he wore dazzled brighter than the sun sparkling off the water behind him. She held back a gasp as her gaze hungrily took him in.

His strong jawline and handsome face made her heart miss a beat. Apparently, it took little attention from him to turn her insides to mush. She squeezed her thighs together to ease the instant ache his attention created and faced the truth. She wanted Sam more than any other man she'd met, dated, or slept with. He was made of potent stuff and their history be damned.

Where had this man come from and what had he done with the Mr.-Know-It-All she'd battled for years?

"Hi." Sam's gaze ran over her before he turned back to the Traeger grill.

She stumbled forward, catching herself on the closest deck chair. Her fingers curled around the smooth wood. She took in a slow, deep breath. "Hi." Her voice came out low and breathy.

"You're just in time. How do you like your steak?"

She wasn't interested in steak at the moment or spending any more time with sexy word play. Whether it was simply by chance, or if their friends had arranged for them to be here, it didn't matter.

Setting aside their past, Evie jumped in with both feet. "What if I said steak isn't what I'm interested in?" Eyeing the open bottle of wine on the table, a Bordeaux this time, she poured herself a glass and sat at the patio table, feet from where Sam watched over the steaks.

Sam's back went ramrod straight at her words. It was the only outward sign that he picked up on the real meaning of her words. Keeping his back to her, he plated the meat, grabbed his glass of wine, and took a deep drink, then turned to face her.

Her gaze immediately went to his exposed chest. His

shirt was unbuttoned, the dips and valleys of his pecs and six-pack revved her pulse. She allowed her gaze to drop to the waistband of his shorts, where a dusting of hair disappeared. And still lower, an obvious bulge behind his fly gave away his body's reaction.

"So, is it the company or the situation that has you refraining from your usual battle pattern and offering me an opportunity to...enjoy each other without endless debate?"

Evie busted out laughing at his formal words. She really had him wondering what she was up to, didn't she? "Oh, counselor you are skilled at this, aren't you? It's a good thing I've never had to be on the opposing side in a courtroom with you. I'm not sure I'd be on the winning side."

"Well, you know what they same about assuming. Even with the fuck me vibes you're throwing my way, I need to be sure before I toss you over my shoulder and take you to bed."

Yeah, there was no going back now, Evie. Finish the game you started or bow out now and pack up and leave. His gaze hadn't left her face since he turned around and his eyes were darker than she'd ever seen them. He wanted her; she wanted him. Years of arguing undoubtedly created the world's longest bout of foreplay and there was nothing left to do but play this out to its conclusion.

"Why do you think it's taken us this long to figure out all our bickering was hiding a mutual attraction neither one of us had the guts to admit?" She asked.

"At this moment, I could give a shit." Sam closed the distance between them and held out his hand. "I'll give you the choice of walking or being carried. So choose fast because I'm so ready to be inside you that if we wait much longer. I'm close to not caring if it happens in full view of anyone passing by."

She liked this side of Sam. Naughty and sexy as hell. The thought of them having sex out in the open was exciting, sending a zap of awareness through her as heat pooled in her core. If the sun had already set, she'd jump at the offer. "Maybe next time. Let's go—"

Sam growled her name, caught her hand in his and tugged her up and against him, kissing her until her head spun. She circled her arms around his waist, spreading her hands over his warm muscled back, pressing herself close. Evie let out a moan when he ground his erection into her. The action created a dizzying wave of desire in her, unmatched by any other man she'd been with.

Without breaking their kiss, Sam dipped down and lifted her under up beneath her ass. She wrapped her legs around his waist, anticipation making her wetter than she'd ever been.

"Hold on tight. I don't want to drop you." Sam's long legs brought them to the room she'd been using. "This good?" He mumbled against her lips.

She nodded and before she could say anything else; he tossed her onto his rumpled bed, whipped off his shirt and grinned at her. "Don't move. Scratch that. Strip. I need a condom." Then he was gone. Scrambling to get undressed before he returned, Evie brushed hair out of eyes and was wiggling out of her sleep shorts when he strode back in. He was beautiful. Shorts gone, his erection straining as he rolled on the condom.

He leaned over her, running his hand from her ankle up her lower leg to her inner thigh, stopping within inches of her heat. "Are you sure this is what you want?" His fast breathing matched hers.

"This. You. Yes, I want it all."

"I'll do my best. But it may take more than once to reach

'all'." Sam brushed his lips against hers. Feather light, he touched her lips again. "I'd be lying if I didn't tell you I've thought about us being together. Like this. Instead of debating world events or which city ordinance should have passed, or—."

"Sam?"

"Hm?"

"You talk too much."

NINE

"Oh, you're going to pay for that." Sam grinned, watching as Evie's eyes went wide at his words. Change of plans. Instead of covering her gorgeous body with his, he kneeled at her feet, holding her gaze as her pupils dilated from anticipation and desire.

He nudged her feet further apart, ran his hands from her calves to the top of her knees and spread her wide. She was on full display, his eyes feasting on his glistening prize. "You're already so wet for me, aren't you?"

She nodded and let out a muffled moan as his hands ventured further up her thighs, then retreating slowly. He watched as she bit her lower lip, chuckling when she let out a puff of air in frustration as he stilled and waited.

"Sam?"

"Evie?"

He'd dreamt of this moment. Of having Evie beneath him begging for him to touch her, that he wanted to take a moment and commit her to memory. "So damn beautiful. You know how many nights I thought of you? Like this?"

Evie shook her head at his words, and for a split second,

he thought he saw tears pool in her eyes. She gifted him with a sexy smile, lifted herself onto her elbows, spreading her legs wider. "What are you waiting for?"

Surprise, then lust, urged him to take what she offered. He bent and licked her satin folds, reveling in her reaction as her body shivered. He repeated the move over and over, increasing the pressure with each pass. Her moans grew louder. Her hips lifted to meet each swipe, then he sucked her bud into his mouth, growing harder at her reaction.

He set aside his need to be inside her. He wanted her shouting his name as she came. Dipping his tongue back between her folds, he flicked and swirled her clit as she pumped her hips against his face, straining and searching for her release.

"Sam, please." Her plea low, raspy, she grabbed him behind his head. "Now!"

He pressed a finger inside her channel, diving in deep, then curling it, searching for the spot that would send her spiraling. He wanted to give her everything she demanded. Her pleasure only increased his. Adding a second finger, he pumped faster, pressing his thumb on her swollen clit as she peaked, her inner walls grabbing onto his fingers.

Sam continued the pressure, prolonging her orgasm. She was glorious as she came. "Tell me what you want, baby."

"Aah...yes...right there...don't stop." Evie arched her back and shouted. "Sam. Yes."

It was music to his ears. He gave her what she wanted until she crested again. He felt her flesh pulsing beneath his fingers. Her cream covered his hands as she rode out another orgasm.

When she stilled, he whispered in her ear, "Evie, I need to be inside of you."

"Yes, please." She cupped his face, looking at him, her eyes filled with need for him and something new, something he'd never witnessed. His heart skipped a beat. A reaction he'd never had with another woman and one he'd think about later. Right now, he couldn't wait. Taking himself in hand, he lined his cock up with her entrance and filled her until he was buried deep within her warmth.

Slow strokes weren't enough for either of them. Evie wrapped her legs around his waist and met each thrust. Her head tilted back, hair flowing on the bed, a look of pure bliss on her face...he groaned her name. It was the most erotic moment of his life.

"I'm coming, and you're going with me." He reached between them, swirling his thumb over her bud, watching as her breathing increased, waiting until she reached her peak again.

"Sam...right...there." Evie shouted.

As she crested, his release hit him hard. She grabbed his ass and held on. Instinct overtook him, thrusting into her over and over, giving her as much pleasure as she was giving him. Making her his, silently giving himself to her.

The moment was...overwhelming. He collapsed into her warm body, silently thanking whoever set them up.

TEN

"So why do you think it took us almost three years to get here?" Sam's raspy voice tickled the nape of her neck, his words and touch waking her the next morning. He kissed his way to her ear and nipped the lobe gently. His left arm already laying across her, he wrapped her tighter to his front, alerting her to his body's readiness for another round.

Evie hesitated a moment too long at the loaded question. Unsure if she was ready for this conversation, she knew a surefire distraction. Arching her back, she pressed her backside into him, eliciting a throaty groan that triggered a rush of warmth deep inside her.

"As much as I want to give in to what we both want..." Sam's hand drew lazy circles on her hip and thigh before resting atop her mound, pressing into the sensitized flesh before resting just beyond where she desperately wanted, no needed him to touch. "...damn it, Evie. Why do you scramble my thoughts to the point that all I can think about is getting inside you and hearing my name on your lips?"

It was too easy to ignore the question and let their

bodies take over. The question would still be there waiting, no demanding to be addressed. Sighing, she wiggled and rolled to her back and met his steady gaze. "I could throw it back to you, but I would be lying if I didn't fess up to wanting you from the moment you opened that sarcastic, combative, sexy mouth of yours. So here it is. One reason I never pursued anything with you was because you didn't make me feel as if my opinion didn't matter simply because I was a woman. And I didn't want to mess things up by letting my hormones take over."

Sam's eyes widened at her confession.

"That shocks you? I mean, it can't be that much of a surprise that women focus more on how men make them feel more than how the guy looks."

He brushed a piece of hair off her shoulder, placing a trail of kisses along her collarbone, then up her neck. "Hm, I've heard rumors, but I've never experienced it firsthand. So, what you're saying is you didn't fall for my charm or good looks, but how I treated you during a conversation where we were on opposing sides?"

Lord, she hoped she didn't just break some unwritten female code or something? Maybe she should have kept that information to herself because he was grinning like she'd just given him the winning lottery numbers.

"Being intellectually stimulated is a huge turn-on. Don't tell me you've never experienced it?"

He pulled back from caressing her, a frown marred his handsome face. Sam opened his mouth to respond, then closed it. Squinting, he held her gaze for a couple of seconds, then flopped onto his back. She loved seeing him squirm, but she missed his heat. Darn it why did they always end up like this? Even after a night spent feasting on each other, she somehow turned it into a debate.

Staring at the ceiling, Sam crossed his arms behind his head. "So, what you're saying is, hypothetically if I don't initially find a woman physically attractive, but because her intellect is so stimulating that would get me hot and bothered for her?"

This is so not how she wanted to start her morning. The morning after being with someone for the first time had always been awkward for her, but this took it to a whole new level. And dang it, she hadn't brought the topic up to make him feel uncomfortable or that he had to defend himself. She needed to get off this topic, and fast.

"Sam, I'm not going to tell you I didn't find you handsome when we first met, because that would be a gigantic lie. If anything, I thought you were way out of my league, and I wasn't sure why you kept talking to me. But if you had a personality that turned me off, there's no way we'd be in bed together right now."

He let out a loud, short laugh. "Me out of your league? Why would you ever think that?" He turned back toward Evie and cupped her chin. "You need to give yourself a bit more credit. And no matter how long it took us to get to his point, it was worth it. You, Evie Nolan, will always be way ahead of me in every way, and I'm so good with that." He captured her lips, kissing her deeply.

She grabbed onto his shoulders and returned the passion he ignited until they both ran out of breath. Pulling back just far enough so she could look into his eyes, she poured out the feelings she'd been suppression for far too long. "I know I've thrown up barriers between us. It's an old habit based on witnessing my parent's loveless marriage and overhearing fights a young girl should never have to hear. I've spent too many years pushing my happiness behind my career goals. As much as I always thought I didn't want to take a chance on building something real with a man, I also know that I'm not built for just a fling, Sam. Not with you."

The sound of her heartbeat thundered in her ears, waiting for him to say something. Instead, he kissed her again. Slowly, thoroughly, never pulling back long enough for either of them to speak as he covered her body with his, nudging her legs apart, pressing his erection against her mound.

"Evie, now that I've had you, and you've had me, there's no way I'm letting you go. We've had years to see each other at our best and our worst and..." He pumped his hips into her, wringing a moan from each of them. "...and now I plan on convincing you to take a chance on us."

Evie's heart skipped a beat. "That sounds an awful lot like a challenge. But what if I've already made up my mind?"

"Either way, I'm going to keep you in bed for the rest of the week. I feel like we have a lot of making up for lost time." In a single motion, Sam entered her, setting a steady rhythm, stroking her inner walls until she felt the sharp tingle of an orgasm. She lifted her hips, taking him deeper, urging him faster.

"Evie!" Sam's husky voice rang out. Coming together, then with a flick of his thumb on her clit, she shattered on his last stroke. Sam held himself over her, rocking his hips slowly as their breathing mingled and slowed. Holding each other tight, their bodies slick and sated, Evie whispered the words she never thought she'd ever say, but now felt she couldn't hold in any longer. "I love you, Sam."

He stilled for only a moment before he dipped his head down and captured her lips. The kiss was demanding, sealing their fate. "Oh, babe. I love you, too. What do they call it when two people fall in love at first sight?"

Evie rolled her eyes at him. "Um, love at first sight?"

Sam tickled her under her ribs. "No, smarty. In the movies and in books, there's a term for it, for what just happened with us over the past couple of days. My sister's always telling me that's how she's going to fall in love. That as soon as she sees him, she'll know he's the love of her life."

She couldn't think of the term he was searching for, certainly not with him still inside of her.

"Huh, I'll text her later. But I think we've definitely set the record for falling in love after years of dancing around our attraction. What do you think?"

Sighing, Evie wound her arms around his neck and placed kisses along his jawline. "As silly as it sounds, I think you're right. And since we're on the topic, I think I know of a good wedding planner. She's about to have her second baby, but for me, she'll do anything."

Sam braced himself up on his arms, gazing down at her with a goofy grin on his face. "Wait, was that your way of proposing to me?"

Evie matched his smile. "Yeah, I guess it was."

"What was my answer?"

"You haven't given it to me yet. And I must say, you're being rather rude. Do you want me to list all the benefits of marriage? And, how marrying me will vastly improve your life and—"

"Yes." Sam kissed her ever so softly, pulled back and stroked her cheek with the back of his hand. "No debate from me this time. Just name the date and time and I'll be there."

Thinking about her brother walking her down the aisle, Evie didn't hesitate. "How do you feel about Thanksgiving?"

I hope you enjoyed Evie and Sam's three-year-long insta love HEA and consider leaving a review! If you're curious about her brother, Cole, check out his story in >>>
WORTH THE WAIT

L♥VING

Goldie

A RESCUED BY LOVE: LATER IN LIFE *steamy* NOVELLA

DEBRA ELISE

ABOUT

GOLDIE

I've been in semi-permanent fight-or-flight mode for almost a decade--searching for a loser ex who doesn't want to be found; watching my only child fight, then thankfully beat cancer; and suffering in silence (mostly) for years with endometriosis.

That last one has kept me from living life to the fullest and giving my daughter what she's always wanted: a family.

Then, at the exact right time, things seem to finally be going my way. After leaving almost every job I've ever had out of boredom, six months ago I landed a new position that could finally be the one.

But there's one obstacle even I didn't see coming.

It's a six-three, nerdishly sexy problem who thinks I'm the one. But I'm not looking for love, just a job that finally challenges me and has a great health plan.

FORD

Work is crazy.

My family is crazier.

And my personal life? I'm not going to lie, it's been pretty dull and a bit lonely, okay, a lot lonely.

I tell my friends I don't have time for love. But what I haven't told anyone, especially my mom or my nosy cousins, is that I'm a romantic at heart. I know *the one* is out there.

And at 42, I may have just hired the woman of my dreams.

Convincing her proves challenging.

But I'm not worried, I enjoy a good challenge. And Goldie is the best one yet. And I'm not giving up until she's mine.

She says she's broken and not interested in love, but all I see are her perfect imperfections.

ONE

GOLDIE

THE RELIEF of being pain free was...well, to be honest, I'm still trying to get used to it. Even the twinge of discomfort I feel almost a month after my surgery has nothing on the years long grip endometriosis had on me, keeping me from so many life events—or myself, but especially for my daughter, Lily Ann.

The saying "New Year, New You," couldn't be more apt. At forty-one years old, and almost four weeks out from a hysterectomy, I was ready for the next chapter in my life. Better health, a new career, and now finally my own home. No more renting.

This new year was going to be our best yet. Even if I couldn't give my daughter the one thing she's asked Santa for since she could talk—a sibling. She'd been forced to grow up too fast without her father in the picture, then having and thankfully beating childhood cancer.

Sighing, I didn't want to go down that particular part

memory lane so I pushed all thoughts of what I couldn't give my daughter and focused on all the positives in my life.

Today was my first official day back to work at Carter Security. I loved my job as a scheduling operator. Right now, I was assisting other account managers, and hoped to gain my own accounts when I reached my one-year anniversary.

We specialized in all forms of security services and protection from high-profile athletes, multi-million-dollar businesses or wealthy clients who required various forms of personal security, on-site services, or system-wide technical expertise.

I finally felt as if I'd found my place with this company. And best of all, it provided an excellent health plan, and the salary was more than I'd ever thought I'd ever earn.

I'd decided to meet Kiersten, one of my closest friends, for lunch. Typically, I brought my lunch to work as the company has a nice break room. But today I needed a boost of her positivity to get me through the nerves of returning to work.

"Hey, sorry I'm late. I offered to drop off a last-minute order not far from here." Kiersten sat down grinning at me, then reached across the table and squeezed my hand. "Hey, I know that look. What's up? I seem to remember you telling me that brooding over things you couldn't change was behind you now that you've had your surgery." Leaning back, she scanned the menu just as the waiter arrived.

Giving him our orders, we declined his offer of a bottle of wine. "Maybe next time, we have to go back to work after this." He gave me an unexpected once-over which left me in a bit of shock. When was the last time a man had checked me out? I mean, he was at least twenty years younger, but still, he was cute. My heart sped up at his attention.

"Look at you. You're practically glowing over there, getting lingering looks from hot, younger guys. I'm telling you, Goldie, this is your year. I'm so happy you're healthy. Lily's happy and healthy too, plus your awesome new job. Now you just need a man."

Head spinning from Kiersten's sudden arrival and optimistic words, I laughed the last part of her statement. Scanning the restaurant, I watched as the waiter walked away, stop at the bar, and enter our order onto a tablet. Definitely too young. He glanced over his shoulder and caught me checking him out. I felt my cheeks warm as I quickly glanced away. Unfortunately, in doing so, my gaze landed on a table full of men which included the owners of the company I worked for. They were with a couple of our soon-to-be clients.

Kiersten's earlier comment about needing a man popped into my head because the one man who would have been at the top of my list, *if* I had a list of men I wanted to date, was the boss I considered totally off limits and out of my league. And he was staring at me. I couldn't look away. Then, in a sexy as sin move, one of his eyebrows lifted, and his full lips lifted in a brilliant smile.

I wanted to melt into the floor. Oh, man he was hot and even more so when he smiled. Women from the age of eighteen to eighty didn't stand a chance around this man. Somewhere around six-one-ish and leanly muscled he was a walking fantasy. And he'd been in mine a little too often lately.

What should I do now? I'd been caught and, knowing Ford Carter, he'd find a way to tease me. He was the laid back of the two owners, who happened to be cousins, and single. But I knew how dangerous workplace relationships could be so I'd had locked down my attraction to him from day one. But a girl could still look.

I'd met Lily Ann's father at work almost eleven years ago and swore I'd never go through that nightmare again. It didn't matter how nice, sexy, and smart he was—Ford was off limits.

I not only needed this job, I wanted this job, and that was a first for me. Unlike past jobs I took only to pay the bills, I could see myself working at Carter Security for a long time.

Ford's look had not only ignited a full body flush but unleashed a swarm of butterflies in my lower belly. Gathering my wits, I shrugged my shoulders and broke eye contact. The waiter's attention had been nice, and it gave my ego a much-needed boost, but the look from Ford, heck any look from him, often produced dangerous feelings within me.

Okay, every time he looked my way.

And maybe I had given in to the "if only" daydreams a time or two where the "if only" became the dream of us meeting when I was younger, healthier, etcetera, etcetera., but I tried to keep them to a minimum since it left me all kinds of frustrated.

"Wait, what'd I miss? Why are you all red?" Kiersten's voice and eyes held concern and confusion. She looked around the restaurant, and I knew the moment she spotted the reason for my reaction. Ford was no longer looking at me, but that didn't really matter. Somehow, she'd picked up on my attraction to him without me ever saying a word. It's what good friends inherently knew about each other. Like how I knew she was holding tight onto her feelings for Dr. Jack Monroe without ever telling me what was going on between them. It made me think perhaps I should find out what was really going on and offer any help I could considering he'd been my surgeon.

"Tell me again why you're not going after that tall drink of water?" Kiersten smirked.

Rolling my eyes, I wiggled in my seat. I couldn't shake that look from Ford. "I really don't know what you mean. He's basically my boss, so he's off limits, even if he was interested in me. Which he's not."

A different person delivered our lunch, thank goodness. I really didn't want to deal with whatever the first waiter might have had on his mind. I was terrible at let downs, hence why I'd stayed with my ex way too long.

Smiling at the server, we waited until we were alone again to continue our conversation. Keeping my eyes forward, I fought the urge to look back over at Ford's table.

"Goldie, you're a beautiful woman. There's no reason to write off finding a man to share your life with. You've been fighting to become healthy again for so long, you deserve to let loose, have fun. So why not him?"

Not wanting to argue, I ignored her question then dug into my meal. Twenty minutes later, after taking the not-so-subtle hint to change the subject, Kiersten was telling me about Holly's, her boss at Just Desserts, whirlwind romance and upcoming marriage to Zane Snow. He was the brother of Noel Snow-Scott, a friend and wife of TS Scott, one of the owners of the Idaho Outlaws, a United States Baseball League team and one of Carter Security's biggest clients. In fact, I'd been working with one of their players before taking time off for my surgery.

"So, you up for going out on New Year's Eve? Harlowe told me she invited you." Harlowe worked for the Idaho Outlaws and was married to Zak, and that meant Ford would probably be there. I wasn't sure I could handle being in a social situation where he would have a date and I didn't.

"Maybe your sitter, Mrs. Baker, can watch Lily?"

Kiersten was seven years younger than me with the drive and energy to still party, but I was more than happy curled up on the couch with my daughter, watching movies or reading one of my cozy mysteries.

"C'mon. All the cool kids are doing it. I bet Ford will be there." Grinning, she reached for the check before I could grab it.

"Hi Goldie. Where am I supposed to be?" Ford asked.

Somehow he'd magically appeared at our table without my noticing. How'd he do that? Even at work, he had a way of sneaking up on me.

"I hope you don't mind the interruption. Zak and I were having lunch with the team from RJ Imports, and I didn't want to leave without stopping by."

His dark brown eyes twinkled, and his smile...darn it, it should be certified dangerous. Another round of fluttering erupted in my belly and even though I no longer had a uterus, the way he was looking at me had me envisioning a baby boy with Ford's dark eyes and dimples and that was not only more dangerous but crazy. I could never give him a child and I had no business thinking anything could happen between us. He was not the man for me.

"Not at all. Ford, this is my friend Kiersten Stafford. She manages Just Desserts."

He took Kiersten's hand, and a rush of jealousy overtook me. *Darn it.* I had no claims on him, but it took me a minute to calm my heartbeat and stop thinking about removing her hand from his—forcibly.

"Uh, thanks for stopping by. I'll be back to the office soon and be ready to—"

"No rush. Enjoy your lunch. We're all glad you're back. You look great, by the way. In fact, you're glowing."

"Right? I was just telling her that," Kiersten said.

What did he mean? Was he just being polite? Was he flirting with me? For a moment, no one said anything. Too tongue-tied to respond, I nodded, then sent Kiersten a pleading look.

She took my hint, saving me. "It was nice meeting you, Ford. Maybe we'll see you at Zak and Harlowe's New Year's Eve party?"

"That would be great. Nice to meet you as well." Ford grinned at her, then turned back to me. "See you later, Goldie." He paused, giving me another quick, but interested look before leaving.

Both Kiersten and I watched him walk away. As soon as he passed through the front door, she turned to me, smirking. "That man wants you, Goldie. If any guy looked at me the way he was just looking at you, I'd be running after him."

Blinking rapidly, I shook my head. "You're wrong. He's that way with all his employees. He's nice to everyone."

"Keep telling yourself that, my friend. But I want an update later on about how the rest of your day at work goes."

A half hour later, as I settled behind my desk, I was still stunned at what happened at the restaurant. Was Kiersten right? Was Ford really attracted to me?

And if he was, what was I going to do about it?

TWO

FORD

DRIVING BACK TO THE OFFICE, thoughts of seeing Goldie flirt with the waiter had stirred a jealously I'd never felt before. And it had me rethinking my choice to hold off asking her out until she'd settled back into work. I wasn't supposed to know anything about her health issues, but things had been said by one of her female co-workers who couldn't keep a secret, so I had a pretty good idea of why'd she been out.

And because of my growing feelings for her, once I understood the long recovery process, the past few weeks had been torture. Every cell of my being wanted to reach out to her, to be there for her while she healed.

I knew Goldie was the one for me halfway through her interview. Technically, all our employees were hired by our Human Resource Director, but I would occasionally sit in on those that needed more of an intuitive decision based on more than what was listed on a prospective employee's resume. In the security field, going with your gut often meant the difference between life and death. Yeah, sitting behind a computer may not hold the same intensity or immediacy as protecting a high-profile client against unseen threats, but that didn't make the position Goldie held in our company any less important.

And Goldie Dupree had that undefinable something that would fit in perfectly at Carter Security—and if I handled things subtly and more importantly, carefully so as not to create a human resource issue—in my bed, and my life.

I hadn't gone all through my twenties and thirties holding out for the right person, only to be discouraged by her all-business aloofness now that I'd found her. She may think that getting into a relationship with me was off-limits since I was an owner, but I'd been wooing her since that first day. She just didn't know it—or at least I was pretty sure she didn't.

For some, love at first sight happened only in books or in movies. I knew better having been struck dumb by not only her beauty, but how she handled herself during the interview and every day since. So, I played it cool in the beginning. I dropped hints here and there to see if she'd be interested in going to dinner, but she always managed to change the subject.

I had been willing to wait until she got to know me better.

But that all changed today. Seeing her at the restaurant, looking healthier and lighter of spirit than at any other time in the past six months, had me contemplating all sorts of ways I could finally get my hands on her. Even now, just thinking about her had me half hard as I awkwardly walked back into our building, hanging back as Zak conversed with our newest clients.

When that twenty-something waiter had drooled all over her, it had made me want to stake my claim. Seeing her smile at another guy had created this crazy vision in my head of pulling the ultimate caveman move—marching over to her table, throwing her over my shoulder and hiding her away from any man who dared even to look at her. Man, I had it bad.

"That was nice of you to stop by Goldie's table to say 'Hi.'" Zak said. He was not only my business partner but my cousin. Pulling me aside as we entered the conference room, his gaze was full of his typical sarcastic humor.

Keeping my eye on our clients, I kept my voice low. "Why do I sense a *but* coming?"

"No. Not this time. Just make sure you're all in with her. She has a daughter and, from what I've overheard, a deadbeat ex. Plus, as you know she just returned from medical leave. It's her first day back, and you looked like you were ready to pounce. At least give her a couple days to ease back into the rhythm of the job." Zak nodded at the two men waiting for us to take our seats.

"You sound like my mom. Except for the pouncing part. Ever since I entered my forties, she and my sisters have been on my case to find a nice girl, settle down. Well, I don't want a 'girl,' I want a woman and I've finally found her."

Zak did a double take at my words. "Huh? You're serious? My bet was on you being a lifelong bachelor. Guess my wife was right. Either way, I'm looking out for our newest and most valuable employee. Goldie is more than a hard worker. She's intuitive and has a real knack for working with our clients. I don't want to see her hurt or have to deal with HR on this if all you want is a little slap and tickle."

At my cousin's words, all I could hear was the roaring of the ocean in my ears. If we were alone right now, I'd make him eat his words. Gritting my teeth, I glanced over to the table where two sets of eyes were locked to us. I lowered my voice. "I'm not doing any such thing. Now let's get this meeting started before I rearrange that pretty face of yours. Harlowe would never forgive me, and your wife is not someone I want to piss off."

In a rough whisper, Zak said, "I'm simply doing my job as an owner, Ford. If Goldie really is the woman for you, I'll be in the front row at your wedding, but until then, make sure she knows you want more than an office fling. Got me?"

Zak joined our clients and began the meeting as I reluctantly took my seat. I'd rather be talking to Goldie once she returned instead of focusing on contract negotiations. I began wondering how he'd figured out my feelings for Goldie. I wasn't sure how I felt about that. I thought I'd done a more than decent job of treating her like any other employee.

Thinking back to this morning, I remembered how I felt when I saw her after she arrived back at the office. I could barely form a coherent response when she'd greeted me in the break room over coffee. Then seeing her at the restaurant, watching her blush over the waiter's attention, had me seeing green.

Determined now more than ever, I spent the rest of the meeting coming up with a plan that would leave no doubt in Goldie's mind just how serious I was to make her mine.

THREE

THE SECOND DAY back at work started off well enough. I was finding my groove again and was in the middle of requesting two background checks when my cell phone beeped, indicating a voicemail. I kept it on my desk in case Lily Ann ever needed to get ahold of me. Texting was quicker for her than having to go through the switchboard.

The caller ID flashed the one contact I'd been waiting to hear from for months, while also dreading it at the same time. "Goldie Dupree speaking." The tremble in my voice had me sitting up straighter and taking a deep, calming breath. *C'mon Goldie, you can handle whatever news he has.*

"Ms. Dupree, it's Ben Sanderson. Looks like your ex has finally surfaced. I've got a location on him. He's in Colville, Washington. Was working at an outfit there that seems to have been legit. But that's not how I found him."

The private eye I'd hired two years ago began coughing after his rapid-fire info dump. Waiting for him to speak again, my mind raced. Mumbling under my breath, I couldn't believe how close he was to Pineville. Why hadn't he reached out to see Lily Ann?

"Sorry about that. I really need to quit smoking. Had the corona virus last month and can't shake this damn cough." Another fit of coughing was so loud I had to pull my phone from my ear. That's when I noticed Ford standing next to my desk, a questioning look on his handsome face.

Damn. Why'd he have to show up now? It was bad enough that every time we bumped into each other; it took me at least a half an hour to settle my racing heartbeat, but now when I was receiving possibly the most important phone call of my life, I wasn't sure I could handle both.

The PI finally stopped coughing. "Okay, so he's been visiting a clinic over in Spokane. I'm close to finding out what for. I've been talking to a gal in the front office who lucky for us doesn't seem to understand the meaning of a HIPPA violation. Says he comes in twice a week. I'm thinking it's for chemo."

Stunned, I almost dropped the cell. Ford moved closer; his features narrowing in concern. My mouth had fallen open...could I be any less attractive right now? Pursing my lips, I locked onto his eyes, seeking a lifeline, but instead my thoughts turned to late nights and seeking hands and lips. My hormones working better than ever.

"Ms. Dupree, you still with me?"

"Uh, yes. Yes, I'm here. You're sure it's the right, Lance Hill? Born in sixty-seven?" I didn't add "with a record a mile long." Something I wished I'd known before I'd become pregnant, hell before I gave in to his non-stop pursuit of me all those years ago. The only good thing that came out of that relationship had been Lily Ann. I was happy to bear the brunt of all the negative impact his abandonment had created if it meant keeping her from his influence. I hadn't been searching for him for years so my daughter could have a relationship with her father. No, I wanted to find him because he was going to pay his back child support even if it meant I had to spend my last dime making him accountable.

"He's the one. I showed that gal the pictures you sent me. It's him. The main reason I'm calling is so I can get the updated documents to serve him. You think you could get them to me by tomorrow morning? I've got a server licensed in this county all set to go."

My gaze hadn't left Ford's. His quiet support was easing my anxiety over finally finding Lily's dad. Was this really happening? Would he finally be held accountable? Could I handle seeing him again. How would I tell Lily Ann? I really wasn't looking forward to that conversation, afraid she'd ask to see him. The fact that he may be ill didn't change my determination to get him in front of the court.

"Yes, I'll call my contact right now and get the updated papers sent as soon as possible. It might take more than a day, though, but I'll keep you updated."

The PI ended the call with an assurance he'd watch the clinic and note Lance's comings and goings. Deep down, I knew the truth. If he was going there, he most certainly had a life-threatening condition. And if it was cancer, I wasn't sure I could muster up any empathy for him. He wasn't there when his daughter had gone through her battle with leukemia and nothing short of him getting on his knees begging for forgiveness plus paying back every cent of child support he owed would make me feel sorry for the bastard who'd run off when his daughter had needed him the most.

My hands shook as I set the phone on my desk.

"Goldie, you, okay? That didn't sound like a client's call."

The question disguised as a statement sounded like he was more than curious, as if he cared about me more than a coworker, and there was something else—something more... primal in his tone. It set off all sorts of tingles along my skin.

Rubbing my arms, I did my best to sound calm. "No, that had nothing to do with a client. It was personal. I'm sorry, Ford. But if you don't mind, I'd like to keep it that way." Dropping my arms, I stood, smoothing my blouse. "I'm going to get some coffee. Excuse me." Running wasn't my typical style, but Ford had a way of triggering all sorts of needy feelings inside me. Once, when he complemented me on an assignment a few weeks after I began, I almost giggled like a silly schoolgirl experiencing her first crush.

I was adding a healthy dose of creamer to a much needed cup of coffee when I heard footsteps behind me. In any other situation, heck, on any other day, his attention would be flattering. Right now, all I wanted to do was settle my overwhelming emotions in private.

"Goldie, you're white as a ghost sweetie, uh...I mean, are you okay? Did that call have something to do with your surgery last month?"

Sweetie? Wow, did I look that bad? There was no way his concern was anything but professional. He'd never shown me any personal interest before today, no matter how much I wished it were different. "No, I'm good. Never healthier, in fact. But it's the kind of news that's double-edged, you know? Good news, bad news and all sorts of complications, but nothing that I can't handle. Please don't worry, I promise it won't affect my job performance. I just need to make a couple calls, then it's back to work." I gave him what I hoped was a convincing smile, then finished doctoring my coffee.

"I'm almost done setting up the team in Boise, so I should get back to it. Thank you for checking up on me."

"Okay. But if you need any help, someone to talk to, I'm here. In fact, let me give you my personal cell number. I didn't mean to eavesdrop, but it was difficult not to overhear what the guy on the phone was saying. If you need any help with the courts, I know someone who could expedite anything you need."

Ford didn't move. As I walked by him and my shoulder brushed his arm as I passed. Sharp tingles of awareness shot through me, stealing my breath. I sensed more than saw his reaction and it made me curse how cruel fate was that I'd be wildly attracted to another man I worked with. Hustling back to my desk, I didn't dare look back to gauge his reaction. It didn't matter anyway because there was no way I would pursue anything with Ford. Yes, he was the total opposite of Lance in every possible way but I'm not sure my heart could take another chance on love.

And wasn't it just my dumb luck that I met him eleven years too late?

FOUR

FORD

I COULDN'T SHAKE how Goldie had looked during and after that phone call. I'm not sure how many times I had to talk myself out of making another trip by her desk to check on her, but it would have been more had I not had to leave for off-site meeting. I knew she was more than capable of handling any situation. Heck, it was one of the reasons I was so drawn to her, but that didn't make it any less frustrating for me when every fiber of my being wanted to protect her.

Walking out of the parking garage elevator, the sound of cursing rang through the air. It was Goldie. Instinct kicked in and I sprinted toward the sound coming to a halt when I found her standing in front of her ancient car, its hood up, her hands on her hips, looking pissed.

"Can I help?"

Without looking at me, she said, "Do you know anything about cars?"

I didn't. But that wasn't going to stop me from helping her. "I know enough that it's better I let an expert handle this. But I can give you a ride home. I'll call a guy I know to take care of this for you. Leave the keys under the front seat and grab your things. I'll go get my truck and be right back." I didn't wait for her to agree.

Ten minutes later, a silent Goldie sat rigid next to me. She hadn't said more than a dozen words, but that was okay. I knew she was dealing with a lot from the mysterious phone call and now her car breaking down. I was just happy I was the first one to discover her.

"That's it. The one with the red trim, up on the left." She already had her hand on the door handle.

Pulling into her driveway, I was prepared for her to jump out as soon as I stopped, so I slowly eased onto her driveway. "I almost forgot. I wanted to talk to you about working with RJI. If it's not too much trouble, could I come in for a few minutes?"

She was so cute, struggling not to be rude. I don't think she had it in her. And I didn't feel any regret at taking advantage of her good nature. The first phase of my plan was all about getting her to drop her guard and to see me as more than a boss, someone only to be seen at work.

"Hey, Mom!" A miniature version of Goldie came running out of the house, her unzipped winter coat flapping behind her.

Setting the truck in park, I switched off the engine and watched as Goldie jumped down from her seat, and embraced her daughter. "What are you doing here? Shouldn't you be at Mrs. Baker's?" Standing on the porch was an older woman wearing a bright pink coat and matching knitted hat.

"Hi, Goldie. Sorry to worry you, but you weren't answering your cell. My sister needs me to pick up a prescription and drop it at her place. I thought it would be quicker if I brought Lily Ann home. And before you lecture me, I'm perfectly fine walking down the sidewalk. I grew up here and I've navigated worse weather and streets than this."

"Of course, Mrs. Baker, thank you. I had some car trouble. You must have called when I was negotiating with an engine that refused to start."

I took that as my opportunity to join the group of ladies. Stepping out of the truck, I rounded the hood, standing a couple feet behind Goldie.

"Hi, I'm Lily Ann. Who are you?"

"Lily, that's not very polite." Goldie admonished her daughter.

"It's okay, Goldie. It's fine. I'm Ford Carter. I work with your Mom."

The young girl skipped over to me and grinned. "Cool. Are you a bodyguard or something? You look like you could beat up lots of bad guys." Lily Ann bounced from one foot to the other.

I chuckled at her enthusiasm. "Not exactly. Although I was in the Army, and I looked out for my buddies all the time. Does that count?"

Her daughter's jaw dropped, then she mouthed, "Wow!" Stepping forward with her hand out, Lily Ann solemnly said, "Thank you for your service."

Gripping her delicate hand, I nodded, unable to speak for the sudden lump in my throat. No other person had ever made me react in such a way, nor feel more appreciated for my time in the military than the sweet sprite had.

"Is he staying for dinner, Mom?"

"Dinner, um no. He's just going to stay for a few minutes so we can discuss some work stuff."

I watched Goldie as she did her best to ignore me as she

said goodbye to the sitter, threw her arm around her daughter's shoulder, and walked her back into the house.

I followed. I hadn't exactly been invited, so I stood outside the front door and cleared my throat. Goldie shed her jacket, took her daughter's, and hung them up in the coat closet before answering.

I could see the wheels turning in her head. I wasn't giving up, though. "I won't take too much time. I promise and you don't have to ask me to stay for dinner."

After another moment, she relaxed and waved me in. "Okay. But I really need to get her fed before she begs me for more time to read. I swear that girl would read non-stop till bedtime, past bedtime, in fact, if she had her way."

Nodding, not quite sure how to answer that, I took in the open concept main floor and instantly felt at home. The entire house was probably less than fifteen hundred square feet, but Goldie had made it feel warm and welcoming in soft earth tones and comfortable looking couches and overstuffed chairs.

Standing on the opposite side of her kitchen counter, I watched as she began removing items from the refrigerator. "So, the new contract. We signed it today and need someone to be the lead scheduler with their in-house security department. Zak and I would like that to be you."

Goldie froze. A package of chicken in one hand and a crown of broccoli in the other, her eyes wide. "Me? But, but I haven't even been with the company a year yet. I'm sure Tanner or Lisa would be a better fit?"

Interesting reaction. I thought for sure she'd jump at the opportunity. "Well, they each have a full client load. Besides, don't sell yourself short. You've really shined since we hired you."

Goldie began moving again, gathering up baking dishes

and other ingredients. It was an unexpected pleasure watching her prep dinner without consulting a recipe as she continued to talk, or rather argue with me.

"Thank you. I appreciate that. I do, but I don't want to take this account away from someone who's been there longer than me."

Walking around the counter, I stopped next to her, placed a hand on her arm and waited until she stopped mixing and looked up at me. "You're not taking anything from anyone else. I appreciate your concern, but you've earned this, Goldie." The urge to dip my head and kiss her was strong, but I didn't want her to think she was being given this opportunity because I wanted her. That wasn't the point of today.

"*Moooom*, I'm hungry. Oh, hi again. Did you change your mind? Are you going to stay for dinner?" Lily bounded into the kitchen, stood next to her mother, and gave me an impish grin.

"That's very nice of you Lily, maybe another time, okay? In fact, if it's okay with your mom, maybe the three of us could go out for pizza next week?"

A strangled sound came from Goldie. And reluctantly I removed my hand and stepped back.

Okay, so maybe I may have overstepped, but really seeing Goldie in her home with her daughter made me want to be a part of her life more than ever. If I had to be a bit sneaky where this gorgeous woman was concerned, then so be it.

"Can we, Mom? Oh, that would be so fun. I'm still on break from school, so I get to stay up later, too."

I saw the struggle in her eyes, and I almost caved. There was a way out of this, I think, but I held firm.

"Sure. But tonight, it's chicken and broccoli, and I need to get it started. Say goodbye to Mr. Carter."

"Yes!" Lily Ann twirled on her toes and hugged her mom. "It was nice to meet you, Mr. Carter. Thanks again for taking us out for pizza next week."

Clearing my throat, I turned to Goldie and said, "That's quite the little person you created."

"Yeah, she's pretty special. So, thanks for the ride home. I, um... I'll call a ride share in the morning and be at work on time. Oh, I need to call a towing company."

"No need. It's already at a friend's shop. He's going to call me as soon as he figures out what's up with it." Not waiting to see her reaction to that bit of news, I made my way to her front door.

"Oh, and you still haven't accepted the new account. If you're thinking that I'm expecting anything from you, personally, for the opportunity, make no doubt that is not the case. But I'm putting this out there, because I think after yesterday, and today there's no denying our mutual attraction. And it has nothing to do with the offer. Take it or don't. It won't change how I feel about you professionally. But personally? I'm going to do my absolute best to get you to agree to see me outside of work. Starting with pizza next week."

"Ford—"

"No, I know. Now is not the time to talk about what I really want to talk about with your daughter in the house. So, say yes to the account, Goldie. You deserve it."

She'd snuck up on me as I made my way to the door. "Ford. Look at me. Please?"

How could I turn down that offer? Almost to the door, I turned to see she was closer than I thought. Too close, because if given any hint from her, my hands were eager to touch her, wrap her up and not let her go until she said yes to all the wicked things I'd been wanting to do to her.

She let out another strangled noise, which made my dick twitch. Flushed, she looked over her shoulder before answering. In a low tone, she said, "I'll take the account, and as far as the other...thing, I'm not sure that's a good idea."

"Great, sounds good. I'll let Zak know and I'll be here say, seven-thirty tomorrow to pick you up." Seeing a flash of defiance in her eyes, I reached for the handle. I wasn't giving her a chance to change her mind.

"I'll see you in the morning." I almost made it. Goldie blocked me and our positions couldn't have been better if I'd planned it.

Heart racing, my nerve endings now on high alert. This woman had no idea what she did to me, but maybe it was time to show her. "You don't want me to leave, I get it. If I were a woman, I'd want to spend more time with me, too."

Goldie's expression went from defiant to confused with a flash of desire and awareness before settling back into defiant with the tilt of her chin. She was so damned pretty, and I couldn't hold back anymore. Snaking a hand around her waist, I pulled her into my chest and captured her lips in a hard kiss, hopefully leaving no doubt how I really felt about her.

Succumbing to months of wanting her, this wasn't my typical move. I expected her to resist, put me in my place. In fact, I don't think I've ever forgotten myself around a woman, taking what I wanted without asking. At first her body stiffened, but then she wound her arms around my neck, molded her body around mine, and kissed me back.

Someone let out a moan. It may have been me, might have been both of us, but it signaled a shift as sparks flew. Tunneling my hands through her hair, I gentled my kiss, feathering my lips against hers, then slipped my tongue inside, slowly driving us both mad with need.

"Mom! Can Maggie come over after dinner?"

Lily Ann's shout was the ultimate bucket of cold water. Springing apart, we stood staring at each other as we gulped in air. Air filled with enough electrical current to light up Pineville. Recovering as best I could, considering my erection was straining against the fly of my slacks, begging me to finish what I started. I shifted for relief, it didn't work. So, I did what any guy would do on the verge of being caught ravaging an impressionable girl's mother—I kissed Goldie on the forehead, stepped around her and opened the front door.

Thankfully, a blast of cold air hit me, cooling my overheated body. But before I left, I wanted to make sure she knew this wasn't over. Nope, this was just the beginning.

She'd followed me out onto the porch, Lily Ann safely on the other side of the door. Leaning down, I kissed her hard and swift before pulling back then turned to my rig. "Seven-thirty, beautiful. I'll see you tomorrow." I didn't dare look back at her as I walked toward my truck. Confirmation of her desire for me turned out to be the hardest thing I've ever had to walk away from.

But by the way she responded to me, I had never felt more optimistic.

FIVE

GOLDIE

LAST NIGHT FORD had left me stunned and needy. I managed to finish making dinner, somehow. But Lily Ann was full of questions about Ford, and I couldn't help but compare him to her father and the news I dreaded to share with her.

"Mom, I'm ready." My daughter had been born full of sunshine and even when she'd suffered from cancer, her positive attitude had barely diminished. She was also a morning person. I was not. Taking another sip of my dark roasted coffee, I let out a long sigh. I had twenty minutes before my self-appointed chauffeur showed up and I still hadn't figured out what to wear or what to say to him.

Maybe I could just pretend that the fireworks-laced kiss hadn't happened. It was the best plan I could come up with after a night spent dreaming of possibilities, of sweaty bodies pressed together, straining for the unicorn of orgasms.

"You okay, Mom? You have that weird face you make

when you eat cheesecake, but we don't have any, so what gives?"

Taking another sip of coffee and keeping my face averted from her prying eyes, sometimes it was quite the trial having such a self-aware kid. I wouldn't trade her for anything even if it'd be years before I could truthfully explain what had put the goofy look on my face or the embarrassment of the flush heating my body at being caught imagining Ford naked.

"Fine. Just running late. I'll see you tonight. Don't forget your gloves." Usually, she spent an hour before catching the school bus with Sissy Baker down the street, a retired schoolteacher and a gift from god. However, during winter break she'd been spending all day with the sitter. When Lily Ann had been declared cancer free and able to return to school, I'd found Mrs. Baker through a mutual friend. I only needed help in the morning and a few hours after school, until Lily was old enough to stay home on her own.

She'd become the grandmother Lily never had since my mother passed when I was in my early twenties and, well, I had no idea about my ex's family. Yet one more reason to curse him. I had been far from young when we met, but he's fifteen years older and told me he didn't have siblings. He lied to me so many times I'm not sure what the truth was anymore. He'd left home when he was seventeen and never returned. In the beginning I felt sorry for him missing out on family, but it had become quickly obvious he had no feelings for anyone but himself, and by then it was too late. I was pregnant within a few months of dating and spent the following three years doing my best to shield Lily Ann from an uncaring father whose only interest in her was sporadic and only given when it suited his needs.

A notification sounded on my cell, dragging me back to the moment. Oh shit, I had ten minutes until Ford would be here. And knowing him, he'd be on time. A habit I knew he possessed and was a running joke in the office. He truly cared about those that worked for him and Zak. I really shouldn't be surprised at how he'd been looking out for me. I knew a lot of his habits, because I'd noted most of them, studying how he interacted with people—he treated them more like family members. *Yeah, that didn't sound creepy at all.*

Nine minutes, fifty-two seconds later, my doorbell rang. Hopping on my right foot as I put on my left shoe, I fast walked to the front door and pulled it open without looking.

Ford had an arm braced on the door frame, the other on his hip, and I swore he was giving me the stink eye. But dang, even with his scolding gaze, I felt the pull of attraction.

"I could have been anybody, Goldie. You should really be more careful."

He stepped across the threshold after I waved him in. I made a childish show of throwing the deadbolt. "You're right. However, I was expecting you. And typically, bad guys don't ring the doorbell first, so...." Letting out yet another sigh in response to his squinty gaze, I chuckled. He must not have any idea that no matter the intent behind his look, my body involuntarily responded to him. A sharp shiver shot through me. He must have noticed that response because his eyes darkened, and when he rubbed his chiseled chin it was all I could do not to let out a sigh.

I thought he might kiss me again. I wanted him to so very much. And if he didn't in the next few seconds, I was ready to do something I never did, make the first move.

"Goldie, unless you want to be late...very, very late to

work this morning, grab your coat and the rest of your things. I'm not sure you're ready for what I'm thinking. But when you are, know this...an hour, even two, hell three, will not be enough for me and the plans I have for us. Because there's no way in hell I'm going to leave your bed just to race back to the office. No, Goldie, when you're ready to fulfill the need I see in your eyes, I'm all yours... after work."

Our gazes remained locked, but when he said the magic word, "work" it pulled me out of the sensual fog. *Damnit.* Why? Why'd he have to go and ruin a perfectly good fantasy? Stupid karma always messing in my love life. Why couldn't I find the mailman or the grocery delivery guy just as attractive as I did Ford? Someone...safe. Because I didn't want safe. I wanted the intense pulse pounding, toe-curling, I might die if I can't have them connection, and yes, even love. I wasn't in love with Ford though. It was too soon for that.

"I've got an update on your car, plus I wanted to discuss the new account with you before we reach the office. They have some interesting ideas concerning how they do background checks on key employees that I want to run by you." Putting more distance between us, he moved in a wide circle around me and walked back outside.

Well, that went well. How could he turn his emotions off so easily? I wanted so badly to call him back inside. For the first time since before Lily Ann was born, my libido was screaming. And then after she arrived, the change in my hormones hadn't treated me very nicely and what had been a minimal case of endometriosis before I had her had flared into debilitating monthly periods, then constant pain every day.

My sex drive had pretty much disappeared for years, but it didn't matter since by then my ex had left us and the last thing I'd wanted to do was date during and after Lily Ann's battle with cancer.

To be honest, I'd never expected to experience ever again a rush of longing as I did from Ford's lustful look—my body had fired up again, every erogenous zone on full alert. Thanks to the health insurance I now had and the low dose hormones I chose to take, it was an incredible feeling. To be desired, to feel desire for someone.

Grabbing my things, I locked the front door, stepped off the porch, and found him holding the passenger door for me. Smiling, he helped me in, and waited until I buckled my seat belt before closing the door.

The beginning of the drive into work was awkward. I pulled out my cell and tried to read the dozen or so emails that had come in since yesterday. Halfway to the office, he slowed and pulled into a drive-thru coffee stand.

"What would you like?"

"Um, you know, we have pretty good coffee at work." I put my cell away and shifted forward in my seat to look at the menu.

"Sure, but here you can get a double shot espresso latte with whip cream, and they have over thirty flavors to choose from. It's one of life's little luxuries I like to indulge in from time to time. Everyone should, don't you think?"

"Hey there, Ford. The usual?" An attractive dark-haired barista leaned out the window and gave him a wide smile.

"Time to time, huh?" Grinning, I scanned the menu again and chose the special of the day.

His face had turned pink. It was cute, and he was sweet.

"Thanks, Kyra. How's business?" Ford took the drinks, then handed over his card.

"Never better. I finally pulled the trigger on that new

location. It should be up and running by March. Thanks again for the tip on the property going up for lease."

Taking a long sip of the best peanut butter and dark chocolate latte I'd ever had, I lifted an eyebrow at her statement, then held back a laugh as his face turned another shade darker.

"Of course. You're welcome. See you next time." Ford gave her a quick wave as he pulled away from the coffee stand.

"Well, well. You're just full of surprises, Mr. Carter. You seem to enjoy offering up all kinds of help, no matter where you go. Which reminds me, you were going to tell me about my car."

Weaving through downtown Pineville, Ford expertly handled the snow-packed streets. "Chester says it should be ready mid-day. It was something in the carburetor, not too serious and he had the part in stock. And he's giving you a discount. He'll have one of his employees drop it off in time for you to drive it home."

Why wasn't I surprised by how deftly Ford seemed to handle any problem? Connections with mechanics, inside information on local real estate for pretty coffee stand owners. What was next? A personal banker that would give me a sweet deal on a home loan. Now that would be nice, especially with the way interest rates were being raised every month. So how did I thank him without feeling like I owed him? And I still hadn't figured out how to handle that kiss from yesterday.

We pulled up in front of Carter Security, entered the ramp for the parking garage, and a moment of panic hit me. What if we ran into anyone? What would they think? "Wait, can you drop me off on the first level?"

"You afraid to be seen with me, Goldie?" Ford didn't slow down at my request.

"That's a silly question. And the answer is yes. I don't want anyone to get the wrong idea about us. And Zak, or the head of HR, are at the top of that list."

He didn't respond, just kept driving. I sunk down in my seat and peered toward elevators praying no one was around or worse looking in our direction.

"Goldie. It's fine. If anyone asks, we just tell them the truth. Your car broke down and I offered to drive you."

Throwing up my hands, I couldn't believe he didn't get it. "Ford, stop the truck now!" I was not going to let anyone else, even him, dictate my choices. I'd left one man because of his alpha-like ideals. I was not going to let another believe he could make decisions for me.

Ford didn't immediately stop, but he did slow and pull over. Placing the truck in park, he shifted toward me. Instead of the anger I expected on his face, he looked confused. "I didn't mean to upset you. What is so wrong with me driving you to work?"

My head was pounding, and my heart ready to burst, I sucked in a couple deep breaths. "Thanks for stopping. I don't expect you to fully understand. I guess only a woman would get why I'm upset. The optics aren't great for me here, Ford. I've just returned from medical leave after only working six months. I mean if I could have held off another half year to have the hysterectomy I would have, but I needed it dammit, and now you've given me this new, high-profile account, so yeah, I'm just a bit worried about what people will think seeing us in your truck arriving for work."

Grabbing my stuff, I didn't give him a chance to respond and maybe that was unfair, but I needed to get out and away from him before someone saw us.

"Look, I'm flattered. And that kiss was amazing, but this thing..." I waved my hand between us before I scooted to the edge of my seat and jumped down. "This isn't going to work for me. Besides, I don't want you wasting your time with me, when you could be someone who could give you.... Anyway, thanks for the ride and dealing with the mechanic."

"What the *fuuuuck*. Goldie, wait!"

———————

I SPENT the rest of the day dodging even the slightest chance of running into Ford. I wasn't proud of how I handled things earlier. He sent me an email with all the details of the RJI contract. Just reading his name on the screen elevated my pulse rate. How had this happened? I couldn't have picked a worse time for this list of brand-new problems. I was so tired of being in constant flight or fight mode.

My car was delivered late afternoon along with a reasonable repair bill I had Ford to thank for and the updated document showing the new outstanding child support Lance owed me was emailed over right before I left. I forwarded it to the PI, closed my eyes, and sent up a prayer for Lance's health. As mad as I was at him for abandoning his daughter, I couldn't wish for his demise. I needed to keep my thoughts positive, and my energy reserved for the things I could control.

Later that evening, after Lily helped me make one of her favorite dinners, spaghetti, and mini meatballs with a ton of parmesan cheese, we were cuddled up on the couch watching her favorite show. During a commercial break, she turned to me and asked about Ford.

"So, are you two dating now?"

I hadn't expected the question. I'd done my best to keep any men I dated out of her life. Unless I thought the relationship would turn long term, I wouldn't introduce her to anyone I dated. There hadn't been anyone who I cared enough about and it had been years since my last date. But now she'd met Ford, liked him immediately, and I was stuck. Because, I really did like Ford. Wished for something real with him, but other than obvious sparks between us, I was pretty sure we were looking for two different things.

It was a slippery-slope, and I needed to be careful how I explained it to Lily.

"Honey, we're not dating. He works where I work. He's a friend who found out our car was broken and drove me home."

She scrunched up her nose and rolled her eyes. "Mom, I'm not a kid anymore. I'm ten and I know he likes you. He invited us to pizza next week."

Oh, she was good, and I forgot about the pizza invite. "Yes, you are getting older. You might think you understand these kinds of things, but it's complicated. Dating someone you work with is not a good choice."

She put a finger on her chin and then began tapping. I did the same thing when I was deep in thought. Lord, I loved this child of mine.

"Thinking hard or hardly thinking?" I raised both my hands as if to tickle her. "I need an answer, or the tickle monster will return."

She just sighed. Oh yeah, the tween years were upon us.

"I don't get it. If you like each other, you should date. Maggie's dad is dating a woman. But I'm not sure where he met her. Maggie says they're always making funny faces at each other. And one time, when they dropped her off at her house, Maggie said her dad kissed the woman for a *looong* time before she went in her house."

Yeah, she was definitely getting older. "Well, that's fine for Maggie's dad. But I don't think Ford likes me the same way Maggie's dad does his lady friend."

Lily started nodding her head at me. "Yes, he does, Mom."

"And you know this how, oh wise one?"

"Because he looks at you funny. Like in that movie we watched last month. The one where the heroine doesn't know the hero likes her, but his eyes go kinda goofy when he's listening to her. And in the end, they kiss and live happily ever after."

Late that night, long after I'd tucked Lily into bed, I lay in mine, going over all the things I wished I could have said differently to Ford. He didn't deserve my outburst. He still needed to hear my reasoning, but I could have been more tactful.

Rolling to my side, I brought my extra pillow into my body and hugged it close. I used to do this often when my abdominal pain was at its worse with a heating pad wrapped around my waist.

Tonight, I guess I just needed the comfort as I thought about my conversation with Lily. She was so adamant that Ford and I should date. And she was right. I'm pretty sure he liked me, and I definitely liked him. The memory of our kiss soon became all entwined with the movie Lily and I'd watched and its eventual happy ending.

I drifted off, wishing if only life were as simple as a movie.

SIX

FORD

THREE DAYS HAD PASSED, and Goldie was still avoiding me. She answered all of my emails, but she'd stopped having lunch in the break room and if I happened to walk by her area of the office she was always busy, never lifting her head or looking in my direction even if I talked to someone close to her desk.

I wasn't sure how much more of this I could stand. I knew how I'd reacted was wrong and I definitely knew why she'd been so upset with me once I'd calmed down. And after I told Harlowe what happened she offered to help me work through a solution. Sometimes a guy needed a woman's opinion, and I certainly knew my cousin's wife would not hold back on the truth. She'd served it up straight because she really liked Goldie and didn't want her to get hurt any more than I did.

"You need to ask her out to coffee or somewhere neutral and apologize for being a guy. And if you're really serious about a relationship with her, you need to know a few things about her. Why I think she's resistant to you." We'd just finished dinner and Zak took their toddler up to bed, leaving us alone and without his input on the situation, thank god.

"I'm not looking for gossip, Harlowe. I realize she just had major surgery. And I've met her daughter. She's a great kid, from what I can tell and I know this may sound crazy to you, but she's the one. I knew it from that first day. And I don't want to mess things up any worse than I already have."

I thought for sure Harlowe was going to give me a hard time, try to talk me out of thinking I was in love with Goldie. Instead, her lips curled up and I kind of began to worry at the strange way she was looking at me.

"Oh, how the mighty have fallen. Confirmed bachelor falls for single mom. I love it. Well, it's about time, and I can't wait to see how your mom reacts to the news." Harlowe reached over and gave me a hug.

"Thanks. But you can't tell her. Not anyone. Well, I guess you and Zak can talk about it since I already told him, but I don't think he believed me. Just tell me what I should do?" I was definitely out of ideas. At least ideas that didn't revolve around showing up at her door and kissing her again, then dragging her off to bed and making her scream. That one wasn't practical, but it was my favorite.

"It's going to be easier than you think. You told me you're pretty sure she's into you, right? I mean, you know this for a fact. It's not just wishful thinking?"

"I'm pretty sure I know when a woman is into me, Harlowe. Thanks for the vote of confidence, by the way. My ego's not bruised, not at all."

She threw a pillow at me, and I caught it before it smacked me in the face. "Good arm."

"Oh, stop. Your problem is you've never been told no by a woman before. But Goldie's not just any woman. You know about Lily, right? She had cancer when she was four, five years old."

Shaking my head, I answered her. "No, I didn't know that. But I do know that something's going on with her father. I overheard Goldie talking on the phone about having papers served to him. Probably child support related."

"Ding-ding-ding. Give that man a prize. Yes, he's a loser who left them shortly after Lily Ann was diagnosed with cancer. From what I've gathered, they never married. But he was someone she met at work, that much I know. And that may be why she's hesitant to start anything with you."

Hmm, another piece to the puzzle. "Okay, so maybe that's a strike against me. I'm sure I can overcome that concern. What else you got?"

Another pillow sailed through the air. I easily deflected it. *Okay, maybe that came out a bit too cocky.* "Alright, in all seriousness. What's your suggestion? How do I convince Goldie to date me?"

"It's simple. Tomorrow night at our party, you treat her like she's the only woman in the room. But don't overdo it in, you know, a creepy stalker way. And every time you catch her gaze, look at her as if you can't wait to get her alone."

Rubbing the back of my neck, I began second guessing asking her for help. "You sound like a guy right now Harlowe minus the off-color description of how I should, um, you know...um, is it hot in here?" What if she went rogue and approached Goldie on her own? It was time to leave. I'd figure it out, somehow.

"Thank you, Harlowe. I definitely appreciate you. I'll

see you tomorrow. Tell Zak I'll catch up with him later and yeah, thanks." She walked me to the front door. I gave her a kiss on her cheek. But she tugged on my coat sleeve before I opened the door.

"One last thing. Soft touches. We women love that."

"Soft touches?"

"Yeah. You'll figure it out. Oh, and when you're next to her, like in a group of people, don't monopolize the conversation. Let her talk and—"

"Okay, okay. Now you've gone too far. That sounds like how you'd want Zak to act. I'm not getting in the middle of that. Good night." Chuckling, I finally made my escape and left, feeling a bit overwhelmed from her extremely specific suggestions.

The information Harlowe shared about Goldie's ex may be new, but one thing was for sure, New Year's Eve was the perfect time to show Goldie exactly how serious I am about her. I was all for the soft touches, longing glances and I was definitely all in on a new beginning.

Almost twenty-four hours later, I was back in my cousin's house surrounded by friends. Across the room was Goldie. She'd arrive about a half an hour ago with her friend Kiersten and she looked as beautiful as ever but also... a bit sad.

Recalling Harlowe's advice, I finally made my way over to her side. I didn't want to pounce on her the moment I saw her, but she hadn't been looking in my direction. I wasn't sure if it was on purpose or not, but the chance to flirt with her, look at her with longing and desire in my eyes was a bust.

Grabbing two glasses of champagne, I made my move. Goldie's avoidance whether intentional or not, was not going to keep me from what I wanted—her.

SEVEN

GOLDIE

I wandered the room, still in a bit of a fog from the news I'd received shortly before leaving work earlier. Ben, the private investigator, called me to inform me that when the process server went inside the clinic to wait for my ex to show up he overheard the nurses discussing a patient who'd no longer be coming in for treatment. Lance. He'd passed the night before. A neighbor had discovered the body. Apparently, his form of cancer had been stage four, and he'd waited too long to begin treatment. There would be no chance at a reconciliation for Lily Ann with her father.

Without thinking, I'd gone into fix it mode after ending the call with the PI, but it wasn't my problem to fix. The courts would receive word from the process server and the local coroner's office would send a copy of the death certificate at some point and the case would be closed. And then I stopped myself. Why was I once again worrying over things out of my control? Hadn't I dealt with enough over the last decade? A part of me would mourn Lance, but not now. I hadn't seen him in years, and he hadn't been a factor in any of my decisions for a very long time. But my heart ached for my little girl. The chance of any kind of relationship with her father was gone.

I'd worked hard this past year, and I didn't need to spend any more time wishing things could be different. I'd learned that if I wanted change, I needed to change how I responded to obstacles put in my path.

When Kiersten texted me to make sure I was still going with her to the Carter's New Year's Eve party, I said yes. I'd already told Lily Ann she could spend the night at her friend Maggie's house, so I couldn't use that excuse when Kiersten showed up at my place an hour ago. She took one look at me, asked me what was wrong, and I burst into tears. The friend that she was, she listened till the end when I had no more tears to spill or story to tell. She convinced me getting out the house was the best thing for me, and I agreed. I knew I needed to get out of my head, forget all my problems, old and new, and enjoy myself.

Tonight would be about me, relaxing with friends and celebrating the new year because god knew the past year had its ups and downs and I was ready to build upon the good things that had come my way. I was still sad that having the hysterectomy, although the best thing for my body, had also taken away all possibility of giving Lily a sibling. But our life was good. And I really was grateful for everything we had.

Plus, I had a hot guy whose kiss had made me feel desirable again. I didn't need forever, and maybe he wasn't looking for that either. And there was only one way to find out.

A voice over the background noise of the party filtered toward me, and I immediately recognized it. Ford.

Avoiding him at work had only temporarily put off what I needed to say to him. To apologize and hopefully repair our working relationship.

My doctor had given me the all-clear for sex at my four-week post-op checkup and if I could convince Ford that we could share one night together, scratch our mutual itch, it didn't have to equal commitment or cause any awkwardness at work.

I knew he was nothing like Lance. It finally sunk in that I didn't need to use him as an excuse any longer. Not in my dating life. Well, my new and improved dating life anyway. We're adults and I'm sure he'd welcome my honesty and besides, what guy would turn down no-strings-attached sex?

"Goldie. Hi. I'm glad to see you could make it."

Ford's low, growly voice sent a wave of shivers through me. He'd managed once again to sneak up to me unnoticed. But my body was on full alert now. At six-three, I had to tip my head back to meet his eyes. The look in them had me wishing we were already alone.

"Ford. I'm glad too, thank you." I took the champagne glass he handed me and took a small sip. I didn't drink much and didn't plan to have more than a couple glasses tonight. "I was hoping we'd have a chance to talk. I owe you an apology from the other day. I overreacted. I let a situation from my past get in the way. I know you would never intentionally put me in a compromising position. I'm sorry."

Instead of responding, he took my hand and led me to a corner of the room where there were few people. I took the opportunity to check him out and build up my nerve for what I wanted to say next. His leanly muscled frame had been in a few of my fantasies since I started my job. Okay, more than a few. And tonight, I really wanted to see what was under the tailored, long sleeved black button down that showed off his physique perfectly.

"I wanted to say sorry as well. I should have immediately gotten what you were saying, but in my typical fashion, I thought my way was better. I will never put you in a position like that again. You have my word." Ford took my free hand, wrapped it in his, then kissed my fingers.

His lips feathered over my skin, sending a direct arrow of need through me. My panties were already wet from the look he gave me earlier, but now they were soaked.

"I, ah...I accept your apology. And I also wanted to let you know how very much I enjoyed that kiss. At my house the other day, I mean. Ugh, this is kind of hard, but I want you to know I don't play games, Ford. But I also don't want you to think I'm trying to make this attraction between us, uh.... Could you stop doing that please? I can't think straight with you touching me and looking at me like you want to eat me up."

His lips lifted slightly at both corners, giving me a final dose of confidence. "Forget what I just said." Lifting up on my toes, I kissed his grinning mouth then said, "Take me home."

EIGHT

FORD

"YOU LOOK GOOD IN MY SHIRT." Slacks unbuttoned, I walked into Goldie's kitchen and the sight greeting me was one I was ready to see every morning for the rest of my life.

"I feel good in your shirt." She pours me a cup of coffee, hands it to me and before she can get away, I capture her lips, cradle her neck and take my first sip of the day. Yup, better than coffee. So much better. I walk her back till she bumps into the counter. Gripping her hips, I lift her up onto the surface and she spreads her legs open in welcome. Bracing my hands on the cool granite, I deepen the kiss, wringing sweet sounds from her. The moment so perfect it grips my heart, taking my breath away.

I'd never get enough of this woman. She'd been so open and giving last night, driving me to the point that I almost shouted "I love you," but I didn't want her thinking my declaration had anything to do with just sex. No, she deserved to hear it from me when I was clear-eyed and stone cold sober. There was no way I wanted her saying my feelings for her had anything to do with the champagne we drank or the heat of our passion.

I couldn't let another day go by that Goldie didn't wake up knowing how much she was loved and that I wanted her in my life forever.

Goldie's fingers dipped between the waist band of my slacks and my skin. Releasing a groan as her hand pulled me free, squeezing my cock, bringing it to her slick opening. Nothing short of a bomb going off would keep me from driving into her right now except not having another condom.

"Sweetheart, last night I used the only condom I had. But I'm clean. Actually, I've never had sex without one." Resting my forehead on hers, I tried to control my breathing, holding myself rigid, waiting for her response.

"I'm clean too." Her frustrated moan let me know she was equally desperate for me. Her seeking lips captured mine, then her mumbled words had me driving home.

"Inside me. Now!"

Had we not already been together last night consuming each other, pressed tightly long after our bodies had settled from a soul shaking simultaneous orgasm, a first for me, I would count this moment inside of Goldie as the best yet.

And hopefully after today, we'd have a lifetime of moments to rival this one.

She lifted her hips, locked her legs around my waist, holding me tight as I thrust into her again and again. The sound of our bodies connecting filled the room, along with the cries of my name was my undoing.

Reaching between us, I circled her clit over and around. I pressed my thumb on her engorged clit. "Come for me Goldie." I whispered against her ear as she fell apart, her body shuddering around mine as I followed, bellowing her name.

Time didn't compute. Setting her gently on the counter without letting her go, I held her close, still buried deep as her body shuddered, aftershocks rocking through us both.

"All I can say, is...Oh. My." She dropped kisses along my jawline before leaning back. "That was incredible, Ford."

"Mm, hm. No words right now." I buried my face into her neck, breathing her in, committing to memory her scent, this moment.

"I need to move and use the bathroom, but I'll be right back."

Stepping back as difficult as it was, I let her go because I needed to get my brain back on track, rehearsing the speech I'd been working on since I first saw her last night across the living room at Zak's place. *Shit, when had I'd turned into a sap?*

Gathering up some bagels, cream cheese, marmalade, butter, I wasn't sure yet what she liked, I reheated my cup of coffee and began boiling some water to press a new batch.

"This is nice. A man who can assemble breakfast. I like it." Grabbing my mug of coffee, she took a long sip.

"You should see how I order takeout." Chuckling, I watched her step out of my reach. A warning bell went off in my head at her action.

She made up her bagel, put it on a plate, and took over making coffee.

"What's on your mind?" I asked, unsure if I wanted to know, but the vibes she was giving off were not what I was expecting after the phenomenal kitchen sex we'd just shared.

"Lots of things. Which one would you like to hear first?"

Warning bell two. Damn, I waited too long. I should have told her how I felt first thing. "Goldie, I've been wanting to tell you something for a while now. Um, how about we sit?" Sweating, I was actually sweating. Shit. I grabbed her plate and lifted her up on the counter. Might as well just go for it.

"Goldie Dupree, I knew you were the one the moment we met at your interview. I thought waiting to tell you was the best way to go, didn't want to scare you off your first week of work." Grinning, I cradled her face and looking her straight in the eye. "I lo—"

She put her index finger over my lips, her eyes filled with tears as she shook her head. "Don't say anything you'll want to take back. Not until you hear me out."

Dazed, what had just happened? The first time I want to tell a woman I love her, and she cuts me off?

"Ford, I should have been clearer up front. I don't want you to feel that you owe me empty words or promises. Last night, this morning, was...perfect. But I'm not looking for a commitment from you or anything else. There's no need to worry about me. I'm good with just having this night with you."

She was smiling. But something was off. She wasn't looking me in the eye any longer. And I wasn't going to let her talk me, or herself, out of this. "Goldie, I don't know what to say. In fact, I'm kind of at a loss. If this has to do with work, I can assure you nothing has to change. I'll make sure no one gives you a hard time about dating one of the bosses."

The shadow of sadness I'd noticed last night at the party returned to her eyes.

"Ford, this won't work between us long term. I'd rather we acknowledge that now so we can be friends. Prevent any weirdness at the office." She gently pushed me back, then jumped off the counter.

"Oh, no. Don't I get a say here? You just decide that things won't work out based on what exactly? Past failed relationships? Because everyone I know has gone through those. That's how you know when someone's right for you. At least, that's how it was for me. How I knew that there's no one else I want in my life other than you."

A single tear fell down her cheek. I reached out to swipe it away, but she backed up, out of my reach.

"I'm okay. Really." Goldie scrubbed her face, erasing another tear. She took another step away from me, crossed her arms, and I felt her slipping away from me.

"You don't look okay. I realize this may be too soon for you, but I need to let you know how I feel about you. We're at a time in our lives where waiting or following some arbitrary pattern of dating before enough time has passed to say I love you isn't necessary. Not when you know you want to spend the rest of your life with someone."

Her smile had disappeared fully. At my declaration, instead of joy on her face, all I saw was more sadness.

"Goldie, talk to me, baby."

"Do you remember what I said to you in your truck the other day?"

"You said a lot of things. Which one am I supposed to remember?" My tone came out sharper than I wanted it to. *But what the hell was going on here?*

Sighing, she ran her hands through her tousled, golden-brown hair. Hair my hands had been wrapped in not that long ago when I was inside her and she was crying out my name, coming all over my cock. I would give just about anything to be back in that moment right now, telling her I love her over and over until she believed it. Until she knew I wasn't going anywhere.

"I told you about my surgery. How I couldn't put it off any longer?"

My hands itched to pull her in close, to comfort her. But I could tell this was a hard subject for her, so the best thing I could do right now was listen. Mimicking her stance, I crossed my arms and nodded for her to continue.

"Having a hysterectomy means more than no more periods. In my case, it also means no more excruciating pain. I suffered from endometriosis for years because I never had good enough health insurance that would offset the cost for me. Until I started working for Carter Security."

"That's great. I'm really happy that we could have helped you out—"

"Without a uterus, it means no babies, Ford." She looked at me now. "You said it yourself. We're at a time in our lives where making choices for the rest of our lives needs to happen now if they're ever going to happen."

Not sure quite where she was headed, I needed to let her know that not having a uterus wouldn't change my mind about her, about needing her in my life.

"That's not quite what I said, and I think you're making an awfully big assumption here, Goldie. If I wanted kids, don't you think I would have by now?"

"What if one day you figure out that you really do want a child of your own? I can't give you one, Ford. And I don't want to be the reason you can't. I need to end this before I fall any deeper, before Lily has a chance to become attached to you—before my heart gets broken."

The word "again" went unspoken. She was worried about the past when all I was focusing on was the future. I could no longer just stand there and not touch her as more tears fell onto her cheeks. I scooped her up and marched back to her bedroom. Placing her gently on the mattress, I joined her, gathering her close. I wasn't sure of the right words, so I just went on instinct.

Placing my hand over her abdomen, I gently circle her flesh and the scar from her surgery. "I did not fall in love with you, thinking you'd give me a kid. This part of you was important, yes. It brought you Lily Ann. And I can't wait to know her better. You're so lucky to have been able to have her, sweetheart. But my love is not conditional. I don't need you to have a baby with me. I just need you. I'm asking for a chance here. To show you, prove to you how much I love you and that you are everything I could ever want. That one day, I'd love to be Lily's stepfather. There are other ways to have another child and if that's what you really want, we can explore those. But know this, for me, I don't need any more time to know that you are the only one I don't want to live without. That we, the three of us, are all the family I need. I love you, Goldie."

EPILOGUE

Eighteen months later

GOLDIE

"Мом, get in here! He's got ahold of my hair and won't let go."

The weekends had never been the same once Ford had moved us into his house on the lake shortly before we got married last year. Now Saturdays were filled with outdoor activities and Sundays with sports on the huge sixty-inch screen in his man cave. Then there was Brutus. I hadn't known he would be part of the deal until after I'd fallen in love with Ford.

His dog wasn't a dog. He was a small horse. He loved Lily Ann and was a fierce protector of everyone in the family. Especially the newest member who relished all the love and attention but was a real stinker when it came to long hair. And dog tails.

Laughing at the desperation I heard in her voice, I

walked into the front room, knowing what I'd find. "Okay, relax. Mama's here. I have just the thing to distract him." Brutus let out a loud woof at my entrance. "Not you, silly. You already got your treat for the day."

Ford walked into the room behind me, his laughter mixing with mine.

I approached Lily Ann and her tormentor. Although he was way too adorable to truly be stuck with that nickname. "Okay, mister. Let go of your sister's hair and you'll get a cookie." I waved the teething biscuit in front of Hudson, and like magic, he lunged at me, releasing the lock of Lily Ann's hair he had wrapped in his chubby little fist.

"I got to hand it to you, Mrs. Carter. Your instincts with our son never ceases to amaze me."

"Stick with me, Mr. Carter. I've got a lot more tricks. And with this little stinker, I have a feeling his teenage years will prove interesting." With Hudson in my arms, happily drooling on his biscuit, I stood on tiptoe and kissed my husband. Lily made gagging noises in the background, but secretly I knew how much she loved her dad. She'd begun calling him that not long after we got married.

Wrapped up in Ford's arms, tears welled in my eyes. They appeared not just from the incredible blessing of being able to foster, then adopt Hudson when I'd confided to Ford last year I wanted to expand our family and he'd wholeheartedly supported me.

No, the tears unlike the ones I'd shed over so many happy moments since I told Ford how much I loved him, were from having the sweetest little boy in my arms, with a chubby little hand full of a now soggy biscuit and his other wrapped around a lock of my hair. Ouch!

This pain, however, I could handle for the rest of my life.

I hope you enjoyed Goldie and Ford's story!
What to read next?
Kiersten and Jack's story: TANGLING WITH THE
DOCTOR

Also, check out Zak and Harlowe's story: TEMPTING
ZAK

Don't miss out on my new releases. Join my newsletter
today and receive a free short story set in my Pineville
World:
https://bit.ly/DebraEliseNewsletter

L♥VE at

Forever

&

56TH

A RESCUED BY LOVE: LATER IN LIFE *steamy* NOVELLA

DEBRA ELISE

ABOUT

LOVE AT FOREVER & 56TH

Falling for someone she works with hadn't worked out the first time around, so why should it now?

Finding love after 50, er 56, seems nearly impossible—or maybe it's just her?

Lois has guarded her heart for so long since her messy divorce that she's not sure if she'll ever find it again.

Well-meaning family and friends all have an opinion on her single status. But she's tried the apps, the in-person speed dating events, and lord help her, blind dates—all with little success.

All she wants is a man in the same stage of life as her.

AND most importantly, she wants a man who gives her full body chills that lead to having the big "*Oh*" that isn't battery assisted.

That's not too much to ask, right?

Unfortunately, she's already met that man, and she's put him in the "don't even think about it" zone.

The sexy, silver fox from her past—who doesn't seem to

remember their almost hook-up back in college—is now everywhere she is.

Her strategy of ignoring him soon backfires—she forgot how persistent he is—can she give him, and love, a second chance?

ONE

IT WAS New Year's Day. The day for nursing hangovers and writing down resolutions. Picking your word of the year. New year, new you! *Blah, blah, blah.*

And today was her fifty-sixth birthday.

She once thought seeing her kids happy, married, and having their own kids would be enough for her. That she had no more wishes left. But it turned out not so much. That was the problem with wishes, sometimes once fulfilled, you realize there should be more to go after, especially when someone, yes, her, tied their level of happy to others instead of themselves.

And when she finally realized she'd put her happiness on the shoulders of others, well, it had been the wake-up call she hadn't seen coming but desperately needed.

After a messy divorce years ago, Lois thought she had all the time in the world to find someone to share the rest of her life with.

She'd wanted a man who shared the same interests, to go on adventures with and who gave her full body chills when he looked at her. She may have her AARP card, but that didn't mean her libido had retired.

Were her expectations too high?

Patrice Holt, her best friend, sat across from her as they sipped wine to celebrate her fifty-sixth trip around the sun.

And yet all Lois could think about was not having a man to warm her bed. Did that make her pathetic, shallow, both? She'd need something stronger than the rosé in her wineglass to come to terms with and admit what she really wanted, the man she really wanted. The man she'd stubbornly banned herself from going after.

"Lois Campbell, why are we sitting back here, hidden from all those handsome men?" Patrice Kade, her best friend, glanced toward the front picture window of O'Malley's Pub, where a group of men, younger men, sat nursing hangover cures.

The drink in their hands was the pub manager's, Slade Johansson's, specialty. He'd created when he first worked as the head bartender years ago and it had become a huge hit. Not that she'd ever had need of it, but her son Sam had sworn by it in his twenties.

At the mention of "handsome men" an image flashed in her mind: a man with piercing blue eyes, movie star good looks, and a runner's leanly muscled body. She tried to vanquish the picture of *him* from her brain, but it didn't work. She'd been trying for months since he came back into her life, and it had never worked—not once.

So, instead, Lois thought of all the reasons Adam Riordan should not be on her mind, and all the reasons he needed to be off limits.

"Don't roll your eyes, Lo. Why not consider someone younger? You're an attractive, vibrant woman who still has a lot of energy for life and, ahem, sexy times. You could have your pick of men. What about trying that *Must Love Silver Foxes* site again?"

Patrice spoke out loud about what she'd been pondering. Finding the person to take a chance on had become a chore and kind of depressing. Were her standards too high? Were there no men her age left who wanted a woman of the same vintage?

Lois had thought turning fifty had been one of her biggest fears. But now that she was staring fifty-six in the face and yearning for that long ago birthday filled with friends and family toasting to her best decade yet.

What a bunch of hooey.

Gah! Who says hooey anymore? Great grandmas, that's who. Not women who still wanted and still had an itch she wanted scratched. So maybe she'd been super picky about whom she'd let snuggle up to her lately, but that didn't mean her desire for intimacy had vanished.

And yeah, so maybe discovering chin hairs and new age spots were now a weekly, if not daily occurrence but that did not mean she would succumb to the silly and outdated image of a woman in her mid-fifties being past her prime or not still a sexual being.

Hell to the no. She was simply going through a hiatus, waiting for the right man.

She'd also decided years ago she would not embrace the go-gray trend. Lois vowed to color her hair until her last day. No shame to those that have embraced the gray because there are women rocking that look, but her hair color was her main form of self-care. It's something that made her, her.

"Lo? Where'd you go? I think one of those cute guys is checking you out." Patrice grinned.

Looking at the group of men, she noticed one in particular was looking toward them. He was cute and looked to be in his forties. But did she really want someone younger? It had been a question she'd asked herself the past few years and if it happened; it happened. She wouldn't say no if a genuine connection was there.

This man looked familiar. Had they already met? He lifted his pint of beer, wearing one of those grins that conveyed he'd been caught looking. And that's when she knew who he was. He worked with her son in the district attorney's office, plus her boss, TS, had introduced her to him a couple of years back at one of his famous Fourth of July parties.

Sighing, she nodded at him, then turned her attention back to Patrice. "That's a big no. He works with Sam."

Patrice said, "Oh, shoot. What a bummer. Oh, well, the Pineville curse strikes again. Three degrees of separation, right? You know it's all TS's fault, right?"

"Amen, my friend." Grinning, they clinked their glasses, then dissolved into giggles. Oh, how she loved her bestie.

Setting her wineglass down, she sighed at having a boss who knew everyone in town, which made it difficult for her to find a guy who didn't want to date her in order to get closer to one of the richest men in America. She loved being the executive assistant to TS Scott, who made his money in tech and was now the majority owner of the Idaho Outlaws baseball team, but it had its downsides too.

She wondered if she could get away with spending the rest of the day drinking her way through becoming closer to sixty than fifty? Images of both her kids, and their significant others, flashed in her mind and, yeah, probably not the best idea. Evie and Sam, and Heather, and Rex were planning a nice dinner tonight for her at *Salvatore's*, her favorite restaurant.

The dinner was just for the grown-ups she'd see her grandkids on Sunday. Owen and Milly were spending the night with Evie's best friend, and Heather and Rex's kids, Sammy, and Lyla, were at his parent's place for the night.

Lois loved how everyone's family still lived in Pineville. Another reason to love Idaho's biggest small town.

"So, okay. How are we going to find a man who has no ties to your boss, or your son, who isn't younger than you and wants a strong, independent woman in her fifties?" Patrice leaned onto the table and narrowed her eyes.

"I know that look. Do you already have someone in mind? Should I be afraid?"

Patrice raised her eyebrows, about to answer her when Lois noticed her besties gaze zeroed in on the pub's entrance, and for the first time since we've known each other, she looked guilty. "Um, no. Just want to see you with a man worthy of you, who not only makes you happy, but adds 'all the things' to your life."

Her closest friend's sincere words made her feel loved, but then she began fidgeting with her napkin, and that was so unlike Patrice. "Thank you for that, but are you okay? Is it the wine?"

"Hello, ladies. Happy New Year."

The greeting rang out from directly behind her. She'd missed the approach of the man who'd been disturbing her sleep and made her feel regret like no other man had. Muffling a groan, she tried to come up with an excuse to make a fast exit before Patrice invited him to join them.

What happened instead shocked her. He didn't stop to chat. In fact, he didn't even look at her. Adam leaned down and gave Patrice a quick hug and said, "I'm meeting Zoe for lunch. I'll see you next week, okay?"

He gave her a brief nod and walked over to an empty table and sat with his back to them.

Talk about a change-up in how he typically greeted her. She wasn't sure what to make of it. Lois had done her best to let the team's new orthopedic surgeon know she was not interested in being friends, or anything else.

They had briefly been in each other's lives because of his friendship with her brother Lance back in college. When it had become clear to her that he didn't remember their last night together all those years ago, she'd made sure to be as neutral as possible whenever their paths had crossed, either at work or in their personal lives.

Somehow, he'd finally gotten the message after months of being on the receiving end of her cold shoulder. But why now? And why did it bother her so much?

TWO

THE NEXT TIME she saw Adam was a week later, back at work after the holidays, and all she could think of when she looked at him was that confidence was sexy.

And, as he stood before her desk, he exuded it like he was born with an extra serving. At any age Lois supposed confidence was sexy, but at fifty-eight, Adam Riordan wore his like a finely tailored suit.

His Romanesque features, striking blue eyes and silver hair only added to his charm and okay animal magnetism. And if her nipples were indicators, their rock hard status confirmed her body's traitorous desire every time Adam was near.

But it had been his boyish charm that she'd fallen for during her freshman year in college. He was her brother, Lance's roommate, and her first major crush. She thought he'd been into her as she was him and had gobbled up every bit of attention he paid her. But Lance always seemed to sense her hero worship and would do what he could to block Adam's interest in her.

Until graduation night.

A night she fought to forget every time Adam spoke to her.

A night he seemed to have forgotten.

A hurt she'd never really recovered from.

It was a memory that was as fresh in her mind today as the day after it happened when humiliation filled her when Adam acted as if nothing had happened as he and Lance left for their summer adventure before med school.

But it had happened, and the kiss they'd shared along with fevered touches and whispered confessions had been the magical moment she'd dreamed for all that year, and it was finally happening. Until her brother calling her name had interrupted them, breaking them apart where they stood grinning at each other like lovesick kids. The memory of it all these years later still heated her cheeks.

"Lois, you okay?" Adam's words snapped her back to the moment.

She plastered a neutral look on her face, reverting to her initial strategy, but after Saturday's party, it no longer felt like a winning one. And she was beginning to believe it was one she no longer wanted to employ.

Stupid menopausal hormones had her all twisted up six ways till Sunday. At least if he said anything about her blushing, she could blame it on a hot flash. He was a doctor, after all, and probably wouldn't bat an eye at her explanation.

"Sure, why do you ask?" Lois scanned her computer screen, trying to appear busy with her boss' schedule. "I'm just thinking about the next meeting TS has and what I need to do to prepare." She felt his intense scrutiny and couldn't stand it anymore. She looked at him with the full intention of saying something uncomfortable to make him stop, but his gaze was full of heat and he wore a look of "I dare you" on his handsome features.

"Adam, we don't have a meeting today, do we?" TS saved her as he exited his office and held out his hand to the team's orthopedic surgeon.

Sending out a silent thank you to her boss for saving her from further stretching the truth and being rude. Something she really hated doing, but she didn't know how to handle Adam's interest.

Lois had worked for TS for just over ten years and had become close to him and his growing family. They had a wonderful working relationship, and she couldn't imagine leaving her position just because seeing Adam on the regular was uncomfortable.

"No, I was on my way out to meet Zoe for lunch and stopped to chat with Lois. How's the prep for spring training coming?"

"Great. And oh, by the way, I have four tickets for you both to attend the Children's Place gala. I hope it's not too short of notice for either of you to find dates?" TS asked with a slight lift at the corner of his mouth.

Lois knew that look, and she didn't trust that look. What was her boss up to?

The men walked away from her desk toward the elevator. Releasing a sigh that she'd escaped answering another unspoken question from the ever-persistent doctor, Lois gave the pair one last glance before grabbing her purse and leaving for her lunch.

Adam's gaze had returned to her and this time, and with TS as a witness, he checked her out as she smoothed her skirt over her hips. Pinpricks of electricity exploded everywhere along her skin, as his roaming glance had touched and damn if the flush she felt develop from her breastbone to her cheeks didn't give her away.

She was spared her boss' reaction to Adam's blatant look as the elevator doors closed. All she saw was the ghost of a smile on the face of the man she couldn't fall for—not again.

THREE

"I NEED A DATE." Adam reluctantly grumbled in answer to his best friend's question. He and Kade had just sat down for lunch at their favorite sandwich place, Evergran's Grill, at the far end of Main Street. It was a new place in Pineville his oldest daughter, Zoe, had recently discovered and couldn't stop raving over.

"Sorry, bud. I promised Patrice I'd stop being your wingman." Kade took a big bite of pastrami on rye and still somehow grinned as he ate. It was two days before New Year's Eve and besides having no one to ring in the new year with,

"Not really in the mood. And before you ask, I'm not taking either of my daughters ever again. Too many people that don't know who my girls are think I'm 'robbing the cradle.' Hell, I had a lady come up to me at last year's hospital gala tell me I reminded her of a character she read in a romance book and that I seemed to suffer from a daddy complex. Shit, it was embarrassing. She at least waited until I was alone to lecture me."

"Whoa, are you kidding me? You never mentioned it. Then again, maybe she was jealous. Was she, uh, an older woman?"

"You don't have to whisper, 'older woman', Kade. It's not a dirty word, besides you know I've never dated women half my age."

"When you date." Kade mumbled, then took a sip of his soda.

"What was that? I date. Just rarely." Or lately, Adam conceded silently.

"Okay, so uptight women with age issues. So why now? And what do you need a date for?"

Adam chewed the last of his sandwich as he debated telling his oldest friend not the why or the what, but the who he wanted to ask. He hadn't wanted to interfere with Kade's wife, Patrice's friendship, with the woman who'd been on his mind for the last three months.

"TS has tickets for the Children's Place gala. It's being held at The Resort and although it's not officially a requirement, everyone brings a date whether or not they're married. He's been on my case the last week about it. I swear he's like a mother hen with his staff. Wants everyone coupled up."

Adam wasn't ready to tell Kade who his boss thought he should ask. One thing that he'd been grateful for since Kade married Patrice was that his friend hadn't hassled him about finding love, too. But since TS had pretty much nailed it on the head with whom Adam had been silently wishing he could be with, it was definitely a strange position to be in.

Taking a chance on Lois Campbell, not knowing how she felt about him, would not only affect the environment at work, but with Kade and his wife Patrice.

It felt like he was starting off with two strikes against him before he even let her know he was interested in her.

Most days, she acted like he didn't even exist, paying him the bare minimum of attention only when absolutely necessary and it was killing him.

"Okay, what's really going on? You've never discussed your dating life or lack thereof with me. Not willingly, anyway. Who do you have your sights set on and why haven't you already asked her out?"

Kade was no dummy. He was a sought-after financial planner in Pineville and handled Adam's investment portfolio, so he knew he wouldn't be able to keep his friend in the dark much longer. But was he ready to announce his interest in Lois?

Kade was driving him back to the stadium when he thought screw it and asked, "What do you think if I asked Lois to the gala next week?"

"Whoa, you're asking me this now? I'm minutes away from dropping you off."

"Stop complaining and just tell me what you think." Adam wasn't sure if he was ready to hear his friend's thoughts, but if he said it wasn't a good idea, would he actually take his advice?

Kade was silent a little too long for his liking. "C'mon, it's not that complicated. You either think it's a good idea or you don't."

"Where have you been the last few years? You know what Patrice and I went through, right? So, you think I'm going to say stay away from a woman you want to date? No way. And the better question is, what's holding you back from asking her?"

Lois's beautiful face flashed in his mind. She'd changed

little since he first met her all those years ago. And as little as she'd gifted it to him recently, he enjoyed the challenge of getting her to forget the irritation he seemed to cause her while coaxing that sweet smile he couldn't get enough of.

"That, my friend, is the smartest thing you've ever said."

FOUR

Lois went over TS's schedule again. He wasn't just an owner but the general manager of the Outlaws and relished the day-to-day running of the team. Some days, she wished he focused on his other projects more. Today was one of those days.

He was meeting with Adam and the head physical trainer and that meant she wound have to interact with Adam.

She'd miraculously avoided him the past week. Unfortunately, not seeing him in person had done little to tame her uninhibited and random thoughts about him. So, to avoid speaking with him when he walked into her office before the meeting, she took the coward's way out. She pretended to be on a phone call. His usually upbeat personality was thankfully focused on the trainer as they waited for TS to come out of his previous meeting.

But she felt his eyes on her. Ignoring her body's reaction to whenever he was close, Lois didn't dare make a move. Not so much as a covert attempt using her peripheral vision.

He'd know that she was checking him out as he checked her out.

Her reaction wasn't because she didn't believe a man would pay her notice. She was confident enough in her appearance as not to wonder why a man would pay special attention to her. That was something she'd learned to worry less about since she turned fifty.

And if a man wasn't into her or judged her too old to date with a dismissive glance, it no longer affected her ego as it had in her forties and after her messy divorce. She'd never been a beauty queen, but she'd kept herself in shape, which bonus was great for her mental health and being able to get on the floor and play with her grandkids.

Why was she letting something that happened so long ago affect her still and, more importantly, how does someone get over their past? It's a question she'd been debating in her head ever since Adam walked back into her life. Sure, there's been odd moments over the years where she'd thought of him, but the long-ago disappointment of what could have been had never been this intense.

We both still lived in Pineville. Our kids were of similar ages, but our circles were never the same, not until her best friend married his best friend.

Now each time Lois saw him, it was as if she was in a play. A production where she was a master pretender or, more accurately, a master ignorer.

It felt childish.

It was childish.

And she wasn't sure how much longer she could keep her real feelings buried.

Plus, Adam was making it difficult to ignore him. Now that he was working in the same building as her, it was as if he used every excuse in the book to stop by her desk and chat. But it never went beyond that. Although sometimes Lois saw interest in his gaze and it made her wonder if he too was holding something back.

He kept it casual and seemed to enjoy trying to make her laugh. And it was becoming damn hard to maintain the wall she'd built up where he was concerned. How long was she going to punish herself and him for not remembering that night over thirty years ago?

She was holding tight onto something that couldn't be changed and it was a damn heavy burden. At this point in her life, she most certainly didn't want to be tied down by her past insecurities.

Was she suffering a mid-life crisis? Breakdown? Longing?

She needed to talk to someone about it fast before she did something stupid like quit her job and move across the country. Because that was not going to happen.

Sending a quick text to invite Patrice to lunch, they met up an hour later and were sitting at a table in The Club located in downtown Pineville.

Lois had just told Patrice about her plan to find a date to the black-tie charity event at the end of the month TS had sprung on her, but they were interrupted by the waitress. After taking their order, she scanned the room and caught sight of a familiar head of silver hair. There he was across the restaurant, having lunch with a group of people from the office.

If Patrice noticed her interest, she hid it well. "You know I'm still confused about why you're thinking of going to the speed date night again, which I know you hated last time, when there's an eligible man who'd love to take you. You really should give him a chance."

"Giving who a chance?" She stopped staring at the back of Adam's head and turned her focus back onto her meal.

"C'mon, Lois. It's obvious that there's something going on between you and Adam. So, why don't you give him a chance? He's quite the catch, you know." Patrice smirked at her own pun.

"Funny, but what makes you think I would be thinking of him?"

"Oh, maybe since TS and Noel's party and every other time you two are in the same space, you clam up. But I think I'm missing something. What's wrong with being interested in Adam?"

"One, we work together."

"Bzzz," Patrice interrupted. "You don't, not really. He may be in the same building, but others there have dated and ended up married. Try again."

"You did not just buzz me. My dating life is not some... some dating game."

"Exactly. So why bother going to O'Malley's and sitting through what I know by experience will be unbearably awkward conversations with strangers when Adam is available and willing to date you?"

Lois rarely argued with Patrice or got mad with her, but she was pushing all her buttons today.

"Willing? Gee thanks."

"More than willing, Lo. Hell, if he looked at you at our wedding reception didn't convince you how he feels about you, I'm not sure what will. So, please tell me what you have against Adam, because I want you to give him a chance. Don't you deserve a good man? A man who, and don't tell my husband, has that sexy silver fox vibe going on. He's the full meal deal, right? Attractive, smart, and still has a lot of good years left."

Right, how could she forget that day in Patrice's back-yard as they celebrated her and Kade's marriage, and every time she felt she was being watched, she'd turn and find Adam looking at her. The heat in his gaze reminding her what happened between them, while also highlighting that he didn't seem to remember it and it had sent her running.

"Good years left? Hold up. Adam isn't that much older than Kade. I'd think your husband would take exception to that description. And I'm only a couple years younger. Neither one of us is ready for the retirement center yet."

"Exactly. I only said all that because I thought some tough love would open you up. Plus, I still feel bad about setting you up with the date from hell last year."

Lois felt her temp return to normal. Patrice was like a sister to her, and she knew she wasn't trying to hurt her feel-ings on purpose.

"Okay, you want to know the reason I don't want to date Adam? The real problem is he doesn't remember me. Or rather, he doesn't remember the night we shared back in college."

Patrice's eyes went round, her jaw dropping. "You've been holding out on me."

Twenty minutes later, her best friend held her hand as she dabbed the last of her tears away. "Thank you for not calling me crazy or dismissing my feelings. You have no idea how good it feels to have this weight lifted." Lois checked her cell phone. She had ten minutes to repair her face and get back to work.

"What kind of friend would I be if I did either of those things? I get it. When we're eighteen, everything seems big and forever when we find someone we love. I'm sure if you told Adam, he'd—"

"Understand? How can he if he doesn't remember? I'm

pretty sure it's not an act. No one is that good. Besides, it was so long ago, and I need to keep it there. We both obviously lived our lives. We're different people now."

Patrice nodded. "Maybe. Maybe not. But time doesn't make those feelings any less real just because they took place in the past."

Lois took a long drink of water and a deep breath. She needed her friend's perspective, but continuing to hold someone accountable for what they didn't remember wasn't fair, and she needed to let it go.

She just needed to figure out how she was going to do that.

FIVE

Adam stood people watching from the edge of TS's great room, where the Super Bowl was projected on the wall, which made it easier for everyone to have a good view of the game. But if anyone really watched him closely, they'd see his gaze had only been tracking one person since she arrived.

"I feel as if I'm in some reverse universe where the woman who was warm and friendly toward me back in college has been confusingly cool and standoffish toward me for months and for no apparent reason." Adam blurted out to his friend before taking a deep drink from his Mexican beer.

She'd incredibly agreed to attend the charity gala with him next week, but she hadn't really changed her overall attitude toward him. His guess was that she hadn't wanted to go to the trouble of finding a date. And one thing he knew for sure was that she didn't have anyone special in her life. He'd thanked his lucky stars for small miracles.

Kade patted him on the shoulder, snagged a bacon wrapped shrimp from the tray their hostess offered.

Noel, TS's wife, paused and said, "Want a woman and a friend's advice?"

Adam tore his gaze from Lois's back, noting how her dress fit snugly around her hips, nipping in at her waist. He'd been itching to wrap his hands around her all evening since she walked in. Hell, yeah, he'd take some insight. He was a man who relied on his instincts and his gut told him Lois was worth the frustration she'd been putting him through.

But the question remained why?

TS's wife sent him a cheeky grin and said, "You need to find a way to spend time with her that she can't say no to. And for what it's worth, I think you two would make a great couple." She kept walking, offering the food to more of her guests.

Adam let out a long breath and mumbled, "Gee, why didn't I think of that?"

Kade busted out laughing loud enough he drew the attention of his wife, and unbelievably Lois, who for once wasn't looking at him with disinterest. Instead, she wore an amused expression. It made her appear more approachable than she had in months, and damn if it didn't give him some hope.

He needed to find a way to get her to direct that look at him.

He needed to make a big move. And soon.

Hell, it might as well be now.

"Hold my beer." He pushed the bottle into Kade's hands and walked over to where Lois was standing with Patrice.

Her eyes flared at his approach, and for the first time, he felt some hope that she wasn't as unaffected by him as she tried to appear. Both women watched him until he was standing a foot away, but it was Patrice who greeted him enthusiastically.

"I think your husband needs you." He kept his gaze on Lois as he spoke. He wanted little doubt left between them about why he was there.

"Um, yeah. Okay." She looked between him and Lois, then quickly walked away.

He'd thank her later. And hopefully he'd be able to soothe any hurt feelings for basically barking orders at her.

"Lois."

"Adam." Her tone was guarded and wary.

Good. He wanted her a bit off balance.

"I was hoping we could talk about some things."

"Things? What things?"

The sounds of laughter and conversation hit him, and he realized this may go better somewhere less crowded. "How about we go into the dining room? It's less crowded." He lifted his arm and indicated the direction of the room he hoped was empty.

At first, he didn't think she was going to move, but then spun on a heel and he had the pleasure of watching her walk away from him.

When he entered the dining room, she'd stopped in front of the French doors leading out to the back patio, staring out into the night. The soft glow of the overhead lights made the space feel smaller, more intimate than it was, and he wanted nothing more than to run his hands over her rigid shoulders so she'd relax in his presence.

"Thank you, Lois. I can't help but feel I've done something to make you uncomfortable around me, and that's the opposite of what I wanted since we're now in each other's lives again."

Instead of his words relaxing her, they seemed to make things worse.

"We were friends once. Sure, it was a long time ago, but I was hoping it could be different. Have I done or said something to upset you?"

She was silent and still for so long, he almost gave up. But giving up had never been his way of dealing with uncomfortable situations. "Lois, talk to me. Otherwise, I'm going to do something stupid and call Lance and ask him if he knows why his sister hates me. And then he's going to ask, 'What the hell did you do to my sister?' and then it's going to be a whole thing, and I'd rather know from you so I can make it right."

Her mouth twisted into a small smile. Then she let out a long sigh and he was transported back to college, where she often reacted the same way to his lame attempts at humor. If only she knew how it wasn't just getting her to laugh that he was after, but being his best friend's little sister, it had been the only way he could interact with her without getting a fist to his face.

"Look, did I insult your choice in music back then, or maybe I made you feel...I don't know, awkward around me? Did I say something recently that ticked you off? Help me out, Lo, because I'd really like to get past this and maybe see if we could be friends again." Holding his breath because he'd like to be much more than friends, Adam couldn't take his eyes off her.

Her expression went from surprise to hope to something unreadable in a flash. His heart hammered beneath his rib cage, and he was instantly transported back to graduation day, where he'd been trying to figure out a way to tell her how he really felt about her. Unfortunately, that night had been the only night he'd ever drunk to the point of passing out, and the next day was a whirlwind of goodbyes and regrets.

"You know how sometimes things work out for the best? But other times you spend so much time wondering what could have been that it becomes almost unhealthy?" Her eyes, now bright, were laser focused on him and the twin reaction of the hair standing up on the back of his neck, and all the blood from his head travelling south raised even more questions.

"Tell me." He whispered.

"I think I need another glass of wine for this." She crossed her arms around her middle and smiled. "But that's probably not the best solution. And you deserve to know why I've been such a b-word toward you. No, don't argue. I have, and I guess I just didn't know how to handle my feelings."

Adam released a relieved laugh, then rubbed the back of his neck. "Well, I wouldn't categorize you that way, but it's been pretty obvious I'm not your favorite person."

She shook her head, which made her hair sway back and forth around her gorgeous face. He reached up and cupped her cheek and brushed a lone tear away.

"Hey, it's okay. Just tell me so I can make things better."

"Wow, I can't believe I did this myself, to you. I promise I'm not usually this messed up. In fact, I'm probably to put together most of the time and could benefit from letting loose, letting things go more often. But when I saw you again after all those years, the feelings just came rushing back."

He reached out and took her hands in his. "Okay, maybe we could both use a drink right now."

"No, I'm just acting like a dramatic teenager, lord this just seems silly now."

"Your feelings aren't silly, Lo. When you're ready to tell me, I'm here."

"You have no idea. Now that we're actually talking, it seems like I've made a mountain out of a molehill. When we were in college, I had the biggest crush on you. Did you know that?"

Wow, not the confession I'd been expecting. "I thought you were annoyed with me most of the time, so no, I didn't know." Talk about surprises. He hadn't seen it back then, probably because he'd been doing his best not to ruin his friendship with Lance.

The intensity of her gaze made him pause. What was she looking for? Then it dawned on him. Something must have happened between us. But for the life of him, he couldn't guess what it had been.

"Okay, tell me."

"You really don't remember, do you?"

Trying to lighten the mood, he said, "I'm old, but not that old. So just do it, rip the bandage off and let me have it."

This time, his humor worked, and she chuckled.

"Okay. And really looking back, it all makes sense, but I was young and thought, well, like a teenager, I thought I knew all about the world, you know?"

"The night of your and Lance's grad party at our house, you and me, we, uh, kissed. It was after our parents had called it a night. You were paying me more attention than normal, and I was walking on air. You walked me back to the edge of the yard where it was dark and we...oh, my lord, why is this so embarrassing? I'm fifty-six years old. I've been married, had two babies, and I'm no prude."

Adam felt a large stone drop in his stomach. "Lois, I didn't..."

"Oh, no, no, no. We kissed, and other stuff, and it was totally mutual. No, I'm so sorry I gave any indication it was otherwise. It was...it was perfect. But I hadn't realized how much you had celebrated and when the next day you and my brother were saying your goodbyes and you treated me like nothing had happened, I was—I was pissed, and then I was devastated. And I kind of alternated between those emotions for the next few years until I met my ex at my very first job after graduation. Plus, it didn't help that we were now working together. And the last thing I wanted was a repeat of a failed workplace romance. So, being around you again, it just dug up all those feelings and memories, and I'm sorry."

Adam squeezed his eyes shut, trying to drum up any memory of that long ago night to no avail. Wow, that was not what he thought it would be.

"You know, I think it best if I go home. I know that was a lot to dump on a person. I'll see you next week." Lois let go of his hands and walked from the room.

He let her go. Because really, what could he have said and how drunk does a person have to be to not remember kissing the girl of his dreams?

SIX

THINGS HAD BEEN awkward between him and Lois since Sunday night, no doubt, but she was more open to having conversations with him as long as they didn't talk about what had happened back in college.

He contemplated calling her brother for like half a second, then thought better. He didn't need Lance's blessing to date Lois. The connection he felt with her now was even stronger than the ever-present hormones whenever she was around back in his early twenties. Even if things had started off on a thorny start between them, tonight he was going to be on his best behavior if it killed him.

They'd agreed to meet at the event instead of driving together, so he made sure he was early. The table they were assigned to already had two couples seated and, if coincidences were like lucky pennies, well, he'd have two pennies. Because it was that much of a stretch to figure out he'd been set up as he greeted TS and Noel and Kade and Patrice.

"Fancying seeing you all here. It's been what, four hours

since I saw TS at work and a day since Kade and I played pickle ball?"

"That's what I like about you, Doc. You're handsome and funny." Noel pointed behind him. "And you have great taste in women. Looks like your date is here."

Adam spun around and took in the sight of Lois walking toward him. The first thing he noticed was how her eyes locked onto him, as if he were the only other person in the room.

She wore a dark blue, form fitting dress that flared slightly around her ankles. She wore her hair pulled up with a few tendrils left down, framing her beautiful face. His fingers itched to pull down the intricate style, but he'd save that for later—when they were alone and if he was lucky enough that she wanted him just as much. He felt confident that now he knew the reason she'd been standoffish in the beginning that they could have a fresh start.

Adam couldn't take his off her as she stopped by an empty chair, then looked around the table at their chaperones. "What do we have here? Afraid Adam and I won't play nice tonight?"

TS spoke first. "Actually, we wanted a front-row seat. Hey, ow." He rubbed his shoulder where his wife pinched him.

"We thought it would be fun if all of us hung out now that you two aren't...well, you know." Kade turned to Patrice, a pleading look on his face.

"Oh, no, you managed to do work yourself into a corner all by yourself. Go on, tell them what you meant, *honey*."

Everyone laughed and any remaining uncertainty or worry about how the evening would play out was quickly replaced with the anticipation of good friends sharing a fun evening.

The announcement for dinner came over the p.a. system and Adam pulled out Lois's chair for her. After she was settled, he took his own seat and when he looked over at her; they shared a smile.

"So, who's the other couple joining us?" Patrice asked TS.

"I'm not sure it'll be a couple. I gave tickets to Archer King. He recently bought a large track of land between here and Cedar Ridge and has been staying in our penthouse condo downtown until he decides where he wants to live permanently."

Kade let out a low whistle. "I've heard of him. His grandfather and mother built the family's fortune through questionable means and he's now using it to create all sorts of good works from rehab centers for vets to affordable housing developments for low-income families and the list goes on."

TS nodded. "That and more. He and a couple of his best friends from childhood are committed to giving back and using their own money. But I'll be surprised if he'll actually show up tonight. He's been grumbling about a local real estate agent giving him heartburn over the last strip of land he needs to secure before the project can begin. Anyway, let's not wait for Archer. If he shows up, he'll understand if we don't wait for him."

TS filled everyone's champagne glass from a bottle he had chilled in a standing bucket next to the table, then offered a quick toast before their food arrived. "To good friends, new beginnings, and the Outlaws going to the championship series this year."

"Here, here!"

"Cheers!"

"Amen to that."

As the evening progressed, neither of them ate much dinner. We spent most of our time talking about major life events, what her brother was doing now, things we had in common, our kids, her divorce, the passing of his wife to cancer and what made him decide to take the position with the Outlaws.

When the auction began, Adam settled back and instead of paying attention to the auctioneer, he watched Lois as she and Patrice cheered on the bidders, then discussed which items they wanted to bid on. It had been forever since he'd seen Lois this relaxed. And then there were the moments when she caught him watching her. He loved seeing the flush on her cheeks and what he hoped was anticipation in her eyes.

He enjoyed every bit of the evening, but he was most looking forward to was dancing and taking her in his arms, holding her close.

After the auction ended, the lights dimmed further, and the band began to play. With the first few notes of a song that couldn't have been more perfect, *Love Story*, if he wasn't mistaken, began to fill the room. He knew most of Zoe's and Berkley's favorite songs during high school. It had been hard not to since their music and their laughter filled the house at full volume, much to their brothers' irritation.

Rising from his chair, Adam held out his hand to Lois. "May I have the first dance?"

Lois accepted with a shy smile, and soon she was in his arms. They fit better than he'd imagined, and he'd spent plenty of time imagining. Sometimes real life is better than fantasy. He was immediately transported to that horny twenty-something with sweaty palms. To settle his nerves, he took in a deep breath and was rewarded with a light, sweet bloom of flowers and a hint of spice.

As they swayed, their combined warmth felt as if they were in a bubble-like microcosm no one else could burst if they tried. Wow, when had he become so poetic even if was in his own head?

Is that what being with "the one" did to a guy?

He'd loved his wife, but it had never been as intense and all-consuming as how he felt toward Lois. And he didn't want to waste any more time debating whether they should take things slow or not, because the answer is *not.*

Their story had taken thirty-plus years to reach this point, and he was ready to give her his heart, but let her decide the pace. Although he'd do his best to advocate for sooner rather than later.

"What are you thinking about?" Lois murmured as the next song began.

This one more up tempo, but they stayed close, neither in a hurry to break the spell. "Just how right this feels. Having you in my arms."

"Hmm." She answered.

"What's 'hmm' supposed to mean?" Brushing his lips against her forehead, he waited.

"You...this...us, it feels bigger than I'd ever thought it could, especially after I told you. I just wish—"

Adam pulled back so he could look her in the eyes and reassure her. "No wishing. We can't go back. We're here now. And, to me, it feels like now is absolutely the right time."

She lifted her chin at his words and the look on her face told him all he needed to know.

"Are you ready to leave? Can I take you home?"

Lois nodded. Her smile made him feel ten feet tall, and the urge to kiss her was so strong he had to step back and break their contact. He wanted that first touch of her lips to be for only them.

SEVEN

"I'm usually not this...er, flustered." Lois' heart was beating triple time and, dammit, why was he so close?

"Maybe I like seeing you...flustered. And flushed. It's quite...intoxicating." Adam's voice dropped an octave.

It was husky, shameless, and sexy.

And Lois swore her stomach flipped from the sound combination. As their gazes locked, she noted the blue of eyes had darkened, but his lips were pursed tight. Was he aggravated with her or was it something else? Something that filled her with need. *A primal wanting passed between us.*

Swift and sharp.

Yes, primal. *Oh, no, she didn't just say that out loud, did she?*

And just like that, Lois couldn't care less about all the reasons she'd come up with to stay away from Adam Riordan.

Adam leaned in, braced a hand over her head on the stone wall beside her front door. His eyes had dropped to her lips and his long, silent pause gave her plenty of time to say no.

There was no way in hell she was saying no.

The kiss was electric. Consuming then less so but no less soul shattering as he feathered his lips over hers before nipping the fullness of her lower lip before easing back and breaking the magic.

A new craving erupted within her, and she was not going to let this moment end without taking what she wanted.

Lois grabbed either side of Adam's face and guided him back down to her lips. Opening herself to him, for him, their tongues came out to play: dueling, sucking and everything in between until breathing became paramount.

The crisp air was filled with their ragged breathing when they pulled apart. Adam appeared as shocked as she felt.

"You kiss all your first dates like that?" His voice sounded nothing like before. It was ragged and filled with need. *Lord, had she done that?*

Yes, yes, she had. She'd made a man lose himself in her kiss and the joy and power of it filled her up even as it stole her breath, leaving her unable to form coherent words. Shaking her head, Lois watched as Adam scraped his fingers through his silver-streaked hair, then release a low whistle as he too attempted to recover from that kiss.

She managed a shaky "no," then wrapped her arms around her middle.

The chill of the night finally hit her, reminding her they were standing on her porch in below freezing temps. Oh, how she wanted to say something provocative like, "Want to come in and warm each other up?" but her vocal cords still weren't cooperating.

"I'm glad. And if I wasn't a gentleman, I'd invite myself in. But I really want to see you again, Lo. There's something here and as much as you've kept your distance from me for months, and I want to find out why, I think it's time we figure out if this is just chemistry or if it could be something real...with chemistry." Adam grinned.

Watching his full lips move and wishing they were back on hers, she finally latched onto the meaning of what he'd just said. Chemistry, oh yeah, they had loads. But what if it burned out fast, just like with her ex, and then they were left with an awkward aftermath? Both at work and with their friends.

Could she move on from another failed relationship and still show up in her professional life?

"I can see those wheels turning. Don't overthink it. I'm not going to ask to come in, but I am asking for a date. And we can keep it to ourselves until we figure out how, and when, we want to let our friends know. Okay?"

Did she want to date Adam? Maybe, maybe not. But did she want Adam in her bed? Most definitely.

Instead of answering him, she did something that scared her. Something that sent excitement humming through her body. Lois unlocked her door, stepped over the threshold, and looked at him with all the pent up wanting since he came back into her life.

"Life is short, Adam. At this point, I think we both know where we'll end up. I don't need to be wooed with weeks or months of nice dinners and small talk. I just want you. Now."

Adam's eyes lit up at her daring words and she swore she heard him emit a low growl. A sound that went straight to her midsection. When he swooped into the entryway, encircled her waist and kicked the door shut with his foot, she wrapped her arms around his neck and held on tight.

Her inhibitions disappeared as he pressed the evidence of his need for her against her belly, backing her up to the wall. What woman didn't want to be wanted, craved like this?

With a desperate touch, then a desperate kiss that stole her breath, it was her turn to moan. The sound reached her ears and, for the first time ever, she wasn't afraid to let a man hear the pleasure she was feeling.

Adam pulled back from her and she immediately felt bereft. But he quickly made up for it by asking, "Bedroom?" He nuzzled her neck with hot, open-mouthed kisses, nipping and sucking her over-sensitized skin, and it was all she could do to nod, then point toward the hallway.

She absorbed the rumble of his laugh. His wide chest pressed against her breasts. Her nipples rubbed against the material of her clothing as she tried to get closer to him. Desperate for his roaming mouth to go lower.

"I...oh, this way." Breathless and impatient, she pulled out of his arms, grabbed his hand, and led him to her room.

Adam captured her around the waist again, this time her back to his front. He placed his lips near her ear, nipping the lobe and pulling her into his erection. The move tore another moan out of her as her hips began to sway against his hardness. He unzipped her dress. She couldn't move fast enough to get her arms out of the sleeves and letting the material fall to the floor.

Bared to him in her bra and panties, she felt a surge of power and need as his fingers dipped beneath the lace waistband, diving between her legs exactly where she wanted them.

"You need to tell me to stop if this is not what you want,

Lo. I brought a condom with me, more in hope than in certainty, but if you don't—"

She didn't let him finish the sentence, releasing a "yes" before smashing her lips on his. Her fingers found his waistband, unbuckled his belt, and pushed down his slacks until they gave way, pooling at his feet.

They both stepped out of their shoes, then necessity had them reluctantly making space between them as they raced to finish undressing.

Looking at his lean form and the evidence between his strong thighs that he indeed needed her as much as she needed him, she threw off her bedsheets and crawled onto her bed. "I'm clean and there's no worry about me getting pregnant, so if you are too...there's no need for the condom."

He chuckled at her words and the sound sent a long spiral of need winding through her.

The sound had been one of the things that had always turned her on back in college and it was no different now, maybe even more so.

"Sweetheart, I'm sure you understand the birds and the bees very well, so I'll let that one pass." Adam crawled over her, leaned down, and began dropping kisses along her neck. She stretched, giving him better access, then ran her hands along his sides, tugging him down on top of her.

"You have me so rattled and you know it, but thank you for not teasing me." Lois whispered against his ear before she nipped and sucked his earlobe into her mouth.

He responded with another, rumbly groan and said, "Oh, I'm going to tease you, but it won't be with words."

Before she could answer him, he captured her lips in another all-consuming kiss. Coherent thought, let alone words, no longer mattered. She lifted her hips until his erection fit snugly against her mound, but that wasn't enough.

Rolling her hips, she pressed their flesh together, shifting her legs and then a loud creak filled the room, and she jerked a bit from discomfort. Stupid knee.

"Dammit, I'm sorry, Adam. My knee...I forgot. It really sucks getting old. I just need to move it...there." Lois heaved a sigh. "So much for being sexy and carefree, huh?"

"Are you okay?" His concern warmed her as he ran a hand over the offending joint. "You know I'm a doctor, right? This type of thing is my specialty." He wiggled his eyebrows, then leaned his forehead against hers. "You are sexy, Lo. So much so that I'm feeling like a randy twenty-year-old right now. So, hold on. I'm going to take very good care of you."

Her heart filled with joy at his humor and his declaration.

Adam's expression went from humorous to smoldering. He placed kisses along her breastbone, between her breasts, then when his tongue licked around a nipple, she shivered from the contact.

He delivered on his promise to tease and what was only seconds but felt like forever. He finally sucked a hard tip into his mouth. Releasing it with a pop, he did the same to its twin, then trailed his lips down the middle of her stomach, stoppling along the way to place open mouth kisses above her mound then on her inner thighs, inches from her now drenched folds.

The first lick stole her breath. The second and third had her humming his name. Adam delved his tongue deep inside, setting a rhythm that amped her higher and higher. When he pressed a finger on her clit and thrummed the engorged flesh, she lifted her hips, needing and reveling in the glorious friction.

But Adam was a man of his word, and he'd pause when

she got close, then begin the delicious onslaught all over again.

When the first sharp tug of her orgasm began, she grasped the bedsheets and called out his name. And did so again when he slipped a finger inside her, deeper and began stroking her until he hit her g-spot at the same time he flicked his tongue against her clit. Over and over the sensation carried her along the wave and when she crested, she discovered a new level of intimacy never achieved with her ex.

It was freeing, and it was addicting. And to have it at her age, with the man she's always loved, had her weeping with joy.

"Sweetheart, please tell me those are happy tears, otherwise you're not leaving this bed until we both pass out from pleasure."

She giggled at the picture his words painted. She could live with that. Needing him on top of her, she opened her arms to him as he crawled back up her body. Lord, he was handsome and her mouth watered at the anticipation of him being inside her. "More than happy tears. Now, no more talking."

Adam lined himself up at her entrance and, with their gazes locked, he thrust inside her, filling her to the hilt. The rightness of it overwhelmed her. She rose up and wrapped her arms around him as he pounded into her. Her moans filled the room, her body sang with the need she saw in his eyes—for her.

Urgency overtook them both and with unspoken need from her, his thrusts became faster, harder. Their breathing and the sounds of their bodies joining, slapping together, created a new memory for her to hold on to, to replace the old hurt with the new.

Her second orgasm built and as she rode out its peak, Adam's followed, and their whispered words filled her with another need. A need to shout from the mountain tops how she felt for him.

"I love you," rang from her lips as they collapsed back onto the bed. She didn't need him to say it back, she just needed him to know and there was no better moment than now.

Unfortunately, old habits die hard, and her intrusive mind began questioning the timing of her declaration.

"I can feel the wheels turning, Lo. Don't you dare take it back. To others it may seem fast, but this is us. Our story gets to move as fast as we want it to. I love you, Lois." Adam curled her tighter against his front. "And, if you give me an hour, this old guy will be ready to show you again just how much."

EPILOGUE

TWO WEEKS LATER

ADAM HAD IT ALL PLANNED. The ring was in his pocket, and he was pretty sure Lois didn't think tonight was anything more than a Valentine's Day dinner with friends and family.

As far as he was concerned, two weeks were long enough to wait before asking her to spend the rest of their lives together.

He wanted Lois's laugh, her perspective on life, her humor, her sighs as he sunk into her body, and he wanted the way she looked at him when she didn't think was watching her. And he wanted it every day, in the same house.

Salvatore's was her favorite restaurant, and he pulled a few strings to make sure they could accommodate a large group. Their family and friends were an important part of their reconnection, and he knew Lois would agree with him.

He'd never been more nervous expect maybe when

each of his four kids had been born. He thought he was holding it together pretty well all through dinner. As they waited for the desserts to be delivered, he smiled at Lois as she bounced her newest grandchild, Heather and Rex's little girl, Lyla, on her lap.

When the waiter finally arrived with the heart-shaped mini cheesecakes drenched in chocolate ganache. Heather scooped up the baby from Lois's arms with a promise she'd get her back after dessert.

When she was distracted, he put a box with a big red bow next to her plate. Lois turned, picked up her fork, and froze. A wrinkle appeared between her brow, then her cheeks flushed a pretty pink.

It was now or never, and Adam's heart threatened to jump from his chest. Reaching across the table, he took both her hands into his and the carefully planned speech flew right out of his head.

"Forever. I want forever with you, Lo. Time is a funny thing, and because we've been given a second chance so many years later...well, we have an epic love story to pass onto our grandkids. Well, yours anyway, since none of my kids seem to be interested, but maybe this will inspire them."

Groans erupted from the table where his two daughters and two sons sat and yeah, maybe he didn't need to get that dig in, but it made Lois smile and he wanted to spend the rest of his life being the one to paint it on her face every day.

"I love you, Lo. I feel it to my soul, and to the tips of my sliver hair, which I know you have a thing for."

A round of laughter and catcalls rang out, but all that mattered was that Lois laughed. But when her eyes filled with unshed tears, he began to get choked up. But as long as she said yes, he'd gladly turn into a blubbering mess—because she was his heart, his forever.

"Do you know what today is, Lo?"

"Yeah, it's kind of hard to miss the decorations everywhere." She grinned, wiping her eyes, then waved an arm in the air.

"It's going to be more than that. Open the box, please?" Adam's gaze never wavered from hers as she pulled the bow loose, then opened it slowly. Tears began to fall onto her cheeks and with shaky hands, she lifted the smaller box nestled inside the issue.

In a room full of people, it felt as if it was just the two of them. He took the box and got down on one knee, opened it and said, "Marry me? Be my valentine forever, Lois."

A low-level chant began around the restaurant. "Say yes...say yes...say yes!"

"Looks like I'm outnumbered and honestly, I couldn't be happier that so many friends and family love our love story."

Standing, Adam pulled Lois from her chair and kissed her long and deep before slipping the diamond ring on her finger.

"So, no concerns that we're moving too fast, huh?" Adam whispered.

"Are you kidding? Now is the best time and I'm all in on forever."

Thank you for reading the RESCUED BY LOVE: LATER IN LIFE series. If you enjoyed these stories, please consider leaving a review on the site you purchased your copy from.

WHAT TO READ NEXT?

Check out Debra's books on her website for the latest stories:

www.debraeliseauthor.com

Make sure you don't miss out on my upcoming books or sales by joining my weekly newsletter >>> https://geni.us/DebraEliseNewsletter Once you sign up, you'll receive a link for a FREE short story set in my Pineville World.

ALSO BY DEBRA ELISE

MOUNTAIN MEN OF PINEVILLE

MOUNTAIN MAN SAVIOR West + Lauren

MOUNTAIN MAN PROTECTOR Ridge + Addison

MOUNTAIN MAN DEFENDER – June 23rd

MOUNTAIN MAN BODYGUARD - August 29th

MOUNTAIN MAN GRUMPY SANTA - December 1st

STAND ALONE STORIES (2025)

GRUMP OF MISTY MOUNTAIN Finn + Sami *Out now!*

TANGLING SERIES

Each short story in the Tangling Series features characters in their 30s & 40s who decide to live their lives to the fullest, and that includes experiencing steamy, sexy times. When each heroine is presented the opportunity to tangle with the one they desire—they go all in.

Set in the Pineville World with interconnected characters. Each book can be read as a standalone.

TANGLING WITH THE BREWMASTER – **Luke + Laci**

TANGLING WITH THE COWBOY - **Lawson + Jana**

WORTH THE WAIT – **Cole + Scarlett**

TANGLING WITH THE PLAYER – **Brock + Thea**

ZESTING WITH ZANE – **Zane + Holly**

RESUCED BY AN OUTLAW – **Dean + Nori**

TANGLING WITH THE MOUNTAIN MAN - **Beck + Taya**

TANGLING WITH THE SILVER FOX **Hayden + Brenley**

MY CUPID HOLIDATE – **Rex + Heather**

TANGLING WITH THE DOCTOR - **Jack + Kiersten**

TANGLING WITH SANTA – **Slade + Kara**

FOR THE LOVE OF CURVES – **Roman + Miranda**

TANGLING WITH THE GRINCH – **Walker + Mazie**

BIDDING ON A COWBOY – **Sawyer + Emma**

CEMENTING HER LOVE – **Colton + Shayla**

COMING IN 2026

SECOND CHANCE, INC. SERIES

The Second Chance, Inc, Series is a he falls first, later in life series featuring friends running a non-profit ranch in the middle of horse country Idaho that specializes in providing support services for those in need from skills retraining to trauma therapy for injured, retired military or first responder personnel.

From a former pro athlete and reluctant billionaire, to a burned-out dot-com CEO to an injured war veteran, these men find not only a second chance at reshaping their life's purpose but find women strong enough to challenge them when needed, and after a hard-fought journey, love them despite their flaws.

PRE-ORDER Book One Now!

ARCHER - Archer +Kelee May 18, 2026

RESCUED BY LOVE: LATER IN LIFE series

Each book is set in Debra's fictional Pineville, Idaho World and features characters in their mid-30s, 40s, & 50s discovering love always finds a way. Sub genres include: insta love, friends to lovers, forbidden/workplace and second chance.

LOVE AT EVERMORE & 39TH – **Evan + Cassidy**

LOVE AT SECOND & 49TH – **Kade + Patrice**

LOVE AT FIRST & 35TH – **Sam + Evie**

LOVING GOLDIE – **Ford + Goldie**

LOVE AT FOREVER & 56TH – **Adam + Lois**

RESCUED BY LOVE series

The first series in the Pineville World and features connected characters tied to the Idaho Outlaws, a professional baseball team and their family and friends.

SAVING MAVERICK – **Maverick + Kelsey**

FULL COUNT - **Luke + Lara**

BASES LOADED - **Connor + Reese**

MANAGING BLAKE – **Blake + Caris**

CHASING NOEL – **TS & Noel**

REDEEMING SCROOGE – **Grant + Sophie**

RESCUING ROYCE – **Royce + Amber**

TEMPTING ZAK – **Zak + Harlowe**

PARANORMAL BOOKS

GODS, MONSTERS, AND MAGIC:

(THE BRETHREN'S LEGACY WORLD)

DRAGON'S GODDESS

WOLF'S MATE

FATED TO THE PHOENIX
FATED TO THE GRIZZLY
FATED TO THE PANTHER
FATED TO THE SHIFTER - 2026

ABOUT THE AUTHOR

Debra Elise, a *USA Today* Bestselling Author, writes steamy contemporary and paranormal romance. She lives with her younger trophy husband and their needy golden doodle, Zander, in the beautiful Pacific Northwest. They also have two young adult sons who have promised to never read her stories.

A self-proclaimed extroverted introvert, when not writing or procrastinating, she enjoys a strong cup of coffee and a good nap.

www.debraeliseauthor.com